THE FINAL BEAT OF THE DRUM

THE FINAL BEAT OF THE DRUM

Paniatowski's Last Case

Sally Spencer

**SEVERN
HOUSE**

First world edition published in Great Britain and the USA in 2023
by Severn House, an imprint of Canongate Books Ltd,
14 High Street, Edinburgh EH1 1TE.

Trade paperback edition first published in Great Britain and the USA in 2023
by Severn House, an imprint of Canongate Books Ltd.

severnhouse.com

British Library Cataloguing-in-Publication Data
A CIP catalogue record for this title is available from the British Library.

ISBN-13: 978-0-7278-5064-5 (cased)
ISBN-13: 978-1-4483-0707-4 (trade paper)
ISBN-13: 978-1-4483-0706-7 (e-book)

All Severn House titles are printed on acid-free paper.

MIX
Paper from
responsible sources
FSC® C013056

Typeset by Palimpsest Book Production Ltd.,
Falkirk, Stirlingshire, Scotland.
Printed and bound in Great Britain by
TJ Books, Padstow, Cornwall.

For Kate Lyall Grant – an outstanding editor/publisher and an all-round lovely person.

PART ONE
Goodbye-Ee

Goodby-ee! Goodbye-ee
Wipe the tear, baby dear, from your eye-ee
World War One song

Wednesday, 3 July, 1985

I n the public bar of the Drum and Monkey, Monika Paniatowski glanced around the table at the two men and one woman who were no longer her team.

Directly opposite her sat Inspector Colin Beresford, who, even in middle age, was a formidable melding of muscle and bone. He had been at Paniatowski's side for what, to both of them, seemed like forever, but actually only dated back to the time that she had been a detective sergeant and he a detective constable. Louisa (Paniatowski's adopted daughter) called him Uncle Colin. At Whitebridge police headquarters, however, he had a nickname which was much less avuncular and referred to the more-than-active sex life he led after he'd lost his virginity at the comparatively late age of thirty-one. The name clung to him (like wet swimming trunks) even after he'd settled down, and would probably travel with him to his grave, so that when people who'd known him read his tombstone, they'd find their lips silently forming the missing word, 'Shagger'.

To Beresford's left sat DS Kate Meadows. Neat, petite and elfin-like, she gave the impression that butter wouldn't melt in her mouth, but those who crossed her quickly learned that she had a gaze intent enough to strip away skin.

And then there was Jack Crane.

Handsome Jack!

Dashing Jack!

One-eyed Jack!

Had Colin Beresford been caught in Jack's situation, he would never have lost an eye. When he'd seen that the woman rushing at him had a screwdriver in her hand, he'd have dropped her immediately. But gentle Jack – gallant Jack – had hesitated before hitting the woman, and that hesitation had cost him not just his eye, but also his career.

They'd all been her team, Paniatowski thought, and she would always be proud of them.

Even the table they were resting their elbows on was part of
the team. It had been at this table that she and Charlie Woodend
had worked on their first murder case together, and when
she had stepped into Charlie's shoes, she had brought her own
team here. Over the years, the rest of the furniture in the bar
had been changed several times, but this table – scarred by cigarette burns, stained by spilled ale – had remained. There had never
been a reserved sign on it, because that hadn't been necessary.
The regular patrons – who took pride in the nerve centre of the
operation being in their local – would see to it that no casual
drinker invaded DCI Paniatowski's territory.

Monika caught herself sighing. The table would not survive
their departure for long, she thought, because if there were not
two pints of best bitter, a still orange and a Polish vodka resting
on it, it would no longer have a function.

'Well, this feels more like a wake than a celebration,' Colin
Beresford said suddenly. 'And why wouldn't it? To be kicked out
after all you've done for this force, boss – well, it's a bloody
disgrace.'

'With respect, sir,' said Meadows, 'there are times when you
put the average wild bull in the china shop to shame.'

'And what exactly do you mean by that, Sergeant?' demanded
Beresford.

Paniatowski suppressed a smile. To anyone eavesdropping, she
thought, this would sound like the opening shots in a bloody war,
but it wasn't like that all. It was no more and no less than the
beginning of a ritual in which Meadows took the piss out of
Beresford, he got annoyed, Meadows expressed surprise that he
was annoyed by what had been intended to be a wholly innocent
remark, and Beresford pretended to accept her explanation. It had
been going on for years, and anyone who reached the conclusion
they didn't like each other would be way off the mark.

'You make it sound like the boss was sacked,' Meadows
explained. 'She wasn't. When the Central Lancs force was amal-
gamated with the East Lancs, there were suddenly too many chiefs
and not enough Indians. So somebody had to go, didn't they?'

'I suppose so,' Beresford conceded.

'And it was decided the officers to go would be those who had
put more than their thirty years in,' Meadows concluded.

'And I was one of those ancient lumbering beasts, so I was

culled,' Paniatowski said. 'And, to be fair, they did promote me to superintendent for the last six months, so I'd have a bigger pension.'

'If anybody had to go, it should have been done on the basis of results, rather than years served,' Beresford said.

'In that case, and taking into account my brilliant record, they'd have had me working for them until I was a hundred and six,' Paniatowski retorted, doing her best to lighten the tone of the conversation. 'Besides, it was about time us old ones moved over, and gave the young ones coming up a chance to prove themselves.'

Crane and Meadows openly grinned, and even the outraged Beresford felt the corners of his mouth twitch with amusement.

Paniatowski caught their expressions. 'Oh, for God's sake!' she said exasperatedly. 'Whenever I talk about younger officers do I *have to be* thinking about my daughter?'

'No, but you usually are,' Crane said. 'How's she doing, boss?'

'She's doing fine,' Paniatowski told him. 'She's on a one-year post-graduate course in the States at the moment.' She paused. 'Another ten years and she'll be a chief con. Just you see if she isn't.'

Why do I always sound like a mother hen when I'm talking about Louisa? she wondered.

She supposed the reason lay in the fact that she *was* a mother hen. And not just to her daughter, but to these people, too.

'Where do you two see yourselves going in this new super-force of ours,' she said to Beresford and Meadows. 'Tell me now – before my influence quite fades away – and I'll drop a few words in the right ears.'

Both the inspector and the sergeant looked mildly embarrassed at the suggestion.

'As a matter of fact, I was thinking of putting my papers in myself,' Beresford said.

'Me, too,' Meadows added.

'This isn't anything to do with me leaving?' Paniatowski asked, tremulously.

'Yes, absolutely it is,' Meadows said. 'Without you to hold our hands, we'd be completely lost.' She grinned again. 'Of course that's not the reason, is it, Colin?'

'No,' Beresford agreed. 'Lynn's started to complain about the hours I work, and I can't blame her for that, because I know I'm spending nothing like enough time with the kids.'

'And I want a job in which I can protect people,' Meadows said.

'But you've already got a job like that,' Paniatowski protested. 'It's called, being a police officer.'

Meadows shook her head. 'The people we're usually involved with are beyond help, because they're already bloody well dead,' Meadows countered. 'I want to get into the process at an earlier point. I don't want to avenge the victims – I want to stop them becoming victims in the first place.'

'And what particular job will give you that?' Paniatowski wondered.

Meadows smiled again.

'I quite fancy the idea of being God,' she said, 'but I'm not sure if they accept women for that job.'

It wasn't her best line ever, but when the others dutifully laughed it was clear that it had done what it had intended to, which was to turn down the increasing tension by a notch or two.

They fell into talking about their old investigations – their triumphs and their failures ('Although we've had damn *few* failures,' Beresford pointed out), then, when the lights flashed for drinking-up-time and the landlord put the towels over the pumps, they made their way to the car park, where there were four taxis idling.

'I thought it was best to order them for all of us,' Paniatowski said, 'because there's not one of us – Kate excepted – in a fit state to drive, and the police around here are well-known to be a bunch of right proper bastards.'

'Especially the CID,' Meadows said.

'Oh yes, especially them,' Paniatowski agreed.

As her taxi pulled away, Paniatowski felt a stab of sadness. She'd had no reason for assuming the team would carry on after she'd left, she thought, but she'd harboured a secret hope that like the Temptations and the Drifters, it would survive personnel changes and continue to be – at least in spirit – the team she had created. Instead, even before the seat of her office chair had had time to grow cold, it was already disintegrating.

She was sad, too, on a more personal level, to be saying goodbye to old friends. It wasn't literally goodbye, of course. They'd see each other around, and might even meet up in a pub once in a while. But it wouldn't be the same. Over the years they had learned to trust and respect each other – yes, and even to *love* each other – but it had been their work which bound them together, and once that glue was gone, they'd be like four strangers who just happened to know everything there was to know about each other.

She sighed.

Well, that was that, she told herself.

She'd filled in all the paperwork, signed along countless dotted lines, and her time as a homicide investigator was over.

She was *almost* right.

PART TWO
The Drowning Woman

ONE

Tuesday, 1 February, 2000

The first people to greet the arrival of the new millennium were the inhabitants of The Line Islands (part of Kiribati, population 131,232). A few hours later, the same event was heralded in the Millennium Dome in London by a distinguished company including the queen and the prime minister, who all linked arms and sang 'Auld Lang Syne'. And between and beyond these two points, there were widespread celebrations including firework displays and street parties.

Then dawn came, and it was all over. We were all in the twenty-first century now, and there was nothing to do but learn to get on with it.

Whilst the rest of the month paled in comparison to its beginnings, it was not without some interest. On the sixth of January, Harrison Ford and Julia Roberts were the film stars voted the People's Choices, and Calista Flockhart won the television award. On the thirteenth, Bill Gates stepped down as Chief Executive of Microsoft. On the thirtieth, the St Louis Rams won the Super Bowl, and on the thirty-first, Dr Harold Shipman, Britain's most prolific serial killer, was given a life sentence for the murder of fifteen of his patients (though he may have killed as many as 215).

There were other events which were not considered important enough to merit international coverage, but were nevertheless of great local interest in Lancashire. On the eighteenth, a man was drowned in the Irish Sea off Blackpool, having gone into the water to rescue his dog, which appeared to be having difficulties (the dog, too, drowned). A ten-year-old maths protégée from Preston was informed by Oxford that the university would look forward to seeing her at the start of the Michaelmas Term.

And on the first of February (the month itself being notable as the first of the century to contain twenty-nine days), a well-known businessman in Whitebridge would come to what could only be called a bizarre end.

*　　*　　*

Overcroft House was a substantial detached dwelling dating back
to the early twentieth century. It was located in that area of
Whitebridge which had once been the province of doctors, solicitors and higher-ranking local government officials. Now, virtually
all the detached houses had been broken up into flats, which were
rented by doctor's nurses, solicitors' clerks and town hall
bureaucrats.

Overcroft House had not escaped this process, but its conversion
had been carried out along philanthropic, rather than commercial
lines, and though it admitted to no such thing on the board outside,
it was a shelter for battered wives and their dependent children.

The house had six large bedsits for its 'clients', a communal
kitchen and living space, an examination room, and a warden's
flat and office. There was a garden around the back, with swings
and a sandpit for the children. A doctor made regular visits, a
psychiatrist called by appointment only. There were two part-time
cleaners, though guests were, as much as possible, encouraged to
keep their own area clean. There were also wardens, one of them
part-time. The full-time warden was Kate Meadows, and she was
the only person to have her name on the board outside.

When civic dignitaries and potential donors cornered Meadows at
fundraisers and congratulated her on running such a stressful
operation with apparent equanimity, she usually pasted a modest
smile on top of the fixed look of amiability she had been wearing
since the function began, and said that most people could probably
manage to find the strength to do what positively had to be done.

Only occasionally, when someone like Councilwoman Mrs
Blossom went just too far, did she feel the carefully-applied mask
begin to crack a little. The councilwoman, who had been wearing
an over-elaborate hat which defied the laws of both taste and
gravity, had laid a podgy hand on Meadows' shoulder, and told
her – every word larded with patronising self-importance – that
she thought dear Kate was such a 'brave little thing to take on so
much responsibility'. And Meadows had felt a strong urge to reply
that this was nothing, and that she had once been mistress of a
house designed by John Vanbrugh – that's right, Mrs Blossom,
the John Vanbrugh, architect and playwright, 1644–1726 – which
had had grounds so extensive that they required the full-time
attention of six gardeners. She didn't do it, of course, because

she knew that revealing an aristocratic background would be just as damaging to her career in Overcroft House as revealing a criminal one would be.

And her position there mattered to her. When she'd resigned from the police force (at a time when promotion had been imminent), she'd *expected* her new job would become an important part of her world. But it had very rapidly become much more than that. The work she did in the shelter had become the very keystone of her existence, and without it, she was a woman drowning in the meaninglessness of life.

It was that quiet part of the afternoon, between lunch being cleared away and preparations for tea yet to begin, a time when residents had a light nap or took some air in the garden. For Meadows, it was a chance (grudgingly grasped at) to catch up on paperwork – and that was exactly what she was doing when the door of her office was unceremoniously (and uncharacteristically) flung open, and she looked up to see Lizzie Grimshaw standing there.

According to the records, Lizzie was twenty-one, though she could easily have been taken for much younger. She was also heavily pregnant and expected to give birth soon – which possibly explained the agitated expression on her face.

'Sorry to disturb you, Mrs Maybe,' the young woman gasped.

A flicker of a smile crossed Meadows' face. She had told Lizzie a dozen times that her name was Kate, or – if she insisted on being formal – Ms Meadows, but Lizzie was adamant that if she was called 'Mrs Maybe' on the board outside, it was official, and nothing Kate herself could say would alter that.

Lizzie did not have a lot going for her. She had been ill-educated and ill-used all her life, yet there was a spark in her – a determination to make the best of things – that Meadows couldn't help but admire.

'You've got to do something. Mrs Maybe,' the girl moaned.

'About what?'

'Jane's husband! He's at the front door, trying to knock it down. He told me I had to let him in, and when I said I wasn't allowed, he said I was a stupid little shit, and he'd have me moved to the nuthouse. Can he do that, Mrs Maybe?' Lizzie crossed her arms, put one hand on each shoulder, and hugged herself tightly. 'Can he have me moved to the nuthouse?'

'No, he can't,' Meadows replied.

But she was not sure she was being entirely honest with Lizzie. Of course, Andrew Lofthouse couldn't do it directly, but he was an important man in Whitebridge, and his unseen tentacles could move hundreds of hidden levers.

Meadows switched on the CCTV screen. Lizzie had been quite right. There was Lofthouse, strolling there up and down by the front door – big and square and angry.

This would have to be dealt with – and quickly.

Meadows left the office through the door that accessed her own flat.

'Where are you going?' Lizzie called after her, in a panic.

'I won't be long,' Meadows promised.

If she was going to handle a large, furious man like Lofthouse entirely on her own, she needed to be wearing the right clothes, and she knew, without even stopping to look, that she had nothing suitable. On the other hand, Zelda, her alto ego, would provide her with just what she needed.

She was wearing flat heels that afternoon, but now she shucked them off and selected a pair of high-heeled shoes from what she always thought of as Zelda's midnight collection.

She returned to the office, where Lizzie was still pacing the carpet.

'Where's Jane now?' Meadows asked.

'In the cupboard,' Lizzie said, in a half-moan.

Jesus, that was bad. For a child who felt threatened, a small, enclosed space, shut off from the world, seemed the ideal refuge, but a woman in her late thirties, who'd had a successful business career, really shouldn't feel the need to hide away from her husband in a cupboard.

'There are a lot of cupboards in this house,' she said. 'Which one are we talking about?'

'The one under the stairs.'

Now that really *was* bad. The staircase was in the main hall, which was entered by the front door, on the other side of which stood a furious Andrew Lofthouse. So while there was no logic in choosing *any* of the cupboards to hide in, it was particularly illogical to choose this one. But then it had been primal fear, not rational thought, which had driven her into the deepest, darkest cupboard the house had to offer.

Meadows strode rapidly down the corridor to the central hallway. Her Zelda heels clicked angrily against the marble floor, and the sound bounced back like ricocheting bullets when it hit the ceiling.

And now she could hear two additional noises. The first was a low moaning from somewhere overhead, the second a steady tattoo of impatience being loudly drummed on the door.

She flicked the switch on the entry phone. 'I can't deal with you until I've calmed things down in here, Mr Lofthouse,' she said, 'and the longer you keep hammering on the door, the longer that's going to take me. So it's really up to you, isn't it?'

The banging stopped, but the face on the monitor seemed to swell with rage.

Meadows turned to deal with the moaning, which was emanating from the two women – Lucy and Joyce – and Joyce's three children – Roger, Joan and little Jake – who were all huddled together halfway up the stairs.

A few hours earlier, they had looked like people who were slowly and carefully putting their lives back together again, Meadows thought – now they seemed closer to victims of the Nazis, who had just been herded off the death train on to the platform in a concentration camp, and were awaiting their inevitable fate.

Andrew Lofthouse had a lot to answer for.

'You've nothing to worry about, ladies,' Meadows called up the stairs. 'I can handle it – but first, I need you to take the kids back upstairs.'

The cupboard under the stairs, like most similarly located cupboards – was wedge-shaped. At one end, it was tall enough to store an upright vacuum cleaner. Then, the ceiling immediately began to plunge, so that five feet from its apex, it met the floor.

Jane Lofthouse had managed to squirm and squiggle her way past the brushes, mops and cleaning materials, and was lying in a space so tight that with the back of her head touching the floor, her nose brushed against the ceiling every time she moved.

'What are you doing there, Jane?' Meadows whispered, and she was not faking the concern in her voice – not even a little bit.

'He's outside,' Jane moaned. 'He's going to get into the house, and he's going to hurt me badly.'

'He can't get in,' Meadows promised her. 'Why don't you go up to your room and have a little rest?'

'No!' Jane said, and she shook her head so violently that she hit the ceiling three or four times, and caused a fine white powder-dust to hover like an aura around her skull. 'No,' she repeated, 'my room is all that I have left – the only thing in the whole world that's *mine*. If he hurts me in my room, it won't *be* mine anymore. So let him punish me down here if he wants to – but I'm not going upstairs.'

'You're upsetting Lizzie, you know,' Meadows said, with just a hint of severity in her tone. 'You *do* know that, don't you?'

'No, I . . .'

'She's waiting to go upstairs with you. Please don't make her any more distressed than she already is.'

'All right,' Jane agreed miserably. She began the slow, undignified process of backing out around bottles of cleaning fluid and wellington boots. 'But you can't let him in. You have to promise me, you won't let him in.'

As Meadows helped her to her feet, she was shocked by how fragile Jane felt, and how old she had suddenly become. Even her smell had changed, and she was emanating the odour of a wounded creature which cannot work out how or why this horrible thing has happened, but knows that death is just awaiting the signal to come and collect her.

'Take her arm,' Meadows whispered to Lizzie Grimshaw. 'Help her upstairs.' But before she let go of Jane's arm herself, she said, 'I need you to tell me you don't want to see him – if that *is* how you feel.'

'I was hiding in the cupboard from him!' Jane exclaimed. 'Doesn't that tell you *anything?*'

'Yes, it does, but I'm afraid that isn't enough,' Meadows said. 'If I'm to be on solid legal ground when I talk to him, I need you to be more explicit.'

Jane nodded weakly, and that part of her brain which still remembered being a logical businesswoman made her say, 'I do not want to see my husband under any circumstances. Is that good enough?'

'It's good enough,' Meadows confirmed.

She waited until the two women had turned the bend in the stairs before she approached the front door.

'Take six steps backwards, please, Mr Lofthouse,' she said to the outline on the other side of the frosted glass.

'I need to talk to my wife,' Lofthouse replied, 'so just open the door and let me in.'

'It doesn't work like that,' Meadows told him. 'Before anything else can happen, you have to talk to me – and before you talk to me, you have to take six steps away from this door.'

There was a hesitation on the other side, then she both heard Lofthouse's angry footfalls on the gravel and read his angry body language as he followed her instructions.

She counted out his six steps, and then she opened the door, though keeping the chain in place.

'I'm not talking to you through a gap,' Lofthouse said. 'I've done what you asked of me, and now I want something in return – which is to speak to you face-to-face.'

'Do I have your word that you won't try to force your way into here if I give you the chance?' Meadows asked.

'Well, of course you've got my word,' Lofthouse replied, exasperated. 'What kind of man do you think I am?'

I think you're the kind who beats his wife, Meadows said silently.

But she opened the door anyway, and they got their first proper look at each other.

He was about the same age as his wife, Meadows thought. He seemed intelligent, dynamic and sporty. What he did *not* look was sensitive, but, even so, anyone who didn't know the Lofthouses well would have taken them for the perfect golden couple.

'Six weeks ago, my wife left our house without so much as a word,' Lofthouse said. 'Anything could have happened to her, and I've been frantic with worry.'

'So why didn't you report it to the police?'

'And make myself a laughing stock? Tell the whole world that I'm a man who has no control over his own wife? No, thank you!'

'If you didn't report it, you can't have been *that* concerned,' Meadows said.

'I still wouldn't know where she was if some thoughtful soul hadn't slipped an anonymous letter in my postbox,' Lofthouse said, ignoring the comment. 'So now I've finally tracked her down, and I want to talk to her.'

'She doesn't want to talk to you,' Meadows replied. 'She's been quite clear about that.'

'And why is that? Is it because you've told her not to – because you've been poisoning her mind against me?'

'No,' Meadows said.

'I don't believe you!'

Meadows shrugged. 'Please yourself what you believe. I only give advice when I'm asked for it, and Jane hasn't asked for any.'

'You are seriously trying to tell me that you're capable of keeping that big fat mouth of yours shut?' Lofthouse asked disbelievingly.

'I'll say this once more,' Meadows told him, with an edge to her voice. 'I didn't give Jane any advice because she never asked for any – but if she *had* asked, I'd have told her to steer well clear of you.'

'Because you think she's a battered wife?'

'Because I *know* she's a battered wife.'

'I've no idea why she should want to tell you such a ludicrous story, but it's simply not true,' Lofthouse said.

'I've seen the bruises,' Meadows countered.

'Oh, I see! You've seen the bruises! And do you know how she got those bruises?' Lofthouse asked, with a supercilious sneer.

'No, so why don't you tell me?' Meadows suggested.

The sneer disappeared like magic.

He thinks he's just made a big mistake! Meadows thought. He's decided he's lost control of this confrontation – that he's given away too much information.

But too much information about what?

'Well, how *did* Jane get those bruises?' she said, to pressurize him.

'They . . . they were self-inflicted,' Lofthouse said uncomfortably.

But Meadows was both an ex-policewoman and a practicing sadomasochist, and she knew the difference between injuries that were self-inflicted and those that weren't.

'There seems very little point in continuing this discussion,' she told Lofthouse.

But he was not a man to give up easily, and the message coming from his cold hard eyes was that he was searching his brain for a new basis on which to launch a verbal attack which would make her crumble.

There was a horrid fascination in watching his mental processes at work.

He ran his eyes quickly up and down her body.

Were there any physical defects he could exploit?

No, her figure was neat, and her face, whilst unconventional, was certainly attractive and could almost be described as beautiful. Besides, even if she had defects, it was obvious from the way she held herself that she was comfortable enough in her own skin for that not to bother her.

Then his glance fell on the brass plaque which was fixed to the wall, next to the doorbell, and a look of almost demonic happiness came to his face.

Overcroft House
Residential Accommodation
Warden: Ms Kate Meadows, MBE
Visits by appointment only

'Is that you?' he asked. 'Ms Kate Meadows, MBE.'

'Yes,' Kate agreed.

He was an intelligent man, but not an imaginative one, and she could almost hear the gears in his brutish brain meshing.

People like her treasure their decorations above all else, he was telling himself. Destroy her belief in its value, and you destroy her own sense of self-worth.

He didn't know – how could he? – that Kate had only accepted the medal because she could see its potential as a fundraising tool for the shelter. He didn't know – because she'd taken pains to hide it from everyone – that she was an 'honourable' by birth and a countess by virtue of a short unhappy marriage.

'I know so many women like you,' he said, 'women who self-lessly dedicate themselves to good works for twenty or thirty years. But it's not selfless at all, is it? Because all that time you spend scrubbing the floors and cleaning up other people's shit, you're praying that one day a letter will arrive inviting you down to Buckingham Palace, to meet the queen. And when it does come, it makes all the work you'd put into your job – all the suffering, all the dispiriting moments – finally seem worthwhile, doesn't it?'

'You're wasting your breath,' she said.

And there must have been real conviction in the words, because for a moment he hesitated. Then, his own self-belief – his own arrogance – was back in control again.

'The great day finally arrived,' Lofthouse continued, in an almost dreamy voice. 'You were whisked to Buckingham Palace to see

the queen. You joined an excited line of people, and when it came
to your turn, she pinned the medal on you herself. Did she say
anything?'

'Yes,'

'What did she say?'

'She asked me if I'd come far.'

'Well, that was nice of her, wasn't it?'

Oh, you bastard, Meadows thought.

'Yes,' she said, looking down at the ground – playing along
with his game.

'And was the Duke of Edinburgh with her?'

'Yes.'

'Did he speak to you?'

Yes, he'd reminded Meadows of the great fun they'd had the
last time they'd met, at a rather prestigious shoot in the Scottish
Highlands.

'No, he didn't speak to me,' she said aloud.

'How long did your visit to the queen last? Twenty seconds?'

'A bit more than that.'

'Let's call it thirty then. If you like, we'll even call it forty. Was
it any longer than that?'

'No.'

'So that's what your lifetime of effort is worth – forty seconds
of their time. And what does that make your precious medal
worth?'

'The medal has its uses,' Meadows said.

'I have an *OBE* myself,' Lofthouse said. 'That's superior to
your medal – and I didn't have to clean out a single stinking toilet
to get that.'

Meadows smiled. 'Well, as long as it makes you happy.'

'Don't pretend it doesn't hurt that I've made you realize how
unimportant you are,' Lofthouse said, furious that his attack was
failing to produce the response he wanted.

'Only people who are really unimportant care about how
unimportant they are,' Meadows told him.

'I can't believe it,' Lofthouse said. 'You're lecturing me, aren't
you?'

Meadows shrugged. 'Well, somebody has to.'

'How would you react if I pushed you out of the way, and went
to see my wife?' Lofthouse demanded.

'I suppose I'd be rather disappointed that you hadn't kept your word.'

'I can live with disappointing a little guttersnipe like you,' Lofthouse snarled. 'So, would you only be disappointed, or would you actually try to do something about it?'

'I'd phone the police.'

'And they'd send round a couple of PC Plods. The plods would ask me for an explanation, and I'd put them in touch with some very high-ranking policemen who happen to be members of my lodge – and that would be the end of that.' He smirked. 'So when you think about it, if you want to prevent me getting in, you're going to have to stop me yourself.'

'I know that,' Meadows told him. 'I've known that since I first opened the door.'

Lofthouse stroked his chin. 'I'm the specified six steps from the door, and you're right in front of it. What you have to ask yourself now is whether you can get inside and slam the safety chain in place before I reach you. Because if you can't – and we both know you can't – I just might hurt you. It will be accidental, of course, but that won't make it any less painful. Do you understand what I'm saying?'

'You're making a mistake,' she said, 'because instead of you hurting me, I might hurt you.'

Such a ridiculous statement obviously called for a dramatic response, and Lofthouse was more than willing to provide one. He threw back his head and roared with laughter at her pathetic attempt to frighten him, just as she'd known he would, and while he was posed in this theatrical position, Meadows made her move, turning sharply back into the house.

His roar changed from amusement to anger, and he flung himself at the door and managed to wedge his foot in the gap between the door and the jamb.

They were both pushing against the door, but Lofthouse had the weight, and the outcome was inevitable.

'If you want to know what a battered woman looks like, you'll only have to look in the mirror,' Lofthouse hissed.

His foot was still in the gap, and Meadows brought the heel of her shoe hard down on it. Once she felt it make contact, she began to rotate her knee and ankle, like a one-legged dancer doing the twist. It was a vigorous movement, and any normal heel would probably have buckled, but this was one of Zelda's shoes, and had been built to withstand such treatment.

Lofthouse howled with pain, and stopped pushing. Then, slowly and carefully, he withdrew his foot.

When Meadows opened the door, she saw he was hopping on one leg and holding the injured foot in his hand. He was probably finished, she thought, but it was better to be safe than sorry, and kicked him in the groin. Fresh waves of agony crossed his face, and he crashed to the ground in a most satisfactory manner.

Meadows admired her handiwork for a second, and then, seeing an old couple observing her over the fence, she called to them, 'Maybe next time he'll remember to use the tradesmen's entrance.'

She smiled at them, to show she was joking.

They did not smile back.

TWO

M eadows had first met Jane Lofthouse at a charity function for Overcroft House, when she was still Jane Bright.

'She started out with nothing, you know,' one of the shelter's board of governors had told Kate, as the attractive, smartly dressed (and obviously energetic) Bright appeared in the doorway of the reception room. 'Absolutely nothing! And look at her now – barely thirty, and she runs her own company.'

Yes, back then, she had been so confident and self-assured that she had almost made Meadows feel like a shrinking violet.

Yet what a change a few years of marriage to the wrong man had wrought. The confidence had gone, and it was difficult to accept that the Jane back then, and the Jane who had her face buried in Lizzie's shoulder, were the same person.

Equally remarkable was the change the situation had brought about in Lizzie. In the previous few minutes she had acquired a strength Meadows would never have believed she was capable of, and the thin waif seemed perfectly comfortable with being the rock to which Jane could anchor herself.

Lizzie looked up. 'Has he gone?' she asked.

'He's gone,' Meadows confirmed.

'You're sure?'

'I'm sure.'

And so she was – from the safety of the house she had tracked his progress as he hobbled down the path, climbed awkwardly into his Rolls-Royce, and drove away.

Jane abandoned the security of Lizzie's shoulder, and looked up. Her eyes were bloodshot, her face had all but collapsed.

'You've only made matters worse,' she moaned. 'I know you didn't mean to, but you have.'

'You need to calm down, Jane,' Meadows said soothingly.

'You don't know him,' Jane said, on the verge of hysteria. 'When he's defied, he goes into a black rage – and he stays like that until he's had his revenge.' She sobbed. 'So he'll be back.'

'The first thing in the morning, we'll get a restraining order sworn out,' Meadows promised.

'It won't happen,' Jane said, fatalistically. 'Andrew has a lot more influence in this town than you could even begin to imagine.'

This was a familiar scene being played out in front of her, Meadows thought. Over time, battered wives often grew to think of themselves as more and more useless, while their oppressors grew into supermen who could never be defeated.

'Your husband's not the only one with influence in this town,' she said. 'He may know which levers to pull, but I was a police officer for a long time, and I know where the bodies are buried. If I want a restraining order, I'll *get* a restraining order.'

For the briefest of moments, there was a flicker of hope in Jane's eyes, then it died and she said, 'It will be too late then. He'll come for me tonight – I know he will. And this time, he won't hold back. This time, he won't stop until he's killed me.'

'He won't be able to get in,' Meadows said.

'He'll find a way,' Jane moaned. 'He *always* finds a way.'

'This is the safest building in Whitebridge,' Kate Meadows promised. 'The glass is bulletproof. The locks on the doors are top-of-the-range. Everything is wired up, so that if anyone breaks in, the police are informed immediately, and they have strict instructions to make this call their number one priority.'

Jane still did not look convinced.

'There's only one way of getting in or out without setting off all the alarms, and for that you need the right key,' Meadows continued. 'There are only two copies of that key. One of them is in the bank, and the other –' she reached for the chain around her neck, and hauled up the key which had been resting between her breasts – 'is here.'

'It's no consolation to me if he can't make his escape after he's killed me,' Jane said miserably.

'Stop feeling so sorry for yourself!' screamed the Black Beast, from the dark void at the very edge of Meadows' soul.

She wanted to grab Jane and shake her. Wanted to tell her that she was not the first woman to suffer like this – that the young Kate's situation had been even worse, but she had fought back and *kept* fighting back, right up to the point at which Clifford had his unfortunate accident.

But that would never do, because these were the Beast's words, not hers, and she had long ago decided that she would no longer allow him to speak for her.

'Maybe if you inspected the security arrangements yourself you might feel a little more confident,' she suggested.

A spark of interest came into Jane's eye – perhaps even a spark of hope.

'I'll get Hadley's to check them out,' she said. 'They could be here within the hour.'

Meadows whistled softly to herself. Talk about aiming high, she thought. Hadley Security was acknowledged to be the best security company in the whole of the north-west. She had tried to employ them herself, but they had demanded a king's ransom before they even walked through the door, and appealing to the philanthropic side of their nature had been a total waste of time.

'You might think of contacting some other firm,' she said cautiously, 'but whatever company you do end up with will probably not consider this an emergency, so you'll have to wait three or four days at a minimum.'

If she'd thought about it, she could probably have come up with two or three possible ways Jane might react to this last statement.

She might have simply shrugged, as if to say, oh well, it was just a thought.

She could have felt crushed, because she'd made a huge effort to be positive, only to have Meadows dismiss it as totally impractical.

Or she could have been angry – with either the security company or Meadows – that they should choose to act like the Levite or priest in the parable of the Good Samaritan, and ignore the fact that she was desperately in need of help.

Meadows would not have been surprised by any of these reactions. What did surprise her was that Jane laughed.

And it wasn't a hysterical laugh – it came from deep in the lungs and showed nothing but genuine amusement.

'My God, you don't know much about business, do you?' she asked.

'I've had no complaints about the way I run this place,' Meadows said, and was shocked to hear a note of petulance in her voice.

Jane noticed it, too, and the slightly mocking amusement drained from her face.

'Look, I wasn't meaning to insult you,' she said. 'You've saved my life here, and I'm sure I'm not the only one. I admire you tremendously, and I'll be grateful to you until the day I die.'

'But . . .?' Meadows asked, because with that kind of sentence there usually was a 'but' hiding somewhere under the clichés.

'But you can't even begin to imagine what's it's like to build a business like mine. It involves developing a complex web of understandings and treaties, an intimate skein of duties and obligations. When I get on the phone to Jim Hadley, he'll agree to help me. We're part of the same tribe, and if he doesn't owe me, he owes someone else who does. So trust me on this – he'll be here.'

She'd transformed herself, in just a few seconds, from a total wreck into a near force of nature. It was almost a miracle, but miracles rarely happened, and chances were, it wasn't so much a transformation as a flashback, which would probably be gone as quickly as it had arrived.

A minor miracle *did* occur about an hour later, when a van from Hadley Security pulled up outside, and the man who had been driving it announced himself to Meadows as Jim Hadley, the founder of the empire.

He was a middle-aged man of average height and average build. His hair was a nondescript brown, and he had the sort of facial features that you tended to forget the moment he'd turned his back on you.

'I'm surprised you came yourself,' Meadows said. 'Are you a close friend of Jane's?'

'Or just a member of the same tribe,' she added silently.

Hadley gave her an embarrassed shrug. 'I'm not really what you might call a friend,' he said. 'I'd run into her at the golf club dinner or my lodge's ladies' night, and we always got on well, but I'd say we were never more than acquaintances.'

'So what made you drop everything and rush over?'

Hadley shrugged again. 'Well, you know . . .'

'No, I don't,' Meadows confessed, 'not really.'

'I suppose I felt guilty.'

'About what?'

'Like I said, I wasn't that close to Jane – but I was close enough to guess what was going on.'

'So you knew she was getting beaten up by her husband?'

'Yes.'

'But you didn't do anything about it.'

'I wasn't the only one, you know,' Hadley said, with a sudden hint of aggression in his voice. 'Everybody could see that was happening, and nobody did anything about it. When all's said and done, what *could* we do?'

He was right, Meadows thought. There were only two possible ways to handle that kind of situation – counsel the victim or report the whole thing to the police. But if you weren't on close terms with the woman already, how the hell did you even begin that conversation? And if the victim seemed to be going along with what was happening to her, what was the point in telling the cops about it, since they could do nothing without the victim's cooperation?

It was a common enough story, but no less depressing, for all that.

'I'm sorry if I seemed to be criticizing you, Mr Hadley,' Meadows said. 'I know there's very little you can do in a situation like that.'

'Think nothing of it,' Hadley said, cheerful enough now.

'But I would appreciate it if you'd do your best to assure Jane that she's safe here.'

'I'll do more than just assure her,' Hadley said. 'I'll go over this place from top to bottom and make *sure* it's safe.'

At half-past seven, Mary Barnes, the assistant warden arrived, carrying a bag which contained her overnight toiletries and her pyjamas.

'It's not often you go out on a Tuesday, boss,' she said.

'I know I don't,' Meadows agreed, 'and I'm sorry to give you so little notice, but I've had a rough day, and I feel like a change.'

'Oh, don't worry about that,' Mary said cheerily. 'I need all the overtime I can get, because our Rose is off to college in September, and even though she'll get a student loan, we'll still have to cough up a fair amount of dosh.' She paused for a moment, then, with an edge of concern creeping into her voice, asked, 'So what was particularly rough about today?'

'Jane's husband turned up,' Meadows said.

Mary nodded. 'Ah!'

But now she thought about it, Meadows couldn't quite see why that had made the day particularly difficult. True, there had been violence, but violence was nothing new to her – she had once been attacked by three lorry drivers, and they'd been the ones who ended up in hospital – and it never left her feeling this kind of lethargic pessimism. True, also, that she'd had two hysterical, terrified women on her hands, but that was really part and parcel of running the shelter.

No, the problem was that she simply couldn't shake off the feeling that something terrible was about to happen – something that would destroy the life she had known and come to depend on.

'Don't go nipping out for a quick drink while I'm out,' Meadows said.

It was a joke, a weak one, but nonetheless still a joke, and it was designed to lighten the mood. They both knew Mary would not leave the building for any reason, because unless you had the master key, it was easy enough to exit through the fire door, but impossible to get back in again. Besides which, as Meadows had explained to Jane earlier, the very act of leaving the house would literally set alarm bells ringing in police headquarters.

'I really can't imagine what you get up to on these nights out of yours,' Mary said, '"but if you can't be good, be careful"!'

Another attempt at humour, so maybe Mary, too, had a sense of the overhanging doom.

'I'll be careful,' Meadows promised.

She always was. She had become an expert at detecting situations which might turn nasty, and even better at backing away from them. She never began without firmly establishing a safe word. And she never went to a club near home, because she knew better than to shit in her own backyard.

Tonight, however, she might break one of those rules, because she was too tired and dispirited to drive all way to Bolton or Preston in search of pain, and she had heard that there was a club right there in Whitebridge which might serve her needs.

She picked up the bag in which Zelda and her instruments lived.

'I'll see you in the morning, Mary,' she said.

She was already feeling a little better, and if fate was laughing mockingly in her ear, she didn't hear it.

THREE

Monika Paniatowski and her daughter, Louisa (née Rutter, and now, for professional reasons, Rutter again) were sitting at the kitchen table they had shared when Louisa was a child. There were two bottles on the table, one a Polish vodka for Monika, and the other a Spanish brandy for Louisa. It seemed strange to some people that these should be their drinks of choice, since Monika had left Poland when she was four (and never returned) and Louisa hadn't set foot in Spain (the birthplace of her long dead natural mother) until she was fifteen. But it made sense to *them*. In a way, they were both orphans, and the drinks brought them a little closer to the past they had been denied.

The conversation that evening (and indeed all the evenings they spent together), focussed on the old days – Louisa's first crush on a boy who didn't seem to even know she existed; the holiday in Spain with Uncle Charlie and Louisa's Spanish family, after which the daughter had helped the mother to solve a murder; the way the arrival of the two totally unplanned baby boys had disrupted their lives . . .

What they did *not* discuss was the daughter's work. From Louisa's side, this was because she wasn't *allowed* to discuss most of it with a woman who, despite her past service, was now no more than a civilian. From Monika's side, it was because she didn't want to appear the old hand judging the work of a younger, less-experienced officer. And sometimes (she admitted to herself) she kept quiet because she would hate to seem like a dinosaur, blundering its way ignorantly through the intricacies of modern policing.

At eight o'clock, Louisa glanced down at her watch and said, 'Derek's picking me up in about fifteen minutes.'

'You don't normally leave this early,' Monika said, trying not to sound disappointed.

'Derek's got a business meeting in Seattle tomorrow, and I'm driving him down to Manchester Airport.'

'I thought he drove himself, and left his car in the airport parking,' Monika said, trying not to sound like the nosy mother-in-law.

'He does normally do that,' Louisa agreed. 'But my car's in for repairs, so I'll need his Jag, and it wouldn't be much use to me if it was left in Manchester.'

'Would you like to drop in for a nightcap on your way home?' Monika asked hopefully. 'I'll still be up.'

Louisa shook her head. 'I've got an exceptionally early start tomorrow.'

'Oh? Why's that?' Monika asked. 'Something special happening?'

And she was thinking, 'There you go breaking your own first rule, Monika.'

'Not exactly special, no,' Louisa said. 'The chief con is off in the Caribbean. He's supposed to be advising his opposite numbers over there on how to do their jobs – but I'm betting most of his advice will be dispensed on the golf course. As for the deputy chief – he's been rushed into hospital with a burst appendix. So what that means is that one of the chief superintendents has to take charge – and I was the one sitting in the chair when the bottle stopped spinning.'

'What about your assistant chief cons?' Monika wondered.

Louisa laughed. 'Assistant chief cons?' she repeated. 'What assistant chief cons?'

'I don't know, but surely you must have . . .'

'We got rid of them during the last reorganization. It's all in the interest of "economy and efficiency". This is the new, streamlined police force. Chief supers are now the third tier of management, and whenever the first two tiers can't fulfil the function they're overpaid for, we're expected to step in.'

Paniatowski chuckled.

'What's funny?' Louisa asked.

'The fact that you grumble about having the job foisted on you, when secretly, you're as chuffed as little apples.'

'Yes, I am pleased – in a way,' said Louisa, sounding a little shamefaced at being found out. 'I'll enjoy the work, and it will be good training for the role I eventually hope to fill – but what I *don't* appreciate is people like the chief con avoiding doing the job they're paid to do.'

Monika tried to avoid smiling again, but a smile inevitably crept to the corners of her mouth.

'Has something else amused you, Mum?' Louisa asked, and there was no annoyance in her voice, only curiosity.

'Sort of,' Monika admitted. 'I was just contrasting the way of the two of us approach the job.'

'And how do we differ?' Louisa asked, treating it as a game, while suspecting it might be more than that.

'Well, I can't know for sure, because I've not been there since your rise to eminence, but I see you as being a bit like an admiral, preparing for battle,'

'Go on,' Louisa said, and now she was grinning,

'You stand on the deck of the flagship, and you take in the whole scene – the deployment of your own forces, and the enemy's forces, the weather, strategies the enemy has used in the past, the effectiveness of our big guns as compared to their big guns – and until you've got a complete picture, you won't even think of making a move.'

'And how were you different, Mother dear?'

'I was a little less cautious,' Monika said.

Louisa's grin widened. 'You can say that again! If I'm an admiral, then you were a bloody *buccaneer*. You'd be as likely to board a ship from a swinging rope as walk up the gangplank. And a lot of the time you wouldn't know *what* you were doing there, only that something on this particular ship didn't *feel* quite right.'

'That's true enough,' Monika admitted.

'It's ironic really, when you consider that the reason I was so keen to join the force was because I wanted to be just like you. It didn't take me long to realize I wasn't. I was competent at questioning witnesses and interrogating suspects, but I had no real flair for it, and I didn't enjoy it at all. And you're right – I couldn't wait to get out of the longboat and on to the quarterdeck. But neither is better than the other. Sometimes your kind of bobby will find the treasure, and sometimes my kind will – so there's room for both kinds of policing,'

Maybe there was, Monika thought, but there were a lot less buccaneers around now than there were when she joined the force.

Louisa glanced down at her watch again.

'There's something else I wanted to talk about,' she said. 'Actually, I should have raised it earlier.'

Her tone was casual, the words innocent, yet Monika felt a shiver run down her spine.

'Go on,' she said.

'Do you remember the annex we built on the garden side of the house?'

'Of course I remember it,' Monika said. 'I'm not quite senile yet, you know.'

'It's rather nice, isn't it?'

'It's *very* nice.'

'Didn't you wonder why we had it built?'

Yes, I did, as a matter of fact, Monika said silently. I *was* rather hoping that you'd had it built to accommodate the nanny you'd need when you had children. I'm *still* hoping that, even as your biological clock makes it less and less probable.

'Did you wonder?' Louisa persisted.

'Not really,' Monika lied. 'I just assumed you needed more living space.'

'We had it built then because we thought we might need it in the future, and now Derek thinks the time is right.'

'So you *are* planning to have babies,' Monika gushed. 'I didn't say anything before, because I didn't want to pressure you, but I can't tell you how happy you've made me – even if you have left it a bit late.'

Louisa looked shocked, then confused, then embarrassed,

'We . . . we had it built for you, Mum,' Louisa said awkwardly. 'Derek's asked me to ask you to move in with us.'

A studied response – a tactful one – was called for here, Monika thought, perhaps something along the lines of; 'It's really very kind of Derek to make the offer, but it wouldn't be fair on him to have the mother-in-law living so close.'

That was what it sounded like while it was in her head. What she actually heard herself say – in a voice so rasping and tremulous that she hardly recognized it as her own – was, 'No!'

'Derek really wants you there,' Louisa told her. 'He'd never have made the offer if he hadn't.'

'It's a granny flat,' the wildcat running around Monika's brain hissed, 'and I'm not a granny!'

Did she sound bitter? It was hard not to. She so desperately wanted to be a grandmother, but Derek and Louisa had ruled themselves out, Thomas couldn't have children without breaking his vows, and as for Philip – well, it would be at least ten years before he was free to even take the first basic steps.

'Was I a good mother?' she asked.

Louisa paused for perhaps half a heartbeat before saying, 'You were a *loving* mother. I couldn't have asked for a more loving mother.'

'Answer the question?' Monika said.

'And you were an understanding one,' Louisa said. 'All my friends were always complaining that their mothers never listened to them, but you listened to me, when you were there.'

When you were there!

Aye, there's the rub.

'I know I didn't spend enough time with you . . .' she began.

'You did what you could,' Louisa interrupted. 'Look, Mum, if you hadn't cared about your job so much, you wouldn't be the person you are – and I love that person. For God's sake, I followed in your footsteps, didn't I?'

No, you didn't, Monika thought. Not really. We might both have served in the police, but you're much more detached than I could ever be.

'I'm sorry,' she said aloud. 'I should never have put you in such an awkward position.'

'It's all right, Mum,' Louisa assured her. 'Think nothing of it.'

'You're very nice to your old mum,' Monika said humbly.

But there was a voice in her head screaming, 'Why won't you give me grandchildren I could help to bring up? I'd do better next time.'

A car horn hooted in the street.

'I have to go,' Louisa said.

'Isn't Derek coming in?' Paniatowski asked, because he always spent a few minutes with her when he came to pick his wife up.

'We daren't risk it,' Louisa told her. 'If there's a traffic jam on the motorway, he could miss his plane.' She stood up, kissed her mother on the cheek and headed to the door. 'You will think about what I said, won't you?' she asked, before stepping outside.

'Yes, I will,' Monika replied, knowing that she didn't mean it, and that Louisa would know that, too.

The kitchen door closed. Louisa had hardly touched the brandy, probably wise, since she would have to drive back from Manchester. When Monika lifted the vodka bottle from the ice bucket, however, she saw she was already well passed her daily ration.

'You don't mind if I have another one, do you?' she asked the kitchen wall.

And since the wall seemed to have no objections, she poured herself a generous shot.

Everyone experienced losses in their lives, she thought, and she'd had at least her fair share: there'd been her father, an officer in the Polish cavalry, who had led a gloriously insane charge against Hitler's tanks; there'd been her mother, whose heart had been broken as she had looked on helplessly while her second husband had sexually assaulted her daughter; Bob Rutter, her lover and also Louisa's father, who had sacrificed his own life to save the reputation of their beloved boss, Charlie Woodend; Charlie himself, who had retired to Spain and whose comforting presence she still missed . . .

She shouldn't complain. If she hadn't always had a happy life, she'd at least had an eventful one. And though many waves of misery and despair had washed over her, they seemed like no more than ripples when held up against her precious moments of joy.

Her retirement, though not sought, had been productive. She worked hard for several charities, lectured in schools and institutions and had become a ferocious bridge player.

So what did she want in the years left to her?

She wanted grandchildren!

Well, it had now been clearly established that wasn't going to happen.

A lover, then?

She had had several affairs since Bob's death, but fate had always determined that they should not flourish, and though, at the time, she had felt bitter regret, she could feel no such regret looking back.

So things had worked out about as well as they could have been expected to.

But late at night, alone in her bed, she would catch herself wishing that she could lead just one more major investigation.

It was just a fantasy, she told herself. It was never going to happen.

Yet not four miles from her house, Kate Meadows, a.k.a. Zelda, was walking down an alley leading to a nondescript door, which was the entrance to a place its clients called the Hellfire Club. And every step she took was a step closer to making Monika's dream a reality.

FOUR

The door was in the alley that ran alongside the direct-sale carpet warehouse, and standing in front of the door was a man.

He was big.

Actually, big was a bit of an understatement, Meadows thought.

He had a head the size of a blacksmith's anvil, and shoulders as wide as a corporation bus. The only thing covering his hairy chest was an open leather jacket from which hung a series of heavy chains. He had a shaven head, and several of his teeth were missing. As a living advertisement for the Hellfire Club, he was more of a deterrent than an inducement – and perhaps that was just what the management intended him to be.

Meadows walked towards him with a slinky swagger. He didn't move – showed no sign that he'd even seen her approaching. She came to a halt in front of him – God, he *was* big – and slotted a cigarette in her mouth.

'Got a light?' she asked.

'I don't smoke,' the man said. 'And neither should you. It's bad for you.'

The words sounded convincing enough, but the fact that he had a cigarette smouldering in his right hand seemed to suggest that he wasn't being entirely truthful.

'I want to come in,' Meadows said.

'Into where?' the man asked.

'Into the club.'

'What club?'

'Don't piss me about,' Meadows said, in a voice which nicely combined exasperation and menace.

The man looked her up and down.

She was wearing her outrageous purple wig, and heavy make-up around the eyes. For her outfit she had selected a tight leather corset, a black skirt and the shoes she had been wearing in her encounter with Lofthouse.

It was clear that he liked what he saw, but not enough to grant her *carte blanche*.

'I've not seen you round here before,' he said.

'Around where?'

'Around the club.'

'Ah, so now there *is* a club.'

'The thing is, the management's a bit cagey about me letting in people I don't know,' the bouncer said.

'Maybe you *do* know me, if only by reputation,' she suggested. 'My name, once darkness has fallen, is Zelda.'

The bouncer whistled. 'Well, I've certainly heard of her, but, you know, you don't look anything like how I expected her to look.'

Meaning he would have expected someone well over the minimum height for a policewoman – someone a little less elfin.

'I'm Zelda,' Meadows repeated, flatly – as if she found the conversation both boring and unnecessary.

The bouncer chuckled, 'Nice try, love, but Zelda is a bit of a legend on the circuit, and—'

'I'll stay here until somebody comes along who can identify me,' Meadows said, 'and when they do, you'll have to let me in, won't you?'

'I suppose I would – if that was what actually happened,' the bouncer conceded.

'But before I go inside, I'll make you get down on your knees and lick my shoes clean.'

A look of excitement came to the bouncer's eyes.

'But you won't enjoy it, because I'll order you not to,' Meadows said harshly. 'And if I do that, you'll never dare to, will you?'

'Do you really think you could make me go down on my knees?' the bouncer repeated, fighting back valiantly.

'I know I could,' the petite woman said with absolute certainty. 'And you know it, too.'

The bouncer bit his lip, then forced a smile to his face, as if to indicate they were old friends, and none of this had been any more than merry banter.

'In you go, Zelda,' he said, indicating the door with one of his great thick thumbs.

'Who do I pay?' Meadows asked.

'There's a bucket just inside,' the bouncer said. 'You're supposed to put twenty-five quid in – but why don't you have this one on me?'

'I'll pay my own way,' Meadows told him, reaching into the concealed pocket in her wig, where she kept her cash.

The club ran the length of the cellar under the carpet salesroom, and was mostly lit by subdued lighting. There must have been ventilation of some sort, but it was of the minimal kind, and the walls dripped with condensation. Nobody there seemed to mind the oppressive, sticky heat, because if it was a cosy, comfortable evening you were after, there was always the Prince Albert bar of the Royal Victoria, and down here they liked it a little rougher.

Meadows walked over to the bar. The counter area was bathed – though perhaps drenched would have been a better word – in a harsh purple light which was the product of a dozen naked neon tubes. The barman himself looked surprisingly ordinary, but may have had hidden depths of kinkiness.

'I'll have a double whiskey,' Meadows told him.

She had no intention of drinking any of it, but if she'd ordered a fruit juice, chances were she'd have scared off any potential partners for the evening.

The barman poured the drink, and quoted her a price which, not too long ago, would have been enough to buy a terraced house in some parts of Whitebridge.

'I'll pay for the lady's drink,' a man's voice said, 'if that's all right with the lady.'

She turned to look at him. He was tall and well-muscled, and, if his bare chest was anything to go, not overly hairy. He was wearing a velvet mask which covered everything but his eyes and mouth, and based on what she could see of him she judged him to be in his late thirties. In a more conventional relationship, the age gap would probably have mattered, but in the world of pain it was how you inflicted or bore suffering that mattered.

'It's all right with me,' she told him.

'Why don't we go into one of the alcoves and talk about what we're going to do to each other,' he said, when he'd bought the drink.

'You want to *plan* it out?' she asked.

He nodded. 'I like to know where we're going, and anticipation is half of the pleasure.'

'Fair enough,' she agreed.

He walked with a slight limp, she noted, but she suspected it was less a disability and more as a result of a recent injury.

When they sat down in the alcove, he said, 'Tell me about yourself.'

This was starting to feel wrong. That wasn't one of the questions he should be asking, and his voice sounded unnatural, as if he was doing his best to disguise it.

'I don't like to get personal,' she told him. 'My name's Zelda. That's all you need to know.'

'So I wonder what you do for a living,' the man continued, as if she'd never spoken. 'I'd guess you were some kind of social worker.'

Meadows stood up. 'Thanks for the drink, but I think we've gone as far together as we're going,' she said.

The man grabbed her arm, and held it in a tight grip. 'Sit down again,' he rasped.

'You're hurting me,' Meadows told him.

'I thought that's what you were here for,' the man replied.

'Not that kind of pain – and if you don't let go, I'll hurt you a lot more than you're hurting me.'

The man released his grip. 'All right, I won't force you,' he promised. 'But I really do think you should sit down anyway, *Ms Meadows MBE*.'

'How did you . . .?'

The man chuckled, though there was very little genuine amusement behind it. 'It was the shoes I recognized first, but until I started talking to you, I couldn't be absolutely sure,' he explained. 'Now, sit down!'

She sat down. 'What do you want, Mr Lofthouse?' she asked.

'We'll come to that later,' Lofthouse said, revelling in the power they both knew he had. 'Don't you find it strange, Kate – I can call you Kate, can't I? – don't you find it strange that a woman whose job it is to protect battered women enjoys being a battered woman herself?'

'It's not the same thing,' Meadows said.

'I know it isn't,' Lofthouse agreed. 'But will your board of governors see the distinction? Will they be willing to accept that the warden of their hostel should visit a place like this?'

No, of course they won't, Meadows thought. If they find out, I'm finished. If they find out, I've lost everything.

But she *said* nothing.

'Of course, they don't have to know,' Lofthouse continued, 'and if I keep quiet about it, it will remain our secret. But I'll want something in return for my silence.'

'I won't betray Jane,' Meadows said fiercely. 'If that's the price, it's too much, and you'd better do your worst.'

'I'm perfectly willing to leave Jane out of this,' Lofthouse told her.

'Then what *do* you want?'

'We can't discuss it here. We should go somewhere private. I think we'll go back to my place.'

'I don't want to go to your place,' she said.

'I know you don't,' he replied, 'but you don't have any choice do you?'

'That's right,' she agreed, 'I don't have any bloody choice.'

FIVE

Wednesday 2 February

When Clara Frisk – a cleaner by occupation and larcenist by inclination – boarded the bus close to her home, it was still dark. As she changed buses at Whitebridge Central Station, dawn was breaking, and by the time she got off the second bus at Cotton Lane it was almost full daylight (or, at least, as full as daylight got in February in Whitebridge).

There were those who claimed that the affluence of a

neighbourhood could be gauged by the width of the grass verges which separated the pavement from the road. Thus, while some of the poorer parts of Whitebridge had no verges (and sometimes even no pavements) Cotton Lane's verges were wide and lush and regularly trimmed by the council.

The verges did not look so lush that morning. An overnight frost had frozen each and every blade of grass into a spike, and glancing down at it was like being given an aerial view of an aging punk's head. The pavement, too, bore witness to the drop in temperature. It glistened most attractively – and offered the unwary the opportunity to lose their footing and go arse over tit.

Clara Frisk was not one of the unwary. She made her way cautiously down the street until she reached the house which she had privately nicknamed Lofthouseham Palace. It was a big place, even by the standards of the street, with windows running almost floor to ceiling and pillars like the ones you saw in the old films about the American south.

'Just goes to show there's money in soft drinks,' she said to herself, not for the first time.

She let herself in through the back door into what she called the kitchen, but had heard her employers refer to as 'the trades-men's entrance'. It was a large room, with an Aga and two dish-washers (one of them exclusively for crystal drinking glasses). It had two internal doors, one of which opened into the entrance hall (a vast area with a sweeping marble staircase which led to a minstrels' gallery) and a second of which led into the back living room (which the Lofthouses insisted on calling a reception room).

Clara Frisk opened the door to the entrance hall and called, 'Is there anyone at home?'

In the old days, Mrs Lofthouse, standing on the gallery at the top of the staircase, would have shouted back, 'I'm just finishing off in the bathroom, Mrs F,' or, 'I'll be down in a minute. Could you put the kettle on, will you?'

But things were different since her sudden, unannounced disappearance. Now, the house was usually empty, because Mr Lofthouse had gone out by this time of day, or else had still not got back from the night before (Clara was never sure which). Still, it was as well to check she had a safe run at it before setting about her business.

Satisfied she had the house to herself, she opened the other door and stepped into the reception room. This room had sliding glass doors which opened into the patio and the barbeque, but more importantly, it was where the bar was located.

The bar resembled the one in the best room of her local boozer, except that this bar's tabletop was made of teak, and the padding that ran along the front was genuine leather.

Clara Frisk let her eyes travel along the rows of bottles of gin, brandy, whisky, vodka and rum. Some she rejected straight away, because they were either unopened or very nearly full. Others, she discounted for the opposite reason – there was so little left in them that one or two more glasses would drain them completely. But that still left quite a number of bottles in the third category – neither nearly full nor nearly empty.

Clara opened her bag, and let her hand feel its way through the several layers of cleaning rags to the bottles concealed under them.

They were all *small* bottles – one had held eau-de-Cologne, another cough mixture and a third shampoo, though they had now, of course, been thoroughly rinsed out. She placed them on the top of the bar, and then produced the last piece of equipment she needed for this operation – a small plastic funnel.

As she reached for a Bacardi bottle, she found herself thinking about the rows Mr and Mrs Lofthouse used to have.

God, they were humdingers, though.

Clara had no idea what they were about, since they always took place in some other part of the house – she could imagine Mr Lofthouse saying, 'Not in front of the servants, dear,' as they did in all those old black-and-white films – but they were certainly loud enough.

Slowly and carefully, Clara filled the eau-de-Cologne bottle with the Bacardi. That task successfully completed, she opened the cough mixture bottle, which would soon be filled with brandy.

Actually, it wasn't quite accurate to call what had happened rows, she thought, because rows were between two people, and the only voice she'd ever heard raised in anger was *Mr* Lofthouse's. Of course, it was always possible that Mrs Lofthouse was rowing in a whisper – but she didn't think it likely.

Maybe it was because of all the shouting and screaming that Mrs Lofthouse had left. Mr Lofthouse tried to explain it away by saying that she had gone to visit relatives, but if you believed that, you'd believe Minnie Mouse was as virginal as she looked.

In a way, Mrs Frisk did miss Mrs Lofthouse, because she had been so much nicer to her than most of the snotty buggers she worked for were. On the other hand, she was much more aware of what was going on around her than Mr L was, and the incidents of petty larceny with which Mrs Frisk enriched her day could never have occurred under Mrs Lofthouse's watchful eye.

The decanting was completed, and Mrs Frisk placed her booty back in her bag.

And now, she supposed, it was time to go and do a bit of cleaning.

Mrs Frisk usually started cleaning upstairs, and worked her way down ('Then I don't have to climb any stairs when I'm starting to feel knackered,' she'd explain to her cronies in the snug bar of the Bull and Bush) so she stepped into the entrance hall with every intention of making her way to the master bedroom.

It was when she was almost at the staircase that she saw the round thing. At first she just assumed it was a ball of some kind, though why Mr Lofthouse should want to have balls in the house was beyond her.

Then she realized that the ball was looking at her, and that the eyes it was using were Mr Lofthouse's.

And that was when she screamed.

In the old days, when Whitebridge had been a thriving cotton town, the Whitebridge–Liverpool canal had played a central part in the town's prosperity. It had been the highway along which countless barges (pulled by countless horses) had carried raw cotton to Whitebridge from the Lancashire port, and returned to Liverpool with the bolts of cotton which the mill workers had produced (sometimes under hellish conditions). But now there were no mills, and the tow path was rarely graced by anyone, other than a few fishermen who could not afford to go further afield to pursue their hobby.

Kate Meadows had not seen a soul since she began her mammoth walk along the canal bank. It had still been dark back then, and several times she had stumbled on the stones – smoothed and rounded by years of horses' hooves – which were embedded in the clay to form the path.

She did not know how far she had walked back and forth, or even how long she had been walking, though from the position of the sun, she guessed it was around half-past eight. What she did know was that her legs ached, and her heart was warning her she had pushed it far enough.

It had been insane to go to the Hellfire Club the previous evening, she told herself for the thousandth time – completely bloody insane. If she hadn't gone, none of it would have happened. If she hadn't gone, her life could have carried on pretty much as it had for the last few years.

But it was pointless to dwell on what might have been. Now, she needed to do all she could to rescue at least something from the wreckage.

She had almost reached the bridge where she had parked her car. It seemed like a sign – but then perhaps she was so desperate that *anything* would seem like a sign.

She drove out of town – using little-used side roads whenever possible – until she reached the moors.

The air was crisp and brisk out there, and the heather, though clothed in its winter dullness, was still reminiscent of a calm purple sea. A sparrowhawk hovered overhead, vigilantly desperate, and the occasional shrew broke cover as it dashed from one clump of vegetation to another.

Meadows noticed none of this. She was there for one purpose and one purpose alone.

She drove off the road and bumped her car over perhaps a hundred yards of rough ground. When she spotted a patch that was heather-free, she drew up beside it and stopped the car. She got out, removed the clothing from the boot of the car, and placed it in the centre of the empty patch. Next, she took a piece of rubber hose out of the boot, stuck one end of it in her fuel tank, and put the other end in her mouth. She sucked, and when she could almost taste the petrol, she took the tube out of her mouth, and held it over the clothes.

The petrol cascaded out, and landed on the clothes. Only when they were completely drenched did she stop the process.

She got back into her car, drove it some distance away from the site, and returned again on foot. She took a lighter out of her pocket, and cautiously lit one corner of her bonfire. At first, it merely seemed to smoulder, but then it burst into flames.

The fire did not last long, and soon all she was left with was a pile of ashes. She picked up a stick and poked the ashes, partly to aid their disintegration, partly to ensure that the fire had left no clues – like a button or a zip – behind. But it had done a good job, and not a trace of anything remained.

A sudden wind blew up, swept down on the bonfire, and carried what was left of the ashes away in triumph. Now, there was only the scorched earth to show there had ever been a fire there.

Meadows got into her car again, and drove back to Whitebridge.

She wondered if she had done enough – and knew that she hadn't.

A dozen police officers had converged on the Lofthouse home, but most of them had been dispatched to the upper floor and the grounds, and only two men were left standing in the entrance hall.

The shorter of the two was DCI Eric Dawson. He was in his early forties and had mousey-coloured hair which he wore off the collar. He had grown a small moustache under his rather pointed nose, but if he had hoped that would make his face memorable, he must have been sadly disappointed. Worry lines creased his forehead, and they were not there merely by chance.

Dawson surveyed the scene with horror: the rope hanging from a rail which ran along the gallery, with a noose on the end; the body lying close to the noose, which looked vaguely uncomfortable without its head; and the head itself, which had bounced across the floor, only coming to a halt when it bumped against the side of the staircase.

'How the hell did this happen?' he asked the man who was standing next to him.

The man in question was tall and gangly, with straw-coloured hair and a face which said it was much younger than his twenty-nine years. His name was DS Daniel Boyd, and the determination that he showed on any case he was assigned had earned him the nickname Dogged Dan.

'How did it happen, sir?' Boyd repeated. 'Well, I can only assume that the body weight to drop ratio was all wrong.'

'And what's that supposed to mean.'

'There's a mathematical calculation which works out just how far any given body mass has to drop if your intention is to break the man's neck. If the drop's too long, as it is here, decapitation can often occur.'

He didn't want this case, Dawson told himself, and he had a very good reason for that.

If the victim had been some local snot rag, the killer would also have been a local snot rag, so while it would have looked good on the records if he'd been caught, nobody would really have given a damn if he hadn't been. Andrew Lofthouse was different. He was an important man in the community, which meant that he was a man who mattered to the *people* who mattered.

'The top floor will expect me to serve up the killer's head on a silver platter,' he said.

Damn it! He hadn't meant to put the thought into words, but it was too late now.

'I didn't realize how black your humour could be, sir,' Boyd said, staring down at Lofthouse's head.

'It wasn't meant to be funny,' Dawson replied, angry with himself for saying it, and Boyd for noticing that he'd said it. 'It wasn't what I meant at all.'

If the chief con had been there, he might have acted as a half-hearted ally, he thought, because, when all was said and done, they were both Masons. But the sod wasn't there, was he? He was basking in the Caribbean sunshine, and instead they'd got Louisa-bloody-Rutter, a woman well-known to be even tougher on herself than she was on everybody else – a paragon who accepted no excuses for failure.

All of which made this case a bloody nightmare on which to be the chief investigating officer, and there was no way out, unless . . . unless . . .

'Do you think there's any chance this might just be a suicide, sergeant?' he asked.

'No chance at all, sir,' Boyd said.

Bastard!

'What makes you so sure?' Dawson asked.

'Well, for a start, there's the fact that victim is naked,' Boyd said. 'People don't normally strip off when they're about to kill themselves.'

'No, they don't *normally*,' Dawson agreed, grasping at straws. 'But there have to be some occasions when the normal doesn't happen.'

'And more importantly, there's the blood spatter pattern,' Boyd said.

'What blood spatter pattern?' Dawson asked. 'There's hardly any blood at all.'

'Exactly,' Boyd agreed. 'And if he'd been alive when his head came off, his heart would have been spurting blood like the Trevi Fountain.'

Now why couldn't I work that out for myself, Dawson wondered.

And then he realized that of course he *could have* worked it out if he'd really wanted to, but most of his brain was still clinging to the idea that it just might be possible to get away with calling this a suicide.

'Do you have any theories as to why the killer may have stripped his victim, sir?' Boyd asked.

'We don't know that the killer did undress him,' Dawson said. 'Maybe he was already undressed when the killer attacked him.'

'I hadn't thought of that, sir,' Boyd admitted.

'So you're not quite as smart as you thought you were, are you?' asked Dawson, who had long subscribed to the view that the best form of defence was attack – as long, that was, as the enemy was clearly weakened. 'Well, are you?'

'No, I . . .' Boyd began, reddening.

'So what's your theory?' Dawson asked.

'The killer may have realized he'd left DNA traces on Mr Lofthouse's clothes,' Boyd said. 'That would argue some basic knowledge of forensics, so he could be a bobby or an ex-bobby . . .'

'Or a criminal who's been caught by his DNA before, or someone who's seen it in an American film,' Dawson said.

His heart was starting to beat faster, and he could feel beads of sweat forming on his brow. He was going to have to treat this as a murder – there was simply no way round it.

'Hey ho, all the usual suspects, I see,' said a cheery voice from somewhere near the front door.

Dawson turned around to address the new arrival. 'Good morning, doc.'

'And a very good morning to you,' Dr Horlick replied.

The doctor was a perfect example of unhealthy living. He drank as if he feared a sudden flashing light which would proclaim pub closing time forever, and was almost never seen without a cigarette in his mouth. He was at least five stone overweight, and had the chins to prove it. His idea of exercise was a good long burp, and it was a generally held view among his colleagues that he would be unwise to make any long-term plans. But no one questioned his competence at his job, and it was said he could have been a brilliant surgeon but for his thick, stubby fingers and his tendency to tire easily.

'So where's the stiff?' the doctor said.

'There,' Boyd told him, pointing to the trunk, 'and there,' indicating the head.

'Well, that certainly makes a change,' Horlick said. He walked over to the head, made a token gesture of willingness by bending his knees, then said, 'You wouldn't like to pick this up for me, would you, sergeant?'

'Be glad to,' Boyd lied.

He'd never actually picked up a detached head before, and he was surprised how heavy it was. He passed it to Horlick, who examined it, then turned it several times, as if it weighed nothing.

'Back of his head's been bashed in with a blunt instrument,' he announced. 'My guess would be a hammer. On first examination, I'd say it was rather a powerful blow. You might find some blood at the spot the blow was delivered, but you might not – most of the bleeding will have been internal.'

'Do you draw any conclusions from the fact that it was a powerful blow?' Boyd asked.

Skilfully balancing the head in one hand, Horlick scratched his nose with the index finger of the other.

'Is this your first murder case, sergeant?' he asked.

'No,' Boyd said, looking down at his feet.

'But you haven't been involved in many, have you?'

'I suppose not.'

'I thought so,' Horlick said. 'You've got what I call "beginner's enthusiasm," an urgent desire to get all the answers immediately. Does the nature of the blow tell us anything?' he mused. 'Well, it might tell us that his attacker was a very strong man. On the other hand, he may merely have been a very angry man. Then again, he might just have been pretending to be an angry man to throw you off the scent.'

Two ambulance men appeared in the doorway. One of them was pushing a stretcher from the back, the other guiding it from the front.

'Ah, the cavalry has arrived,' Horlick said. 'Tell me, boys, can you spot the dead man?'

The lead ambulance man, who was obviously used to his banter, grinned. 'I'd say it was the feller without a head,' he said.

'Excellent!' Horlick exclaimed. He sounded pleased. 'You have listened to my words of wisdom, and have learned much. And this,' he continued, holding up the head for them to see, 'completes the picture. If you want to do this by the book, we will require two stretchers – one for the trunk and one for the head – but if you're willing to cut corners, I'm more than willing to look the other way.'

'So when can you do the PM, doc?' Dawson asked.

'Well, aren't we an eager beaver today,' Horlick replied. 'I suppose I could do it as soon as I get him back to the mortuary. Will you be observing it yourself, or will you be sending one of your minions?'

'I'll come myself,' Dawson said, without a great deal of enthusiasm.

'That's a date, then,' the doctor replied, as he waddled after the stretcher. 'Be there in half an hour. I'll be the one holding the nasty sharp scalpel.'

'Pillock,' Dawson said, when Horlick was out of earshot.

The longer Clara Frisk sat in the back of the patrol car, the more her sense of injustice grew.

'Is there a reward?' she'd asked the uniformed bobby who'd opened the door of the car and gestured she should climb inside.

'I wouldn't know about that,' the bobby had replied.

'I was the one who found the body and phoned the police, you know,' Clara had said. 'If it hadn't been for me, who knows how long it would have been before he was found? If that doesn't deserve a reward, I don't know what does.'

'Just get into the car, madam,' the constable had said, guiding her gently but firmly on to the back seat.

'I demand to see your superior officer,' she said.

'You will, madam,' the constable had promised. 'But it may be a while, because he's quite busy at the moment.'

After ten minutes, Clara began drumming her fingers on the seat in front. After twenty minutes, she tried the door, and was disgusted to discover that it was locked. After thirty minutes, she reminded herself that she had something in her bag which would help her deal with the boredom.

DCI Dawson took his packet of cigarettes out of his pocket, then remembered that the latest decree from on high was that there should be no smoking at crime scenes. As he returned the cigarettes to his pocket, he noticed that Sergeant Boyd had been watching the whole manoeuvre.

'Stupid bloody regulation,' Dawson said.

'I think the idea is to avoid contaminating the crime scene, sir,' Boyd said mildly.

Bloody smart-arsed sergeant!

'We haven't seen Mrs Lofthouse. Don't you know where she is?' Dawson asked, sulkily.

'I do know, actually, sir,' Boyd replied. 'According to the station, she's registered as living in a shelter for battered women called Overcroft House.'

'So he was a wife beater, was he? He had a bit of a temper – and then he lost his head completely.' Dawson chuckled, because now he meant it, it *was* funny, and Boyd did his best to create the impression that he was joining in. 'Still, battered wife or not, I suppose she'd better be told he's dead,' Dawson continued.

'Do you want me to do that, sir?' Boyd asked.

Did he? Dawson wondered.

It was often a good idea to have a trained observer there when the news was broken to the nearest and dearest, because a lot could be learned from their reactions. But if Lofthouse's missus had been living in terror of him, it did not take much thought to work out what her reaction was likely to be. She'd probably be useless as a witness too, since anything she told them would be so coloured by her own bias that at best it would be a waste of time, and at worst it could send them up a real blind alley.

'You've got better things to do with your time,' he said. 'Get a couple of uniforms to do the job.'

Boyd nodded. 'At least we've had one lucky break, sir,' he said.

'And what might that be?' Dawson asked.

Does he really not know, or is he just testing me? Boyd wondered.

'Well, the fact that he was decapitated,' he said.

'And how is that a lucky break?'

'It will be very useful when we come to interrogating a possible suspect.'

'Go on.'

'If it becomes obvious during the course of the interrogation that the suspect has no idea how the victim actually died, then we can rule him out. Conversely, if you have a suspect who admits to knowing that Lofthouse was decapitated, then he's our man.'

'Assuming we can keep that fact to ourselves,' Dawson said.

'Exactly, sir.'

'I think your chances of keeping a decapitation secret are approximately nil,' Dawson said.

'The paramedics won't dare talk about it because it would cost them their jobs, and our lads won't do it because that would open them up to criminal prosecution,' Boyd said. 'And even if the newspapers got a whiff of it, they wouldn't run the story, because they know that if they did, we'd never cooperate with them again.'

'And what about the cleaner – this Clara Cluck?' Dawson jeered. 'How are you going to shut her up?'

'I'll find a way,' Boyd said, sounding more confident than he actually felt.

Clara Frisk had polished off her little bottle of Bacardi and was attacking the gin when she heard the door click open, and saw the lanky streak of wind and piss slide in beside her.

'How d'you manage to get the door open? It wouldn't budge for me,' she said, and on hearing herself speak she realized that she was – at the very least – tipsy.

'What's that you're drinking, Clara?' Boyd asked. He took the bottle off her, and held it up to the light. 'Eau-de-Cologne? You shouldn't go drinking scent. It's not good for you.' He held the bottle under his nose. 'Actually, it smells more like gin than scent.'

'It's cold in this car,' Clara said. 'You have to do something to keep warm.'

'But why put it in a scent bottle?' Boyd wondered. 'Do you mind if I take a look in your bag, Clara?'

'Yes, I bloody do mind,' the cleaner said, clutching the bag close to her scrawny chest.

'Fair enough,' Boyd said philosophically. 'We can always leave it till we're down at the station.'

'What do you mean?' Clara demanded.

'Well, if you don't let me look inside, I'll just have to arrest you,' Boyd explained.

'Here, take the bloody bag,' the cleaner said, thrusting it into his hands.

Boyd discovered two more bottles, and looked especially pleased when he found the funnel.

'Naughty, naughty!' he said.

'I should think you've got more important things to worry about than me enjoying a few perks of the job,' Clara said petulantly.

'Is that what you call them, "perks of the job"?' Boyd said. 'I'd be more inclined to call them stolen property.' He paused. 'But you're right, I do have more important things to worry about – so I'll make a deal with you.'

'What kind of deal?' Clara asked suspiciously.

'When people ask you what you found in the house, what will you tell them?' Boyd asked.

'I'll tell them I saw Mr Lofthouse, with his head in one place and his body in another,' Clara said.

'No, you won't,' Boyd said, wagging his finger. 'You'll tell them that you found him hanging by a noose from the gallery.'

'And if I do that . . .'

'If you do that, then I'll forget I ever saw these bottles. But if you tell one person – and I mean just one – what you really found, then my memory will start coming back. Do we understand each other?'

'Yes,' Clara agreed, 'we do.'

'There is one more proviso though,' Boyd said. 'You have to promise me you've learned your lesson and you'll never steal again.'

'I've learned my lesson, and I'll never steal again,' Clara told him.

'Good, then that's settled,' Boyd said.

He didn't believe her and she knew it, but she also knew that he didn't give a toss whether she kept her promise or not, as long as he got what he wanted. And that was the kind of language she could understand.

SIX

It was bloody cold outside, and nobody knew that better than PC Janice Robinson, who had been filling in for a lollipop lady off work with the flu. But now she was back in police head-quarters, and it was going to be an almost indescribable pleasure to hang up her coat and allow the central heating system to run wild over her chilled bones.

It was not to be. She had not even reached her coat peg when the duty sergeant, Arnold Collins, called out, 'Have you got anything on at the moment, Robinson?'

She stopped dead in her tracks. 'Well, I was hoping to take a few minutes warming up again,' she confessed.

'Keeping busy, that's the key to keeping warm,' the sergeant said, his voice thick with genial encouragement. 'There's a fatality notice needs delivering, and that's just up your street, isn't it?'

'Is it?' Robinson asked bleakly.

'It certainly is,' the sergeant confirmed. 'I always prefer a woman to a man for that kind of job, because women are much more sympathetic.'

More sympathetic! Robinson thought with contempt.

It wasn't that at all. The truth was that men simply didn't have the stomach for unpleasantness – their delicate nerves simply wouldn't take it – so as usual, it was a case of sending the woman to do the dirty work.

'Who is it, and where do I go?' she asked, giving in to the inevitable.

'The dead man is Andrew Lofthouse,' the sergeant said. 'Have you heard of him?'

'No.'

The sergeant shook his head despairingly. 'You young girls,' he said. 'You've no awareness of the world around you. All you care about is putting on a show for the fellers.'

Robinson, who was the Mid Lancs female javelin champion, had a sudden vision of the next police sports' day, in which a javelin might accidently go off course and score a bulls' eye through Collins' navel.

'What are you grinning about?' the sergeant asked.

'Nothing,' Robinson said. 'So what should I know about this Lofthouse feller?'

'He's becoming something of a local big wheel. There's talk of him becoming mayor in two or three years,' Collins said. 'Well, there was anyway, but I don't suppose there's much chance of that now that he's bloody well dead. Anyway, his cleaner found him hanging from the banister.'

'Suicide or murder?' Robinson asked.

'Nobody's saying – but from the number of bobbies involved in the investigation, I'd put my money on murder,' Collins said. He glanced down at the work sheets on his desk. 'PC Charnley is free at the moment. Take her with you for company.'

Take her with you in case the widow turns hysterical and needs restraining, Robinson translated.

'You never said where we'll find Mrs Lofthouse,' Robinson pointed out.

'Didn't I?' the sergeant asked. 'You'll find her at Overcroft House.'

'The battered wives' shelter,' Robinson mused. 'Well, it doesn't look like Mr Lofthouse is going to be much of a loss.'

Michael O'Casey and Paul Mason were SOCOs. The acronym stood for Scene of Crime Officer, and while it was true that they did work at the scene of the crime, the word 'officer' was misleading, because they were not policemen at all, but civilians employed to collect data. Generally speaking, their relationship with the force was based on amiable contempt. The CID officers view the SOCO staff in much the same way as they might view migrant fruit pickers – folk who did a valuable job they couldn't be bothered to do themselves. For their part, the SOCOs regarded the detectives as Flash Harrys who lacked the necessary brain power for forensics. And since each side acknowledged that it needed the other, it all worked out rather well.

The two men had begun their work in the entrance hall of the Lofthouse home, taking samples from the blood splashes on the floor, and then searching – to no avail – for fingerprints.

'Looks like our man's been very careful,' Mason said.

'He'll have made a mistake somewhere or other,' O'Casey replied cheerfully. 'They nearly always do.'

Yes, but the key words there were *nearly always*, Mason thought, and he had a nasty feeling that this could turn out to be one of the exceptions.

They dusted the gallery rail for prints, and found none.

'Wiped clean,' O'Casey said.

'Wiped clean,' Mason repeated gloomily.

They entered the bedroom. It was a large room, with double French doors which opened on to a terrace. Hanging over the bed was an elaborate chandelier.

'How the rich live!' O'Casey said, his voice an uncomfortable blend of disgust and envy. 'Looking at that chandelier, you'd think you were in the Palace of Versailles.'

He could see his partner's point, Mason thought. The chandelier, with scores – possibly even hundreds – of crystal pendulums, was extreme, and might even have been described as gaudy. And yet, at the same time, there was something beautiful about it.

'Do you think we need to dust that bastard for prints?' O'Casey asked.

Mason made no reply. In fact, it was doubtful if he even heard his partner, because he seemed absorbed in a study of the chandelier.

'I said, do you think we need to dust it for prints?' O'Casey repeated, louder this time.

'What?' Mason asked, startled.

'Do we need . . .?'

'. . . to dust it for prints? I don't think so, unless you can come up with a reason for the murderer standing on a chair to deliberately leave his prints.'

'So what's the big attraction then? Were you picturing in your front parlour?'

'No, I was wondering about the hook.'

'What hook?'

'The one on the ceiling. It's right there, in the middle of the chandelier, but if you don't look at it from the right angle, you don't even notice it.'

'A hook on the ceiling,' O'Casey mused. 'Now why would they put a hook there?' He chuckled. 'I know – it's because they got tired of holding the chandelier up by hover power, and decided to anchor it to the ceiling instead.'

'I was always worried about being lumbered with a comedian as a partner – but fortunately, it hasn't happened yet,' Mason countered.

O'Casey pretended to look hurt. 'Your cruel words cut me to the quick,' he said.

'The thing is, the hook's quite separate from the chandelier's mounting, so why is it there at all?'

'Maybe it was part of a previous fitment,' O'Casey suggested. 'Do you want to go up there and have a look, or should we . . . you know . . . search for clues and things?'

Mason grinned. 'Let's look for clues and things.'

They found brown stains on the carpet near the French windows.

'Blood!' O'Casey said, in his best horror movie voice.

'Blood,' Mason agreed.

So this, in all probability, was the spot at which the murder actually happened. It wouldn't take them long to ascertain whether it really was blood, Mason thought, pushing all thought of the hook to the back of his mind.

Arthur Cox, the operations manager at the Whitebridge Bottling and Distribution was wearing a smart suit, but looked as if he'd be much more comfortable in overalls, DS Boyd thought. Cox's hands, too – hardened by years of manual work – proclaimed that a collar-and-tie environment was not his natural habitat.

They met in the operations manager's office, high above the factory floor. From here, they had a bird's-eye view of the thousands of bottles being marshalled like well-trained soldiers along the conveyor belt. Boyd was surprised to find that he was fascinated by the whole process, and it was only by an effort of will that tore his eyes away from it and focussed on Cox, who was sitting at the other side of the desk.

'I'm afraid I've got some bad news for you,' he said, gravely. 'Your boss, Mr Lofthouse, has been murdered.'

'That's terrible,' Cox said – but though his face registered surprise, there was very little evidence of distress.

'Didn't you like him?' Boyd prodded.

Cox shrugged. 'As bosses go, he was all right,' he said. 'And now, apparently, as bosses go, he went.'

It was an attempt to use humour as a diversionary tactic, Boyd thought, but he was not about to be sidetracked.

'So you didn't like him,' he persisted.

For a few seconds, Cox seemed to be struggling for a short, sharp answer, but then he gave up.

'The way I feel won't make any sense to you unless you know a little bit about the history of this place,' he said.

'Then give me a history lesson,' Boyd suggested. 'I'm all ears.'

'I was here even before Miss Bright arrived . . .' Cox began.

'Miss Bright?'

'Mrs Lofthouse – but she wasn't married back then. Anyway, when she bought the business off Mr Hardcastle, it was on its last legs, because we'd lost a couple of important contracts, and it didn't seem likely we'd ever win any new ones. The first thing Jane did was to call us all together and tell us there'd be no pay rise that year, or the next year, but if you could stick it out three years – and things worked out as she planned – she'd give us a massive bonus. Well, there were some staff that left then and there, but the rest of us stayed on, and over the next few months we really started to believe the business had a future – and that was mainly down to the fact that we had faith in Jane. And, to tell you the truth, several of the younger lads had more than just faith – they'd fallen in love with her. So anyway, we—'

'You were supposed to be telling me about Andrew Lofthouse,' Boyd reminded him. 'What was he doing while all this was going on?'

'I've no idea,' Cox said, 'because he wasn't around.'

'Well, then . . .'

'Have a bit of patience, laddie, and we'll get to him,' Cox said. 'We all worked our arses off for them three years, but nobody worked as hard – or for such long hours – as Jane. And at the end of it, the business wasn't just doing well – it was a runaway success. And that's where Andrew Lofthouse comes into the picture.'

'Ah!' Boyd said.

'Up to that point, we'd been subcontracting distribution, but then Andrew turns up and suggests Jane might be better off going into partnership with an experienced distributor who owned a first-class fleet. Jane agreed – or rather, she was charmed into agreeing – and the deal was done. But it wasn't an equal deal by any stretch of the imagination. Andrew got a share of a thriving bottling business, and in return Jane became part-owner of a fleet of lorries that were held together by prayers and chewing gum.'

'The trucks I saw in the yard didn't look as if they are held together by prayers and chewing gum,' Boyd said.

'That's because they're not,' Cox told him. 'They're all new, bought with company money – *bottling* company money.'

'Mrs Lofthouse seems to have let her husband walk all over her,' Boyd said.

'I think she was infatuated by his good looks and charm,' Cox said.

'And did she ever regret it?'

'If she did, she didn't tell me,' Cox said guardedly.

'But you must have been able to tell from the way she looked at him and the way she acted.'

'I mind my own business,' Cox said, despite the evidence from the earlier conversation that he clearly didn't. 'I don't know how she felt.'

'Maybe I'll ask her myself what her feelings are,' Boyd said. 'Where can I find her?'

Cox looked down at his desk. 'I don't know,' he said.

'Could she be in her office?'

'No.'

'At home?'

'You won't find her there, either.'

'How can you be so sure?'

'Her husband said she was feeling very tired, and she'd gone away for a rest cure.'

'Where did she go?'

'I don't know. It could have been Bournemouth, or it could have been the South of France.'

He was so obviously – and awkwardly – lying, that Boyd almost felt sorry for him.

'Have you ever heard of Overcroft House, Mr Cox?' the sergeant asked.

'No,' Cox replied, then added a totally unnecessary, 'never.'

'Are you the only one of her original team who knows that she's in a shelter for battered wives – or do the rest of them know, too?' Boyd asked.

For a moment, it actually looked as if Cox was about to burst into tears, then he said, 'The next time I talk to you, I want the company lawyer present.'

Mary Barnes looked at the monitor by the front door, and saw that there were two women in police uniforms standing the other side of it. They appeared to be the real thing, but until it was clearly established that was actually what they were, Mary had no intention of opening the door.

'What do you want?' she asked.

'We want to come in,' said the taller of the two.

'Then you'll have to post your warrant cards through the letter box,' Mary said.

The two women looked at each other questioningly, then the taller one took out her card and pushed it through the slot. The second woman followed suit.

Mary examined both cards carefully, because in the past estranged husbands had tried all kinds of sneaky tricks to get into Overcroft House, and while none of them had gone so far as to hire women to impersonate police officers, there was a first time for everything.

The cards looked genuine enough, and Mary opened the door.

The one whose warrant card identified her as PC Robinson glanced at the brass plaque to the right of the door.

'Are you Ms Kate Meadows MBE?' she asked.

'No,' Mary said, 'I'm her deputy, Mary Barnes.'

'So where's Ms Meadows?'

I wish I knew, Mary thought. When she goes out for the night she's usually back by the time I wake up in the morning, so that I can be away from here by nine. But it's early afternoon now, and she's still not back – and that's just not like her.

'Ms Meadows is out,' Mary said, 'but I'm in charge, and I can deal with any enquiries you might have.'

'We'd like to talk to Jane Lofthouse, if she's here,' PC Robinson said. 'Is she?'

'May I ask you what it's about?' Mary said.

'It's a confidential matter,' Robinson replied, 'I can't tell you anything about it – but I can assure you that it is important.'

Well, if that was how it was, that was how it was, Mary decided.

'I'll take you through to the consulting room,' she said. 'You can wait for her there.'

DCI Dawson and Dr Horlick were sitting in the staff rest room at the mortuary. Horlick was smoking an exotic cigarette which Dawson thought was so revolting that even the stink of the chemicals in the dissecting room would have been an improvement.

'So now you've finished, what are your conclusions, doc?' he asked.

'Basically, they're pretty much what I told you at the scene of the crime,' Horlick said. 'Death was instantaneous – or as near as damn it – and was the result of a blow to the head. It occurred sometime between midnight and four o'clock in the morning.'

'Was he clothed or naked when the blow was struck?' Dawson asked.

'It's impossible to say, although it would have made the killer's task much simpler if he'd been naked, because undressing a dead man is never easy.' Horlick took a drag on his cigarette and exhaled again, filling the air with the essence of low-grade Turkish brothel at closing time. 'The body was carefully and thoroughly washed in a disinfectant or cleanser,' he continued. 'I can't tell you exactly what it was off hand, but the lab should be able to tell us. Anyway, whatever it was, it ensured you'll not be lifting any DNA from that particular corpse.'

'You mentioned the other injuries,' Dawson said.

'Ah yes. They were inflicted several hours before death. They occurred in two areas – the left foot and the groin. I couldn't tell you exactly what instrument was used to inflict the foot injury. Perhaps it was the end of a thin iron bar, or the point on the thin arm of a pickaxe. It could even have been a stiletto heel, but I can't see a big man like Lofthouse just standing there while a woman did that to him. Can you?'

'No,' Dawson agreed, 'I can't.'

'The bruising in the groin area emanates from a small central point, which would seem to support the iron bar theory,' Horlick continued, 'unless, of course,' he chuckled, 'our hypothetical "lady", having trodden on him with her heel, kicked him with the toe of her shoe.'

'Thank you, doctor, you've been very helpful,' Dawson said.

Well, you had to say that – whether it was true or not – he thought.

Kate Meadows had designed the consulting room herself. It was a cross between a police interview room and a psychiatrist's office – both of which Meadows had extensive personal experience of. Thus, there was a table, should this be a formal interview, and a set of easy chairs around a coffee table for discussions of a more casual nature. PC Robinson suspected that the easy seating would be more appropriate for this particular situation, but clung to the security of the table anyway.

When Jane Lofthouse arrived, she was not alone, but instead was accompanied by a pale, nervous young woman who could almost have been called a waif, and was certainly highly pregnant.

'And you are Mrs . . .?' Robinson said.

'And I am Mrs what?' Lizzie Grimshaw asked.

Robinson sighed. 'What's your name, madam?'

Lizzie glanced over her shoulder, as if looking for the madam that the policewoman was talking to, and then, realizing she was the madam herself, said, 'I'm Lizzie Grimshaw.'

'Well, Mrs Grimshaw, I'm afraid you'll have to stay outside while we talk to Mrs Lofthouse,' Robinson said.

Lizzie's bottom lip trembled, and it was obvious that she was finding being so close to a police officer a frightening experience. Then she took a deep breath, and said, 'No!'

'No?' Robinson repeated.

'I'm not leaving,' said Lizzie, in a voice which trembled, but somehow also demonstrated absolute determination. 'It's never good talking to the bobbies, and I'm not letting Jane do it on her own.'

'You *must* leave,' Robinson told her.

'She wants to stay,' Jane Lofthouse said, looking at the pregnant girl with compassion. 'Please let her.'

'I'm afraid I can't,' Robinson said, though she didn't sound very regretful at all.

'Then I don't want to talk to you either,' Jane Lofthouse told her.

Why did they never cover this kind of thing in training school? Robinson thought. And aloud, she said, 'All right, she can stay. But I won't be answerable for the consequences.'

'That's fine with me,' Jane Lofthouse said.

She sat down, and Lizzie sat next to her.

'I'm afraid I have some bad news about your husband,' Robinson began.

'He's dead, isn't he?' Jane said.

'What makes you say that?' Robinson wondered.

'They wouldn't send two police officers round here to inform me he'd got a splinter in his thumb, now would they?' Jane asked. 'How did he die? Was it an accident?'

'I think we'll need to wait for the post-mortem report before we can be certain about the cause of death,' Robinson said cautiously.

Up until this point, Jane had seemed quite calm, but now tears appeared in her eyes. 'He was murdered, wasn't he?' she asked, in a quivering voice.

'Or it may have been suicide,' PC Charnley said.

Robinson gave her less-experienced colleague a look of annoyance, but the damage had already been done.

'He would never have killed himself,' Jane said, sobbing in earnest now. 'Whatever happened, he would never have taken his own life.' She gulped in air as if she thought it was the last breath she'd ever draw. 'What am I to do?' she moaned. 'How will I ever manage without him?'

It was incredible that a woman who had run away from her violent husband should react like this on hearing of his death, Robinson thought.

Or maybe it wasn't! She remembered watching a documentary about the death of Joseph Stalin, the great Russian tyrant who had more than matched Hitler for the number of people who he'd had brutally killed. There had been newsreel film of the inmates of one of his notorious Gulag prison camps. They'd stood in the prison yard – half-starved and badly underdressed for the cruel Siberian winter – and when they heard the news, they had wept and wept until they could weep no more.

At first, Robinson had thought the newsreel must have been faked, but a friend of hers – who had studied such things – had promised her that they were real. These people might have hated Stalin, the friend explained, but he had so dominated their world that the thought of that world without him terrified them even more than thoughts of their own deaths.

So maybe that was what had happened here. Maybe Andrew Lofthouse was Whitebridge's own version of Joseph Stalin, at least in the eyes of his terrorized wife.

Jane had quietened down a little, and was hugging herself and sobbing quietly.

Lizzie Grimshaw had one hand on Jane's head, and was gently stroking her hair. She looked up at the two police officers.

'Does Jane need to identify the body?' she asked.

'Yes,' Robinson said.

'But does she need to do it *right now*?'

'I suppose not,' Robinson conceded. 'As next-of-kin she will need to formally identify the body at some point, but since she's so obviously upset . . .'

'Then I think you'd better go,' Lizzie said. 'I can handle it from here.'

It was incredible that this waif – who didn't look like she could even handle *herself* – could take control of the situation, Robinson thought, but she quite clearly had.

'We'll be in touch,' Robinson said.

'Yes,' Lizzie replied, but it was an abstract acknowledgement at best, because all her attention was now focussed on Jane Lofthouse, and when the two police officers left the room, she probably didn't even notice.

SEVEN

I f there had been a sun, it would have set at four thirty-two, but all that actually happened was that the dark sky which had been hanging over Whitebridge all day got even darker.

Monika Paniatowski went over to the fridge, and removed the bottle of Zubrowka Polish vodka, which had been chilling since lunchtime. She took a glass from the cupboard, poured herself a small shot, and knocked it back immediately. She would slow down after this – she always did – but that first drink hitting her stomach, and announcing that there was a new sheriff in town, was a sensation not to be missed.

She looked down at the glass in her hand, and smiled. Her ancestors, she supposed, would have immediately slung the empty glass into the fireplace, but she would have looked pretty stupid flinging *her* empty glass against the radiator. Besides, it would make a hell of a mess, and unlike those ancestors of hers, she didn't have a small army of *moujiks* waiting to clean up after her.

She could have had another drink within the rules she had set herself, but she didn't. Instead, she returned the bottle to the fridge, and walked back to the kitchen table. Her photograph album sat squarely in the centre of the table. She didn't know why she had taken it out of the drawer – she almost couldn't remember doing so – but there it was, and she supposed there could be no harm in looking at it now.

It was by no means a comprehensive visual biography of her life. There were no photographs of her earlier childhood in Poland, because they had all been abandoned (along with everything else the family owned) when the Germans invaded and her father was killed in battle. There were no pictures of the years that followed, because she and her mother had been refugees in wartime Europe (often hiding in ditches and living off raw turnips straight from the fields) and there had been little opportunity to collect souvenirs.

The third part of her story was also totally unrepresented – those years between her mother marrying her stepfather, Arthur Jones, and her mother's death – those years when, once she had reached puberty, Jones would force his attentions on her nearly every night. Such pictures had existed, because her mother and Jones had put up pretence of being a normal loving family, but Monika had burned all the prints and all the negatives the day they came into her possession – and she had never regretted it.

And so the albums actually started a few weeks after Bob Rutter's suicide, when the formal adoption papers had been certified, and she had become – in the eyes of the law – mother to Bob's daughter Louisa. Monika's excitement – her sheer bloody joy – was reflected not only in the obvious loving care behind each shot but also in the amazing number of pictures of a grinning Louisa there were.

There were a few photographs of her old boss – solid dependable Charlie Woodend – and his wife – the solid, dependable, Joan Woodend – and a couple of shots of Colin Beresford, but there were none of . . . none of . . . none of any other adults.

'None of my *lovers*!' she said aloud, annoyed with herself for trying to avoid the words.

But it was hardly surprising she had not chosen to retain those memories. She had not had many affairs in over three decades – less than could be counted on the fingers of two hands – yet three of her lovers had taken life (she refused to call any of the three of them truly murderers, though, strictly speaking, that was exactly what they were).

None of the other affairs had ended exactly well, either.

Had that been her fault?

Or had God – her all-forgiving God – been punishing her for that first affair with Bob, a married man?

If that was the case, she had no complaints, because she knew that what she had done had been a terrible thing – and what was even worse was that she could not bring herself to regret it.

She turned the page, and there were the twins. Everyone who

knew her back at the time of her pregnancy had wondered who the father was, but only three people had actually known the truth – which was that they had been conceived when she was raped by three bikers.

The first person to know had been her gynaecologist, who had initially kept it secret because he had sworn a Hippocratic Oath to do so, and now kept it secret because he was dead.

The second was Dr Shastri, the police doctor. She had urged Monika to report the rape – had pointed out that it was her duty. Paniatowski had known that, but had said nothing, because she also knew that if word ever got out, her career would effectively be over. Now Shastri had moved back to India, and taken her part of the secret with her.

And the third person who had known had been Kate Meadows. When it had become plain to her that her boss planned to keep quiet about the attack, she had jumped on her motorbike and ridden away. She was gone for two days, and when she returned she brought with her three already-withering skin sacks which contained the bikers' testes.

Paniatowski had not been entirely sure how she felt about this. She was against vigilante justice in principle, but somehow, when you'd been the victim of a brutal and cowardly rape, your convictions were not always quite as strong as they had been.

But one thing she *was* sure of – whether Meadows had been right or wrong, there was no doubt that she had risked her career (and possibly her life) to avenge her boss, and for that, Monika would feel forever in her debt.

She had decided to have the twins aborted. She had convinced herself she could do that with a clear conscience. And then the same God who she felt had abandoned her when Arthur Jones began to climb the stairs to her bedroom, was back – and this time He had been pleading for the life in her womb, and she had not been able to refuse Him.

She flicked through a few pages covering the early life of Thomas and Philip. They were the children of rapists, she reminded herself – the product of bad seed. Was it any wonder, then, that she had watched them grow with apprehension, dreading the moment when the mask of childhood innocence was ripped off, to reveal the raging monster beneath the skin?

It hadn't happened – or, at least, it hadn't happened as dramatically as she had imagined it might.

Thomas had chosen his course in life, and though it was not one she would have chosen for him – one, in fact, she had actually campaigned against – it was his choice, and she respected him for it.

And Philip, she was forced to admit, could have turned out worse. He hadn't tortured any small animals when he was a child – if he had, Thomas would have let her know – and though he was violent, he tended to restrict his violence to men well capable of defending themselves, and . . .

It wasn't much to be proud of in a son – the fact that he didn't beat up women and children – now was it? And indeed, she *wasn't* proud of him in any way.

She turned her gaze back to the album – to a younger Philip, looking up at her and smiling.

Had there ever been a time, she wondered, when it would have been possible – by saying or doing something differently – to have ensured a better outcome?

Or had the bad seed from which he had been born, been firmly affixed in his soul from the very beginning?

She did not like Philip. She did not respect Philip in the way she respected Thomas. If she was honest with herself – and she really was trying to be just that – she despised the slightly-younger of her two sons.

Yet at the same time she loved him – deeply and desperately – and there was nothing she could do about that.

In Whitebridge Central, DCI Dawson's team of detective constables were seated in the centre of the CID suite, getting their final briefing of the day from DS Boyd.

'Firstly, the house,' Boyd began. 'The SOCOs are going through it now, but it's a big place, and they're being careful, so they'll be finished by tomorrow evening at the earliest.' He turned to Dawson. 'Are you happy with that, sir?'

'Happy isn't the word I'd choose, but they're right to be careful,' the DCI said.

'The next point is Lofthouse's clothes. The SOCOs have made an initial search of the house, and haven't found them. Of course, it's always possible that the killer hung the shirt, jacket and trousers neatly up in the wardrobe and put the underwear back in the drawers, and when O'Casey and Mason get round to doing a more detailed search, they'll check that out. Our theory, however, is that the killer took them with him and destroyed them.'

'Because he was worried his DNA might be on them,' Dawson said, as if to remind the rest of the team that he was there, and – despite appearances to the contrary – was in charge.

'Exactly, sir,' Boyd agreed. ''Casey and Masey haven't found the murder weapon, but they're putting their money on it being a ball pein hammer. They can be bought at any ironmonger's, and tomorrow I'll get the uniforms to check on each and every one, in the hope that our killer only bought it recently. It's a bit of a long shot, but very often, it's the long shot that actually makes the case.'

'Tell them about the rope,' Dawson said.

I was going to, if you'd given me a second, you bastard, Boyd thought.

But aloud, he said, 'The rope is the same sort of hemp the official hangman used to use back in the good old days when we hung people for sheep stealing and pickpocketing. There are, however, two things about it worth noting. The first that, judging by the wear and tear, it's not the first time it's been used. So one of the many questions we need to ask ourselves is where it's been used before, and why it was left behind this time.'

'Maybe the killer was so revolted by the head coming off that he just wanted to get out of the house,' suggested a keen young detective constable, whose name actually was Keene.

'That's a possibility,' Boyd conceded, 'but given just how careful he seems to have been about everything else connected with this murder, I just can't see him as the kind of man who panics.'

'Tell them about the skin,' Dawson said.

'There were traces of skin on the noose, but they all came from Lofthouse, which is rather strange, considering that we're almost sure the rope has been used before,' Boyd said.

'Maybe he normally cleans it after use,' Keene suggested.

'The lab says it would be impossible to eradicate all traces of skin without damaging the rope,' Boyd said. 'But though there were no traces of skin, there were traces of black velvet.'

'The fabric, not the drink,' said DCI Dawson, and all the constables chuckled at what was obviously a previously prepared attempt at humour, because when all was said and done, Dawson was the boss.

'We think the killer put the velvet on the rope before previous hangings,' Boyd said. 'There could be a number of reasons why he did that. Maybe it was part of some weird ritual which he omitted to follow when he hung Lofthouse. Or maybe he was eager not to leave traces of their skin on the rope, though I couldn't even begin to guess why that might be important to him. Basically, we have more questions than answers, but at this stage of the investigation, that's not necessarily a bad thing.'

'First thing tomorrow, I want somebody checking on hangings nationwide in the last five years,' Dawson said. He turned back to Boyd. 'Tell us about the neighbours, sergeant.'

'As you'll already have gathered, the layout of the area works against us, because the houses are so spread out that somebody could be screaming blue murder next door, and you probably wouldn't hear a thing,' Boyd said. 'On the other hand, it's also an area that gets very little traffic, which means that people notice it more than they would on an estate. And what three of the neighbours have told us is that two cars drove down the street sometime after ten o'clock, and probably parked in Lofthouse's driveway.'

'Do we know what make and model those cars were?' Dawson asked.

Boyd shook his head. 'They heard the cars, rather than saw them. Maybe these people are too posh to be nosy.'

'Nobody's too posh to be nosy,' Dawson said. 'Have them questioned again tomorrow, will you? Let's see if we can jog their memories.'

Boyd nodded and took a note. 'One of the neighbours heard one of the cars leaving again,' he continued. 'She was a bit vague about the time, because she was already in bed, but she thinks it was at least an hour after the two cars arrived.'

'If it was the killer, it would have been later than that, because, according to the doc, Lofthouse had been home for several hours before he was killed,' Dawson said. 'What else have you got?'

'I talked to the general manager at the bottling plant myself,' Boyd said. 'It's obvious that he resents Lofthouse for elbowing his way into the business, and that he knows that Lofthouse was beating up his wife.'

'What makes you so sure of that?' Dawson wondered.

'I asked him if he knew where Mrs Lofthouse had gone, and he said he didn't, but when I mentioned Overcroft House, his face gave him away. So if he knows where she is, he also knows why she's there. And I got the distinct impression that the rest of the old staff know, too.'

'I can see where you're going with this,' Dawson said, 'but is it likely that one of them would kill Lofthouse because of what he'd done to his wife?'

'I wouldn't give that a definite yes, but I wouldn't dismiss it as a possibility either,' Boyd said. 'From what Cox told me, several of the workers feel a great sense of loyalty to Jane Lofthouse. I think that what Andrew did to her may have made them very angry.'

'Well, there are certainly indications that our murderer was an angry man,' Dawson said. 'It's obvious why he stripped the body and washed it down – that was just being cautious – but hanging him would suggest that he didn't think killing Lofthouse once was enough. So it's possible he was killed because of the way he treated his wife. But it's equally possible he was having an affair, and that the woman's husband killed him. Or that somebody he had done business with felt he had cheated them. We need more information. Wouldn't you agree, Sergeant Boyd?'

There was only one answer to that question.

'Yes, sir, that's what we need,' Boyd agreed.

'Today, we've got an overall view, tomorrow I want us zooming in,' Dawson said. 'I want all the neighbours reinterviewed, and this time I want to know *anything at all* they can tell us about Lofthouse's life. I want everybody at Whitebridge Bottling interviewed, and their alibis for last night checked out. By the end of work tomorrow, I expect to have been told where Lofthouse was last night, and I want a list of possible drivers of the other car that arrived at the same time as Lofthouse's but left a couple of hours later. And I really would be very interested to learn who beat up Lofthouse earlier in the day. Are we clear on that?' He waited until everyone on the team had nodded, then said, 'Right, people, get off home and get a good nights sleep. Tomorrow could make or break this case.'

He watched his team file out with some satisfaction. He had sounded like a DCI who really knew what he was doing, he thought – and it had not been entirely an act. He had not wanted this case, but now he was starting to get a good feeling about it. He was

reasonably certain that with a sergeant like Boyd by his side, he
had a more-than-fair chance of catching his killer. And if he did,
he would have made a friend for life of Louisa Rutter. When she
rose to dizzying new heights – as she was bound to – his help in
assuring her ascendancy would not be forgotten.

'Superintendent Dawson,' he said to himself.

He liked the sound of that. He would have a nice big desk in
a pleasant office, and would sit there and work on budgeting and
manpower projections.

No more robberies to deal with, no more murders to solve. The
stink of criminality would be forever banished from his world.

Oh yes, if he could just hold it together for this case, a rosy
future lay ahead.

What he did not know was that down in the car park there was
a man waiting for him – a man who would hold up his dreams,
and shred them before his very eyes.

After a day of driving aimlessly around Lancashire, Kate Meadows
had finally forced herself to return to Overcroft House, and now
was sitting in her office, her head in her hands, wondering just
how much the police investigation would uncover – and how
quickly it might do it.

If she was lucky, they would never find out that Andrew
Lofthouse had been to the Hellfire Club that night, and if they
didn't uncover that basic fact . . .

She heard a knock on the door, and looked up to find Jane
Lofthouse standing there. But it wasn't her Jane – the Jane she
had got to know over the previous six weeks. Her Jane was quiet,
withdrawn and – to be brutally honest – as scared as a rabbit
caught in headlights. This Jane was the Jane she'd briefly glanced
the day before – a confident Jane who had assured her that if she
wanted Hadley Security, she would get Hadley Security. And
though she was wearing clothes Meadows had seen her in previously – Armani jeans and a Dolce and Gabbana cashmere top – this
new self of hers seemed to transform them into a power-dressing
business suit.

'I'm leaving,' Jane said, 'but before I do, I want to thank you
and to give you this.'

She laid a cheque on the desk. It was made out to Overcroft
House and was for ten thousand pounds.

'It's a lot of money,' Meadows said. 'Are you sure you can afford it?'

Jane smiled. 'There won't be much of my share dividend left when I've covered it,' she said, 'but yes, I can afford it – easily.'

'And I'm not sure it's wise for you to leave just like that,' Meadows cautioned, pushing her own worries aside only by a huge effort of will. 'You've not stepped outside Overcroft House for nearly two months. You should move out in stages.'

'I've no time for that,' Jane told her. 'Now Andrew's dead, I have a business to run – two businesses, in fact, mine and his.'

'I can't believe there aren't any good people there you could delegate to,' Meadows said.

'You're sort of right,' Jane said. 'There are people who could *probably* run the business for a while, but I daren't risk trusting them with it, because if I'm even a little bit wrong about their abilities, the competition will eat us alive.'

'We all think we're indispensable . . .' Meadows began.

'When I made Amos Hardcastle an offer for Whitebridge Bottling, he virtually ripped the cheque out of my hand,' Jane said. 'Because, you see, he thought I had no better chance of saving the business than he had himself. *Most* people thought it was doomed, but I had a few loyal staff who believed in me, and in themselves, and by hard work and self-sacrifice, we managed to pull it off. And I can't let those people down now, because they've got commitments – which I encouraged them to take on – and they can't meet those commitments without their monthly salary.'

'Even so . . .'

'Andrew may have been a brute in our private life, but I trusted him to run the business more than competently, and look after our employees. The only other person I trust to do that is me.'

'Very well,' Meadows conceded. 'I suppose, when all's said and done, it is your choice.'

But she was thinking, 'And there goes my last chance of keeping my connection to Andrew Lofthouse quiet.'

'You're worried that when I talk to the police, I'll mention the fact that Andrew came here yesterday afternoon, aren't you?' Jane asked.

'No, not at all,' Meadows lied – because the last thing she needed was Jane telling the bobbies that Meadows tried to talk her into holding back information.

Jane smiled. 'You don't fool me. I know you have your reasons for wanting me to keep quiet, and I understand them completely.'

'You do?'

'Of course! If I tell them, they'll be up here in a flash, questioning anything that moves, and bagging anything that doesn't. The fact that they'll be dealing with battered wives won't bother them – but it will definitely bother me. Can you imagine what being questioned by the police might do to Lucy's delicate mental balance? Or how Joyce's three kids are likely to react? And it would be even worse for Lizzie, whose been a very good friend to me, because she's already terrified of the cops. They've all been through enough already, and I don't want to be responsible for subjecting them to any more. Besides, Andrew's visit had nothing to do with his murder, did it?'

'No, of course not,' Meadows agreed.

'Well, I'd better be going, then,' Jane said, and though she sounded casual, they both knew it was not a casual decision she was taking.

Meadows rolled her chair over to the small bank of monitors. 'Better check out the grounds before I open the door,' she said.

'Is that strictly necessary?' said Jane, who was now obviously impatient to leave.

'Yes, it is,' Meadows told her.

'But there's not likely to be anybody out there, is there? I mean, we don't exactly announce the fact that this is a home for battered women, do we?'

'Your husband found us,' Meadows pointed out. 'Why wouldn't some other violent man – Lizzie's boyfriend, for example?'

Jane laughed. 'That's rather unlikely, isn't it? After all, Andrew was an intelligent chap, and Gary's just a mindless thug. And besides, isn't he in hospital?'

'He's just come out,' Meadows told her. 'You should never underestimate the cunning of a wife beater, Jane – and you should know that better than most.'

'Point taken,' Jane said, sounding a little shamefaced.

Meadows tapped out commands on the keyboard, and the CCTV cameras did a broad sweep of the grounds.

'Your husband told me that he knew you were here because he got an anonymous letter, and I've been wondering who might have sent it,' she said. 'Who did you tell you were coming here, Jane?'

'I didn't tell anyone. I suddenly couldn't take it anymore, and

I just packed a bag and ran away from home. I wasn't even sure I was coming here until I found myself on the front doorstep, ringing the bell. The leak must have come from one of your staff.'

'It didn't,' Meadows said fiercely. She took a deep breath and grinned self-consciously. 'Sorry about coming on so strong.'

'There's no need to apologise,' Jane told her. 'You're loyal to your staff, like I'm loyal to mine.'

'I just can't believe the leak came from here,' Meadows said. 'I trust Mary and I trust the doctor. And the cleaners don't even know your surname.'

'What about the police?' Jane asked.

'The police?'

'Don't you register your inmates with them?'

'Yes, we're required to . . .'

'Well, there's your leak,' Jane said.

That was possible, Meadows conceded, and under normal circumstances she would have raised that possibility with Louisa Rutter – but these were not normal circumstances.

She scanned the monitors again. 'I can't see anything out there to worry about,' she said.

'Is everything we can see on the screens taped?' Jane asked, sounding slightly troubled.

'Why do you ask that?'

'Because if it is, I'd get rid of yesterday's tape – you know, the one where you kick Andrew in the balls.'

Meadows heard a car pull outside, and glanced down at the screen. 'Your taxi's arrived.'

'Don't you agree – the tape has to go?' Jane persisted, with a hint of urgency in her voice. 'It's your interests I'm thinking of, you know.'

'I think it's safe to let you out now,' Meadows replied, standing up and heading for the door.

Detective Chief Superintendent Towers' nickname was 'Tiny' which meant, of course that he was anything but. In any group of officers, he was always the tallest by half a head, and there were those who claimed – only half-jokingly – that Towers was not his real name at all, and he had only adopted it to underline the fact that he towered over everyone else.

DCI Dawson had an uneasy relationship with his superior. The men were friends within the cultural confines and limitations of the police force, which meant that Towers might invite the chief inspector out to his place in the country for the occasional Sunday barbeque, and Dawson might be allowed to call the chief super-intendent 'Ben' once or twice during an evening of boozing – but Dawson knew that he must never forget which of them was the big chief and which was the humble Indian, and was careful never to step over the invisible line.

Thus, when Dawson saw Towers lurking in the police car park – and lurking was the only word for it – a sudden iceberg announced its arrival in the pit of his stomach.

Towers smiled his 'matey' smile – which was a very bad sign.

'Knocking off for the night, are you?' he asked.

Dawson shrugged awkwardly. 'Yes, well, you know what it's like with a murder inquiry, sir. I'm going to grab a few hours' kip before things start really hotting up.'

'Come and have a drink first,' Towers suggested.

The iceberg in Dawson's gut was reaching Titanic-sinking proportions.

'I don't really think I should, sir,' he said weakly. 'I'm feeling really knackered and—'

'It's always good to talk a case over with a more experienced officer,' Towers said, as if he'd never spoken. 'Where do you fancy? The Grapes?'

'The Grapes would be fine,' Dawson said, with a resigned sigh.

EIGHT

J ane Lofthouse and Kate Meadows walked down the corridor from Meadows' office to the front door.

'Just before I came to see you, I felt this almost overpowering urge to get out of here as quickly as possible,' Jane said. 'It was almost as if the fire doors were calling me: "Come on, Jane, straight through here. Nothing could be easier".'

Meadows smiled. 'But you obviously managed to resist the temptation.'

'Only by thinking about what a lot of bother it would create for you – the alarms going off, and police cars, with their sirens blaring, pulling up outside,' Jane said.

Meadows took the key from the cord around her neck, and inserted it into one of the security locks. When she heard it click, she removed the key and went through the same procedure with the second lock. That task completed, she opened the door.

A blast of cold air hit her, and though she had been expecting it, it still made her shiver.

She turned to Jane and gestured towards the outside. 'There you are,' she said with forced optimism, 'the wider world awaits you.'

Jane did not move. Instead, she stood staring into the dark night, her earlier confidence gone and a look of sheer horror filling her face.

'Maybe you were right about it being too soon, Kate,' she said. 'It's a long time since I've been out, and now I'm not sure that I want to go.' She let out a small sob. 'What shall I do? Whatever shall I do?'

'Take a deep breath, and consider your alternatives as calmly as you can,' Meadows said, in a soothing voice.

But she was thinking, 'You've already said you were going, so why don't you just piss off and give me a little space to deal with my own problems.'

'It was only Andrew I was frightened of, and now he's not a threat anymore, is he?' Jane said.

Well, he wasn't a direct threat, Meadows agreed silently, but he could still do immeasurable damage from beyond the grave.

'I'm going,' Jane said, suddenly decisive again. 'I can't tell how grateful I am to you.' She bent forward and kissed Meadows lightly on the cheek. 'Let me know when Lizzie is about to have the baby, and I'll drop whatever I'm doing and rush over here. I do so want to be with her when the baby is born. I really do.'

'I know. I'll make sure you get the word,' Meadows promised.

Jane turned, and walked quickly through the garden. The taxi driver took her suitcase and opened the back door for her. She got in without looking back.

Meadows stood watching as the taxi made its way along the street and turned the corner.

It felt as if a part of her world had slipped away, she thought, and that was probably because it had.

She wished that she drank or took drugs, but she didn't do either of those things. Her only real distraction in life was a little harmless S&M, but that wasn't possible at that moment. And anyway, it was starting to look as if it wasn't that harmless after all.

She took a deep breath. She wanted to get into her car and drive away into the night, just as she had after that terrible thing that had happened at Lofthouse's home, but she knew that was a luxury she could not afford. What she had to do – even though just the thought of it was enough to set her stomach churning – was return to her office, play the surveillance tape, and see for herself just how bad things looked.

Chief Superintendent Towers selected a table in the saloon bar of the Bunch of Grapes, and called the waiter over.

'What's your poison, Eric?' he asked. 'Scotch?'

'I think I'd better stick to beer tonight,' Dawson said.

'Sod that for a game of soldiers,' Towers replied. 'Two glasses of Bells' please, waiter. And you'd better make them doubles.' He waited until the waiter was out of earshot, then continued, 'So how's the investigation going?'

Maybe this wasn't such a bad idea after all, Dawson thought. Maybe Towers could actually advise him on a couple of things that were really bothering him.

'It's early days yet,' Dawson said, 'but it looks like it could get quite tricky.'

'Tricky?' Towers repeated. 'How?'

'Well, the killer's been so careful not to leave clues that we're starting to think that maybe a police officer—'

He got no further, because Towers hand shot across the table and grabbed his wrist.

'It would be a big mistake to start investigating your fellow bobbies,' Towers said, his thumb digging down into Dawson's wrist. 'A very big mistake. Have you got that?'

The pain was excruciating, and all Dawson's instincts screamed at him that he should either tell Towers to stop or punch the bastard in the face.

He didn't do either. Instead, speaking through clenched teeth, he just managed to gasp, 'Yes, sir, I get it.'

Towers released his grip immediately.

'Sorry about that,' he said. 'I just get a bit worked up when anybody talks about the possibility of there being bent bobbies. There are some, of course. I know, logically, that a few police officers do take bribes, and an even smaller number kill other people, but, you know . . .'

He let the sentence trail off, and Dawson, whose wrist was still smarting like hell, felt he had little choice but to say, 'Yes, I know.'

'In fact, this should never have happened, and it's entirely my fault,' Towers continued. 'The main point of inviting you out was to give you a bit of time off from the case, yet the first thing I do is to ask you how the investigation's going. Stupid!'

'It's always good to talk a case over with a more experienced officer,' he'd said in the police car park – but that was then and this was now.

The waiter returned with the drinks, and without asking how much they cost, Towers casually threw a few notes on his tray.

'That's payment in advance, laddie,' Towers told the waiter. 'Every time it looks like we might be running out, bring us another round. And if you do a good job, there'll be a pony for you at the end of the session.'

'You're going to give him twenty-five pounds!' Dawson mused, as the waiter walked away. 'That was very generous of you, sir.'

'It wasn't generous at all,' Towers told him. 'The secret of getting on in life is working out what you need to pay to get the result you want, and then being prepared to pay it. If I was drowning in the river, and that waiter happened to be walking past, he'd probably pretend he hadn't seen me, but while I'm here, that tip ensures that he's my willing slave, and he'd trample over his own grey-haired granny in order to serve me.'

Though the little speech purported to be about the waiter, it wasn't about him at all, Dawson thought. The message – or perhaps the warning – had been aimed squarely at him.

'We're off to Jamaica for our holidays this year,' Towers said. 'Where are you and Cissy going?'

'Tenerife,' Dawson said, thinking, even as he spoke, that he sounded almost as if he was ashamed of it.

Towers grinned. 'Not very adventurous of you, is it?' he asked.

No, it wasn't, Dawson thought, but then he *wasn't* adventurous. His whole life had been guided by caution and the avoidance of conflict, and the fact that he had somehow achieved his present rank was a constant source of amazement to him.

'Why don't you consider going further afield next time?' Towers asked.

'We can't afford it,' Dawson said, which was at least half true. 'What with the mortgage and . . .'

'My Caribbean holiday has turned out to be quite cheap,' Towers said. 'Do you know why that was?'

'No,' Dawson said dutifully, because that was what was expected of him. 'Why was it quite cheap?'

'Because I've got lots of friends who want to do me a favour,' Towers explained. 'And that's your problem, Eric – you haven't got enough people in your debt. But that could change – if you play your cards right.'

'Oh,' Dawson said, inadequately.

Towers looked down at his glass. 'Enough of drinking this rubbish,' he said, grandly. He signalled to the waiter, 'Bring us a couple of Glenmorangie twelve-year-old malt whiskies.'

'I'll get these,' Dawson said, reaching for his wallet.

'That you will not,' Towers countered, clamping his hand on the other man's arm (though gently this time). 'Tonight's entirely on me.'

'Oh Jesus,' Dawson moaned softly to himself.

'Do you know how I got my master's degree?' Towers asked.

'No, sir,' Dawson said.

But he was thinking, 'and why should I give a shit, anyway?'

'It took me three years of night school and two summer schools,' Towers said gravely. 'And that's not because I'm a stupid man . . .'

'Nobody was suggesting you were, sir,' Dawson injected quickly.

'Three years' night school and two summer schools is how long it takes most people. It's bloody hard work, and you even have to pay part of the fees out of your own pocket.'

Ah, now he was starting to get a sense of which way the wind was blowing, Dawson thought.

'But there's some who have it easier than that, aren't there, sir?' he said, taking a tentative step in what he hoped was the right direction.

'Yes, there's some who have it easier than that,' Towers echoed him. 'There's some who get to go to America for a whole year

– six months in Georgetown University, six months in FBI headquarters – and it doesn't cost them a penny.'

Dawson could have pointed out that it hadn't cost Mid Lancs
Constabulary a penny, either, since Louisa Rutter had been awarded
a Georgetown-FBI scholarship. He could have added that there
was a great deal of prestige attached to the scholarships, and that
most officers on the force had been really chuffed that someone
from a relatively obscure authority like theirs had been able to
win it. And to round it up, he could have reminded Towers that
one of the conditions attached to attending the course was that
once Louisa Rutter returned to England, she had been obliged to
sacrifice one weekend a month for two years, to giving unpaid
seminars on what she'd learned on the other side of the pond.

He could have pointed these things out – but he didn't.

'There's going to be a new regional crime squad,' Towers said.
'Have you heard about it?'

'No,' Dawson admitted, 'I haven't.'

'Of course you haven't,' Towers said dismissively. 'You've let
yourself get so far out of the loop that you know less than
the station cat does.'

'I . . . I . . .' Dawson mumbled inadequately.

'Anyway this new squad will be totally independent of all the
authorities whose patches it operates in, and answerable only to
its own governing body, which, as far as I can tell, will be made
up of county councillors and solicitors.'

He paused. He was obviously expecting a comment, and Dawson
wracked his brains as to what the expected comment should be.

'Amateurs,' he said finally, crossing his mental fingers.

Towers nodded encouragingly, but said nothing.

'Whoever's in charge of the squad should be able to run rings
round them,' Dawson ploughed on, praying he was reading the
signs correctly.

'Smart lad,' Towers said, patting him on the shoulder with the
force of a small sledgehammer. 'This new squad will work out of
a new purpose-built headquarters near Preston – a complete break
with the past, you see. Whoever is chief super will have more
power than a chief constable. If he's got political ambitions, he
couldn't find a better launch pad. If all he wants to do is feather
his nest, the opportunities are there for the taking. But the most
important power he'll have, at least as far as you're concerned,'

he paused for dramatic effect, 'is that he'll be allowed to pick his own team.'

'I see,' Dawson said – because he had to say something.

'It's the job I've been waiting for my entire career,' Towers continued, 'and there's only one other really viable candidate.'

Click! Now it really all fitted together!

'You're talking about Chief Superintendent Rutter, aren't you?' Dawson asked.

'None other,' Towers agreed.

'You've got more experience than she has, sir. You're bound to get the job.'

It had meant to be reassuring, but from the frown which now filled Towers' face, it was clearly not the answer he wanted.

'I've rung Whitebridge General, and they told me that they'll be keeping Droopy Dave, our beloved deputy chief, for at least a week,' Towers said. 'As for the chief, well, he's already made it plain that his golf tour is far more important than keeping Mid Lancs safe, so it looks as if Chief Superintendent Rutter is going to be in charge for a while longer.' He took another sip of his scotch and smacked his lips with pleasure. 'You see what I'm saying here?'

'No,' Dawson said – though he had a terrible feeling that he did.

'This Lofthouse murder is an important case because Andrew Lofthouse was an important man in Whitebridge. So if we don't get a result, who do you think it will damage?'

'Me.'

Towers made a sweeping gesture with his hand, as if brushing that possibility aside as a mere irrelevance.

'Yes, you probably would take a bit of a knock,' he admitted, 'but you're only a minor cog in the machine, and I've already found a way to more than generously compensate you. But who will really suffer? Who will be crucified in the press – especially if I whisper the right word in the right ear? And who will those people who can make or break a simple bobby's career be pissed off at?'

'You're . . . you're saying you want me to sabotage my own investigation,' Dawson said.

'Oh, no, no, no,' Towers replied, wagging his finger. 'I would never ask you to do that. But if you didn't get a result, I certainly wouldn't hold it against you, whereas if you did get a result, I might not always look on you favourably.'

Well, that was certainly clear enough, Dawson thought. What he was being presented with was a scale, with the possibility of conducting a proper investigation (and thus earning brownie points) on one side, and the certainty that if he did do that he would make an enemy of Chief Superintendent Towers on the other. It was impossible to make the scale balance, so the only question was which way he would allow it to tip.

'As I said, I'll be given complete freedom to select my team for the new squad,' Towers continued, almost dreamily, 'and when I'm deciding who to select as my number two, I'll obviously bear in mind the history I have with the men I'm considering.'

So there it was – the bribe for being a good little bobby – out in the open at last.

'It's really in your hands whether I consider you or not,' Towers said. 'Do you think it's likely that I will be able to consider you?'

Dawson swallowed hard.

'Very likely, sir,' he said.

Towers smiled. 'Good,' he said. 'In that case, I'd better order another two shots of that expensive whisky.'

The black-and-white image of the soon-to-be dead man stands five feet from the front door of Overcroft House. The door itself falls within the camera's blind area.

It is clear from the man's body language and gestures that he is confronting someone, and he is very angry with that person. Then the man suddenly rushes forward, so only the backs of his legs are visible, though it is possible to infer what is happening, because the position of the legs reveals that the man is leaning forward – using his bodyweight to force the door open.

For a second, the man goes off screen, but when he appears again, he is hopping backwards and holding one foot in his hands. And now someone else had joined him, and that someone is clearly identifiable as Kate Meadows. For perhaps two seconds, she does nothing, then she lashes out with her foot, catching the man squarely in the groin. The man doubles up, topples backwards and hits the ground. Kate Meadows disappears from the screen, and so is no longer one of the stars of this nasty little movie.

Kate switched off the machine, and took out the tape.

'*If I were you, I'd get rid of that tape,*' Jane had said.

It made sense, because although it wasn't exactly a smoking gun, any halfway competent barrister could make it *seem* as if it was.

She ran her finger around the edge of the tape.

It would be so easy to get rid of it.

She could burn it in the basement furnace.

She could drop it in the canal.

She could even unroll it and feed it through her shredder.

It was the wise thing to do – the only safe thing. Yet she couldn't bring herself to actually do it, because her police officer gut – so long dormant she had almost forgotten it was there – had come back to life and was telling her – was *insisting* – that destroying the tape would be a very bad idea.

You're wrong, she told the gut – but the gut would have none of it.

Very well then, if she was not going to destroy it, what was she going to do with it?

'It has to go in the secret drawer, you idiot!' said an inner voice.

The secret drawer! Another relic of her past she had almost forgotten about.

She pressed the concealed button on her desk, and the drawer slid open. It was not a deep drawer – it would have been much too hard to disguise a deep one – but it was wide, and so much of the history Meadows had chosen to leave behind her was on display. She saw the royal charter, passed down through generations of Clifford's family, and next to it the newspaper accounts of his death. There was the passbook to the Swiss bank account she had never used, and the ring which the Aga Khan had presented her with on her marriage. There was . . .

There was a lot of stuff it was best to ignore. She placed the tape in the drawer and slid it closed.

She stepped back. There was no indication that the drawer had been there, and it would take a real expert to locate it. The tape could remain hidden forever, if that was what she wanted.

How long would it take the police to find her, she wondered.

If the old team had been on the case, it wouldn't have taken them more than a day to track down the woman with the huge purple wig.

So what should she do – just sit there and wait?

She picked up the phone, and dialled a number she had not

used for years, but still knew by heart, and when the woman at the other end answered, she said, 'It's Kate, boss.'

Boss?

Boss!

She'd never meant to say that!

'This isn't a social call, is it?' Monika Paniatowski asked. 'I can tell from the tone of your voice.'

'No, it isn't a social call,' Kate agreed. 'Can you spare me half an hour, boss?'

'Well, of course I can,' Paniatowski replied. 'When and where?'

'Now would be good. At your house, if that's possible.'

'Yes, that's possible,' said Paniatowski, sounding troubled.

'Then I'm on my way,' Meadows said, dropping the phone back on its cradle and heading for the door.

NINE

K ate Meadows and Monika Paniatowski sat facing each other across the table in Monika's kitchen. Kate Meadows had a glass of water in front of her, and took small nervous sips from it, like a thirsty wild bird recklessly refreshing itself from a garden pond, yet always on the alert for the cat. Monika Paniatowski, in contrast, had a large glass of vodka in front of her, and had thus far taken at least three deep swallows.

'So let me see if I've got this straight,' Paniatowski said. 'You broke all your own rules by going to a club so near to home, and the reason you let that happen was because you felt so much under stress.'

'That's right.'

'*Why* did you feel under such stress, Kate?'

Meadows shrugged awkwardly. 'I can't exactly say. It was just that after the fight with Lofthouse at Overcroft House, my brain kept sending out messages that something was about to go badly wrong.'

So you helped it along the way by doing precisely what you shouldn't have done, Paniatowski thought.

'What precisely did Lofthouse say to you in this Hellfire Club?' she asked aloud.

'He said I had two choices. Either I accepted that he was going to expose me to Overcroft's board of governors, or we could go back to his house and discuss alternative arrangements.'

'And you agreed to go with him.'

'Yes, because the way I saw it, there was really no choice at all.'

'How did you get there?'

'He went in his car, and I went in mine.'

'And were you still being Zelda?'

'Yes.'

'So what happened when you arrived?'

'He tried to treat it like a date at first, but I wasn't having any of that. I told him to come straight out with what he had on his mind.'

'And did he?'

'Yes.'

Paniatowski sighed. 'You came to me, you know,' she said. 'It was you who wanted to talk. It really shouldn't be necessary for me to conduct an interrogation.'

'Sorry,' Meadows said. 'It's not easy to talk about it.'

'No, but it still has to be said.'

'He described a number of things he wanted us to do together, and I said I wouldn't do them, even if that did mean he'd tell the board of governors all about me. And then I left.'

'What was it he wanted you to do?' Paniatowski asked.

'I don't want to talk about that,' Meadows said, looking down at the table.

'I need to know,' Paniatowski insisted.

'It's not important,' Meadows exploded in a sudden burst of anger. 'Move on.'

'Did you see anybody else who might have recognized you in the club?'

Meadows shook her head. 'When I'm Zelda, even you wouldn't recognize me.'

'Did you see anyone who knew Zelda?'

Another shake of the head. 'The Hellfire is a third division sort of club. Zelda only ever plays in the first division. But I told the bouncer I was Zelda, and word will have got around, like it does when any celebrity visits a place.'

She wasn't boasting, Paniatowski thought. Zelda was famous – if that was the right word for it!

'You're in deep trouble,' Paniatowski said. 'But you already know that – which is why you're here.'

'Yes,' Meadows admitted. 'I had both the motive and the opportunity to kill him. In addition, there was a prior act of violence just a few hours earlier.'

'There are police forces that would look no further for their murderer, but this isn't one of them,' Paniatowski said. 'And you're particularly lucky this week – although that's perhaps not the best way to phrase it – because Louisa's in charge. She won't let her Auntie Kate be banged up for something she didn't do. She'll see to it that a proper investigation is carried out, and the right man tracked down.'

'So you're saying I should surrender myself at the police station?' Meadows said, in a dull, flat voice.

'Well, yes,' Paniatowski replied, surprised that she even needed to ask.

'I can't do it,' Meadows said determinedly.

'What!'

'I can't do it. If I admit I was there, I'll also be admitting I'm Zelda. And if I admit I'm Zelda, I'll lose my job. And I can't live without that job, Monika.'

There were tears in Meadows' eyes. It was the first time Paniatowski had seen her cry in all the years she'd known her.

'So what are you planning to do instead? Just sit it out, and hope the investigating officers never learn that you were involved?'

'I did think of that,' Meadows admitted, 'but it wouldn't work, because I've left behind so many clues that even the most blundering detective in the world couldn't miss them. And in a way, that proves my innocence, doesn't it?' she asked hopefully.

'Does it?' Paniatowski asked.

'Yes, because if I'd been the killer, I'd have made sure I left no trace of myself behind.'

'On the face of it, that sounds like a sound argument – but *only* on the face of it,' Paniatowski said. 'Over the years, we must have heard suspects make exactly that claim a couple of dozen times, and the fact that it's you saying it rather than one of them doesn't make it any more reasonable.'

'You're right,' Meadows conceded, 'and even if you weren't, it would involve me admitting to going to the Hellfire Club, and I can't do that. So it just has to be Plan B.'

'And what's Plan B?'

'I have to find out who killed Andrew Lofthouse before the police find out I was ever involved.'

'You mean *we* have to find out,' Paniatowski said angrily. 'You mean I have to break the law – turn my back on everything I've ever worked for – to get you off a hook that you're only hanging on because of your own stupidity.'

'You're right,' Meadows said, sounding both regretful and pained. 'I couldn't possibly ask you to do that.' She stood up. 'I should never have come here. Please forget I ever did.'

'Just a minute,' Paniatowski said, as Meadows reached for the door handle. 'You'll never manage it on your own, you know.'

Meadows nodded again. 'I do know,' she agreed, 'but Plan B is all I have, and I've got to give it a try.'

'Even the two of us couldn't swing it,' Paniatowski mused. 'We'd need the full team to have even a slight chance.'

'Colin Beresford would never—' Meadows began.

'You're wrong,' Paniatowski interrupted her. 'Colin just might.' She forced a grin to her face. 'He's very fond of you, you know – in a can't-stand-that-bloody-woman kind of way.'

'I can't ask him,' Meadows said.

'I know you can't,' Paniatowski agreed, 'but I can. I can ask Jack Crane, too.'

She ran her eyes up and down Meadows' body. The woman looked shattered – and that was a first, too.

'Would you like to stay the night?' she suggested. 'I can make you up a bed in Louisa's old room.'

'Chief Superintendent Rutter's old room, you mean,' Meadows said, and grinned weakly, to show she could still make a joke.

'Chief Superintendent Rutter's room,' Paniatowski agreed.

'I'd like to, but I can't,' Meadows said regretfully. 'One of my clients left today, and that always unsettles the others. Besides, Lizzie Grimshaw's expecting her baby any day now, and I need to be around when her water breaks.'

And what happens if you're in a police interrogation room when her waters break, Paniatowski thought – but she said nothing.

'Here's how it will work then,' she said. 'Be in the Drum and Monkey at two o'clock tomorrow afternoon . . .'

'The Drum and Monkey!' Meadows repeated, with something like wonder. 'Are you sure it's still there?'

'It's still there,' Paniatowski replied. 'I've walked past it several times.'

And wished I was inside, doing what I did best, she added silently.

'So we meet in the Drum—' Meadows began.

'I didn't say that,' Paniatowski interrupted her. 'I said that's where you should be.'

'What's the difference?'

'We may be there – which will mean that the whole team has decided to put its neck on the line for you. Or we may not be there.'

'And if you're not there, it means that I'm on my own, and you're all keeping as far away from me as possible, to avoid even a hint of complicity.'

'Yes,' Paniatowski agreed. 'I'm sorry, but that is what it will mean.'

For a moment, it looked as if Meadows was about to cry again, then she threw back her head and said, 'That's the way it has to be. I can see that. I wouldn't have it any *other* way.' She opened the door and stepped into the backyard. 'So I'll see you tomorrow – maybe.'

'So you'll see us tomorrow – maybe,' Paniatowski agreed.

TEN

Thursday, 3 February, 2000

Monika Paniatowski had never been a relaxed sleeper – those early years on the run through enemy territory had cured her of that habit – but some nights were worse than others, and the one that followed Kate Meadows' visit was one

of the worst in a very long time. All the usual dreams were there
– the German soldiers (who were terrible); the Russian soldiers
(who were even worse); her stepfather lying on top of her, his hot
stinking breath on her face almost as bad as what he was doing
down below; her one true love, Bob Rutter, driving over the cliff
and plunging to his death. But that night there was something new
– that night she had what, in a more whimsical mood, she might
have called a Biblical blockbuster dream.

*She is in a park of some kind, and since she can see a number of
olive trees, she guesses it is on the Mediterranean.*

*She is not alone. A number of men dressed in robes are there,
too.*

Twelve – she counts them and there are twelve.

*And suddenly, she knows where she is. This is the Garden of
Gethsemane, and one of these men is Jesus Christ.*

*She hears the heavy, regular footfalls of a number of men,
drawing ever closer. Some of the men are holding flaming brands
to light the way, and as they trot, the flames go up and down,
continually changing the pattern of shadows by the side of the
path.*

*They are almost there, and she knows what she has to do. She
steps forward. Jesus is standing with His back to her, but she taps
him lightly on the shoulder, so He will turn around and she can
deliver the kiss of betrayal.*

*The flaming torches draw ever closer, and as Jesus turns, she
can see that it is not Him at all, but a woman!*

And she knows her!

It is Kate Meadows!

No, it is Louisa!

No, it is . . .

*Then the temple soldiers move in, enclosing their target, and
though Monika implores them to let her through, they don't listen.*

*She has to see who it is she was about to kiss – about to betray
– but she can't, even when she stands on tiptoe.*

But she has to know – she has to.

By the time she'd had two cups of coffee, and three Silk Cut
cigarettes, she was starting to feel a little better. The weather
helped. When she had gone to bed, thick clouds had shrouded the

moon, but now the sky was almost a perfect blue, and the air (which she tested through the open window) was remarkably mild for early February.

It was pointless to allow mere dreams to affect you, she told her herself. It was pointless, too, to deny that though she had woken up weighed down by a blanket of dread, that blanket had been overlaid – ever-so-lightly – with a dash of excitement at being back in the game.

Monika Paniatowski was the proud owner of a white MG MGA Twin Cam sports' car. It could accelerate from zero to sixty in nine point one seconds, and once she was behind the wheel, Paniatowski thought of herself as the queen of the road. It was also a gas-guzzling monster, especially at speed, but as she pulled out of her garage and listened to the eager roar of the engine, she knew it was worth every penny she spent on it.

Paniatowski crossed Whitebridge and headed out along the Preston Road. The road was a dual carriageway, convenient for anyone wanting to get to Preston in the shortest possible time, but very boring for a woman driving an MGA, and the moment she had the opportunity, she turned on to a country lane, where it was possible to do some real driving.

This was the second MGA she had owned. The first had been back in the olden days, when the only mobile phones you saw belonged to Captain Kirk and Mr Spock on *Star Trek*, and when DNA, while an interesting curiosity, was still a long way from being of any use in police work. The car had been her pride and joy, and she had only sold it (with a great many sighs and not a few tears) for practical reasons, when she gave birth to the twins.

She had bought the new one when she retired (though new was scarcely the right word for it, since the last one made had rolled off the production line in 1962).

This one required considerably more effort to keep it roadworthy than the previous one had, partly because most of the mechanics who understood the intricacies of its engine were either retired or working in the Great Garage in the Sky. Thus, Paniatowski had been forced to enrol in an enthusiast's course – Mechanics for MGAheads – in order to be able to do some of the work herself, and had been surprised to discover that she quite enjoyed it.

Parts were also a problem. However careful a driver you were

– and Paniatowski had never been one of those – parts did tend to get worn out after more than forty years of use. New parts were no longer being made, so replacements could only be obtained by cannibalizing one of the 5869 other MGAs which had been sold in Britain – and these sad old wrecks might be rusting away anywhere from a scrap yard in southern Cornwall to a decaying barn in northern Scotland.

Paniatowski did not mind the hassle. After so many years of dealing with the tangled mess which people (including herself) had managed to make of their lives, she thought, it was a relief to have nothing more to worry about than the engine misfiring or the carburettor getting blocked.

Dealing with the tangled messes which people had managed to make of their lives! she repeated to herself.

She really thought she'd left all that behind her, yet here was a new one – and, like the MGA, it was a real classic.

To protect Kate, she – and the rest of the old team – would have to break the law (or ignore it, which, in practical terms, was just as bad) and that was almost unthinkable. To protect Kate, she would be forced to indulge in some actions which might very well undermine her own daughter. And that was unthinkable too. Yet after the way that Kate had supported her all these years, it was equally unthinkable to simply throw her to the wolves.

It was a relief – or at least a distraction – to turn off the country lane on to a dirt track which had the MGA bouncing up and down and releasing mechanical howls of pain.

'It's only like this for about eight hundred metres,' Monika promised the car, and then, remembering how ancient it was, she added, 'that's about half a mile in old money.'

The old house she was approaching was made of dressed stone blocks, and hunkered close to the ground under the pressure of a heavy slate roof. It was surrounded by other stone buildings, all of them too small to presume to call themselves barns, and it was towards one of these that the woman carrying two enamel pails was heading as Paniatowski pulled into the yard.

The woman placed one of the pails on the ground, and waved. She was a good-looking blonde in her late fifties, and had what, in Central Lancs, was often referred to as 'a pair of prize-winning knockers'. The rest of her figure was in good shape, too, and if Paniatowski hadn't known it for a fact, she would never have believed that the woman had given birth to five children.

'If you're looking for my lord and master, he's repairing the fence in the upper field,' the woman said.

Paniatowski grinned. The idea that Colin Beresford should be the 'lord and master' of Lynn Beresford was beyond funny.

When they'd first met, she had been a murder suspect, and 'Shagger' had been a man who leapt from woman to woman as if they were nothing but stepping stones in the hedonistic journey which was his life. And now here he was, a married man with five kids, repairing the fence in the top field.

'If you want to see him, we'd better take the tractor, because driving up there in your Dinky car could just about rupture it,' Lynn added.

'OK,' Paniatowski agreed.

'I'll just feed the pigs first, if you don't mind,' Lynn said, picking up the pails again.

'I don't mind at all,' Paniatowski told her.

Kate Meadows was sitting in her office – doing her best to pretend that this was just a normal day – when Ruby Watkins, the midwife, tapped lightly on her door, and said, 'Could you spare a few minutes to talk to Lizzie?'

'Is anything wrong?' Meadows asked, feeling a prickle of alarm.

'Not wrong exactly,' Mrs Watkins replied, 'but Lizzie is a little upset, and I thought it would be better if you handled it.'

'What's she upset about, exactly?' Meadows asked.

'As you know, I've arranged for her to give birth in the maternity wing of Whitebridge General,' Mrs Watkins said. 'Up until now, she's been perfectly happy with the idea, but when I mentioned it today, she became hysterical.'

'Do you know why?'

'She says she wants to have the baby here. She won't even discuss the possibility of going into hospital.'

Meadows sighed. 'Then I had better go and talk to her,' she said.

The residents' rooms in Overcroft House had a standard layout – brown carpet, pale walls and white bathroom suite – but Meadows had established a small fund which allowed each guest to accessorize her room to suit her personality. Some of the guests chose pastel fabrics and pictures of pastoral idylls, the better to blend in with the already muted style of the room. Others, seeking a complete break from the life they'd known, selected tasselled scatter cushions in bright sumptuous colours, like the Hollywood idea of a Turkish harem.

Lizzie had gone in neither of these directions, preferring instead to be guided by the principle that pink was good, and pink and fluffy even better. Thus she had pink curtains, a pink bedspread and a pink nightdress. The cuddly toys she had bought for her expected child were all pink, too. And since she had been crying, her eyes, when she looked up, matched her surroundings perfectly.

'I won't go to hospital, Mrs Maybe,' she said. 'I won't! I won't! If I can't have my baby here, I'll kill myself.'

'If you killed yourself, you'd be killing the baby, too – and you wouldn't want that, would you?' Meadows asked softly.

'I'll kill myself. I swear I will,' Lizzie said, as if she hadn't heard. She held out her arm. 'I'll slash my wrists and bleed to death.'

'Please excuse us for a moment, Lizzie,' Meadows said, signalling to the midwife that they should step out into the corridor.

'I've never seen her like this before,' Mrs Watkins said.

'Neither have I,' Meadows said. 'She's normally so calm and sensible.'

'And cooperative,' the midwife said.

'And cooperative,' Meadows agreed. 'Is there any reason she couldn't have the baby here?'

'Not really. There are obvious advantages to a hospital birth, of course – there's a team of medics available to instantly deal with anything that's going wrong – but I've delivered scores of children at home. The mother has to be reasonably strong, but after a few months of being built up in here, Lizzie is certainly that.'

'Then given her obvious mental fragility – at least on this matter – I think we should give her what she wants.'

'Agreed,' Mrs Watkins said.

They went back into Lizzie's bedroom.

'If you want to give birth here, then that's what we'll do,' Meadows said.

Lizzie sniffed. 'Thank you, Mrs Maybe.'

'Is there anything else I can do for you at the moment?'

'I want the wardrobe,' Lizzie said.

Not *a* wardrobe, but *the* wardrobe, Meadows noted.

'Which wardrobe are we talking about?' she asked.

'The one I saw in the basement.'

'What were you doing in the basement?' Meadows wondered.

Lizzie shrugged. 'Just looking around,' she said unconvincingly. 'I wasn't doing anything wrong, was I?'

She seemed as if she was about to cry again.

'No, you weren't doing anything wrong,' Meadows assured her, 'but I'd still like to know why you went down there.'

Like a wild animal that realizes it's been trapped, Lizzie glanced frantically around the room, as if looking for an escape.

'Gary!' she gasped with relief.

'What about him?'

'That's why I went down to the basement. To find a hiding place in case Gary came looking for me. So can I have the wardrobe?'

It was a monstrous thing, huge and clumsy, with a walnut veneer which was chipped away at the edges. It would have fitted in – maybe – in the offices of an old-fashioned undertaker, but anywhere else it would look distinctly – and uncomfortably – out of place, and it was no great surprise that its previous owner had left it behind when he moved out. Meadows had tried to sell it at first, and when that failed, to give it away. But no one would have it – not even as a gift. And so it sat there in the basement, waiting for the warden to find the time to arrange for it to be taken to the dump.

'That old wardrobe would take up far too much of your living space,' she said looking around the room. 'You'd be banging into it all the time.'

'I don't care,' Lizzie told her.

'And you really haven't got enough clothes to need a wardrobe of that size.'

'I will have – eventually.'

'Listen, if you want another wardrobe, I'll buy you a nice light modern one – one that will blend in with this room.'

'Don't want a new one – I want the one in the basement,' Lizzie persisted.

'But why are you so keen on it?'

'It reminds me of when I was growing up,' Lizzie said. 'I had one just like it my bedroom.'

Meadows, who had read Lizzie's social worker's notes, didn't believe for a second that Lizzie would want to have *anything* that reminded her of her childhood, and if this situation had cropped up a few days earlier, she would have stuck at it until she'd learned what was really on Lizzie's mind. But this wasn't a few days earlier, and she wasn't the conscientious warden she'd been back then. Now, she was a woman drowning – exhausted and consumed by fear for her future – and she did not have the energy to pursue the matter any further.

'Please, Mrs Maybe, can I have it?' Lizzie said.

Meadows sighed. 'Yes, you can have it.'

'Thank you, Mrs Maybe. If my baby's a girl, I'll call her after you.'

Despite the nip in the air, Colin Beresford was stripped to the waist, and was holding a sledgehammer which he was using to drive a wooden post further into the ground. His naked torso was not as impressive as it had been twenty-five years earlier, but it was still impressive enough, and it was clear that farming – albeit part-time – was suiting him.

Lynn brought the tractor to a halt a few yards from where he was working. 'I've got a lot to do, so I'll leave the pair of you to it,' she said.

Paniatowski climbed down. Her bones were still vibrating from the ride, and she wondered how anyone ever managed to stay on a tractor for more than half an hour.

'Well, look what the cat dragged in,' Colin Beresford said cheerily. 'It's good to see you, Monika.'

He squatted down, picked a bottle which was leaning against the fence, and poured some of its contents into a mug, which he offered to Paniatowski. 'I've only got the one mug, so we'll have to share,' he said. 'Sorry about that.'

Paniatowski peered into the mug. The liquid inside was a sort of muddy green. She took a tentative sip.

'Well, tell me what you think of it,' Beresford said.

Paniatowski grimaced. 'It tastes like a diabetic tomcat has peed on a dead hedgehog,' she said. 'What is it?'

'Nettle beer,' Beresford said. 'I make it myself.'

'I'm not surprised. I certainly can't see anyone else having the nerve to give it to you,' Paniatowski replied.

The old Colin had been a drinker and a womanizer, but he had always been discriminating in both areas. There were men who would have sex with any woman who had a pulse (and a few who would even waive that qualification) but Colin had been choosy about his amorous encounters, even if they were only a one-night stand (as they invariably were). And he'd been even pickier with his beer: he drank only pints of Thwaites' Best Bitter, and would send them back to the bar if he decided that whoever had pulled them did not have sufficient expertise to serve up a really good pint. And just look at him now. He was monogamous for a start (and Paniatowski was sure of that, because if he hadn't been, Lynn would have killed him long ago), and drank a nettle beer which it would have been charitable to describe as toilet fluid.

Was there any point in asking this new Colin to sail with her on the good ship Probably End Badly?

Beresford took a gulp of his nettle beer, and wiped his mouth with the back of his hand.

'You've never been one to mess about, so why don't you tell me what's on your mind,' he suggested.

Paul Mason and Michael O'Casey were well aware that other people called them Casey and Masey – as if they were a pair of old-fashioned, end-of-the-pier comedians. It didn't bother them at all. In fact, they could be said to have earned the name by their habit of delivering their oral reports as if they were enacting comedy routines which were sometimes so old and feeble that they should never have been allowed to leave the intensive care unit. Occasionally, a new detective might rebuke them for their frivolity, but he would soon learn that they were the hardest working, most competent SOCOs in central Lancashire, and decide that their corny humour was well worth tolerating because of the information it carried within it.

On this, day two of the investigation into the death of Andrew Lofthouse, the team were lifting prints in the master bedroom when Mason looked at his watch and said, 'When are we expecting the other teams to arrive?'

'What other teams?' O'Casey asked.

'The other teams that Sergeant Boyd promised us would be shouldering some of the workload,' Mason said.

'Oh, them,' O'Casey said. 'They won't be coming. DCI Dawson phoned me and said something else had come up, and he couldn't spare anybody else.'

'You could have told me that earlier,' Mason said.

'I could,' O'Casey agreed, 'but I so hate to see you disappointed.'

'So there's just the two of us,' Mason mused.

'Why would you want more people around?' O'Casey asked in a mock-offended voice. 'Aren't I enough for you, anymore? Have you stopped loving me?'

'Of course I haven't stopped loving you,' Mason said scornfully. 'How could I, when you have everything a man could want – dandruff, bad breath, varicose veins, bunions—?'

'That's a dirty rotten goddam lie,' O'Casey interrupted him in a fake American accent which would have been embarrassing if it hadn't been deliberately bad. 'I do *not* have varicose veins.'

'Seriously, though, why are there only the two of us?' Mason asked. 'I could understand it if we were working in a terraced cottage – put more than two of us in a place like that and we'd be forever getting in each other's way – but this house is big enough to keep three or four teams busy.'

'Ours not to reason why, ours just to dust and pry,' O'Casey said whimsically. 'If I were you, I'd let the matter drop.'

But Mason was not prepared to do that.

'Just what case have they put the other teams on?' he demanded. 'Has there been another murder?'

'Not that I've heard about,' O'Casey admitted.

'So this case should be given top priority. We all know that the first forty-eight hours on an investigation are the most crucial, so why are they pissing us about?'

'It is a bit concerning when you put it like that,' O'Casey admitted.

'It's almost as if they didn't want this case solving,' Mason said.

'Yes, it is,' O'Casey agreed, suddenly sounding rather worried.

ELEVEN

The University of Central Lancashire had been established in the 1960s. In its youth, the campus had seethed with excitement and a belief that here was a place in which radical new ideas could be discussed, and previously hidden truths uncovered. But many newer institutions had sprung up since then, elbowing it out of its avant-garde position, and now it had entered a more sedate middle age – not quite a grandmother yet, but at least a maiden aunt.

Paniatowski walked across the main piazza (why couldn't they call the bloody thing a square, she wondered) to the lecture hall where she had been told she would find the man she was looking for.

The lecture was already underway, and she slid quietly into a seat at the back of the hall. The lecturer was a tall man in his mid-forties. He was handsome in a dashing romantic sort of way, and this impression was only heightened by the black patch which covered his left eye.

'So here we have Scene Two of Shakespeare's *Twelfth Night*,' Jack Crane was saying. 'What do you make of it?' He looked around his audience. 'You, Miss Bains, what's your opinion?'

'I think it's good, professor,' the girl said confidently.

She was the sort of girl who wouldn't exactly make an effort to trade on her looks, since she'd know she had no need to, Paniatowski thought sourly. She had that kind of gentle, almost characterless beauty which made boys hang around her like dogs on heat, and men treat her as if she were a combination of favourite daughter and approachable deity. And from the way she said 'professor', it was plain she thought she had Jack Crane exactly where she wanted him.

'Good?' Crane repeated, incredulously. 'You think it's *good*?'

'It's *very* good,' the girl amended,

'We have read the same scene, you and I, haven't we?' Crane asked, sounding genuinely puzzled.

'Er . . . yes . . . we . . .'

'Viola asks the sea captain what country they've been ship-wrecked in, and he says it's Illyria,' Crane said. 'Now they've been there for quite some time, so you'd have thought she might have asked that earlier, but we'll overlook that for the moment. She says her father once told her it was ruled by a Count Orsino, and that he was unmarried then. He's unmarried now, the captain tells her, although he is wildly in love with a lady called Olivia. Does that strike you as a normal conversation – one with a natural flow – Miss Bains?'

'No, not exactly,' the girl said, stumbling over her words. 'But it is Shakespearean.'

'Ah, that explains it then,' Jack Crane, 'Is there anything else about the scene we should discuss? Oh, yes! Viola says, I think my brother, Sebastian, died in the storm. I wonder why she hadn't mentioned *that* before? And the captain replies that he doesn't think he *is* dead, because before the ship went down, he saw Sebastian tie himself to the mast – another fact it's been rather insensitive of him to hold back for so long.' He paused, 'Still think it's good, Miss Bains?'

'Well, er . . .'

'Am I saying Shakespeare's rubbish?' Jack asked, speaking to the hall in general. 'No, I'm saying some of what he wrote is rubbish. Let me read you the opening of a play that isn't – the first scene of *Othello*.'

He read through the whole scene, playing all the parts himself. Paniatowski found it magical. He took her on a journey through the dark, damp streets of Venice. He made her shiver at the evil in Iago's words and share in Brabantio's anger and fear over his daughter's fate, and when he'd reached the end of the scene, she was exhausted.

'I could marry him,' a girl sitting close to her whispered to her friend. 'I'd do it tomorrow.'

'In case you haven't noticed, he's an old man,' her friend replied. 'But I know what you mean.'

An old man! Paniatowski thought.

Jesus, what did that make her?

'I wonder what happened to his eye,' one of the two whisperers said.

'I heard he lost it in a bar fight in Tangiers – over a woman,' the other girl told her.

Paniatowski chuckled softly to herself. Lost it in a bar fight in Tangiers! How much more romantic that was than the truth – that it had been gouged out with a screwdriver by a woman who was out of her mind on drugs.

'The whole essence of the play is contained in that one scene,' Crane was telling his students. 'It's brilliant, and I can't think of any other writer – living or dead – who could have done it.' He turned to the girl he'd addressed first. 'Do you feel I'm deliberately persecuting you, Miss Bains?'

'No, not at all,' the girl replied, unconvincingly.

'You certainly shouldn't,' Crane said softly. 'Virtually everyone in the hall would have reacted as you did to the text, but there are very few with the strength of character to come through the third degree like you did. I recognized that quality in you – and that's why I selected you for the verbal battering.'

Still the same smooth-talking bastard you always were, Jack, Paniatowski thought admiringly.

'Right, that's it for the day,' Crane continued. 'Go away and have sex or get high or do whatever else you do in your free time. And if you get bored, you might even think about reading a book.'

The students filed out, but Paniatowski stayed where she was. Crane showed no surprise at seeing her there, which meant that even though he'd given no sign of it, he must have spotted her much earlier. She gave herself a mental pat on the back for training him so well.

'Hello, boss,' he said, as he drew level with her. 'You're looking well.'

'So are you,' Paniatowski replied. 'Still not got a glass eye, I notice.'

Crane grinned. 'When you reach my age, it helps having a gimmick when you want to pull women,' he said. 'The patch gives me a certain air that certain women find intriguing.' He paused, and looked around him, as if to make sure that they were quite alone. 'So tell me about the Andrew Lofthouse murder,' he continued.

'How did you know . . .?' Paniatowski began.

But it was obvious how he knew. If she'd wanted to see him socially, she'd have rung up and made an arrangement. The very fact that she was there in the middle of the day meant she had something she needed to discuss with him, and given their past together, what else could it be but the murder that was currently dominating the newspapers?

'It has to be one of the old team that's somehow got tangled up in it,' Crane said, 'and my guess would be DS Meadows.'

'It's her,' Paniatowski confirmed.

'Given the way she is, something like this was bound to happen sooner or later,' Crane said.

True enough, Paniatowski agreed silently.

'I'm willing to do all I can to help her, and so is Colin Beresford,' she said. 'How about you?'

'Who could resist the opportunity to be in their very own Shakespearean tragedy?' Crane asked.

Louisa Rutter looked across her desk at DCI Dawson. He wasn't the man she would have assigned to this murder, she thought, and it was just bad luck that he'd been the one on call when the murder was reported. Still, she was stuck with him, so she supposed she'd better make the best of it.

'I notice you've only put one SOCO team on the case, Eric,' she said.

'That's right,' Dawson agreed, shifting uncomfortably in his seat.

'As far as I'm concerned, this is a priority case,' Louisa told him, 'which means that you can have whatever resources you need.' She smiled. 'Within reason, of course.'

'Yes, ma'am,' Dawson said, returning her smile with only the barest flicker of his own.

'Specifically, it means you can have a couple more SOCO teams on the case, if you think it will help,' Louisa amplified.

'Masey and Casey are a good team,' Dawson said.

'I know they are. I've worked with them myself, and I'd go so far as to say they're an *excellent* team,' Louisa replied, 'but it's a big house, and I would have thought time was of the essence.'

A look which could almost have been called relief came into DCI Dawson's eyes.

'If you don't have confidence in me or my judgement, then I'm more than willing to withdraw from the case, ma'am,' he said.

'That won't be necessary,' Louisa assured him hastily. 'You're the man on the spot, and if you say that one team is enough, then I'll take your word for it.' She glanced at her watch. 'Is there anything else?'

'No, ma'am, that's it,' Dawson said.

'Then thank you for your time, and if you have any problems, please feel free to contact me immediately,' Louisa said.

Dawson stood up. 'Thank you, ma'am.'

When he'd gone, Louisa did her best to make some sense out of what had just happened.

Dawson knew as well as she did that it would benefit the case to have more Scene of Crime officers on the job, so why had he resisted her attempt to assign him some?

Maybe the SOCOs weren't the main issue at all. Maybe they were only an excuse – a mechanism – which he was using to get himself thrown off the investigation. But why would any DCI want that to happen?

She was tempted to remove him from the case, but unless she could prove he had been guilty of gross negligence, that would reflect very badly on her.

She felt as if she were caught in a tunnel, and though she didn't want to go forward, it was impossible to turn back.

Paniatowski looked around the saloon bar of the Drum and Monkey. The tables and chairs had changed since her day, as had some of the advertisements on the wall, but other than that, this was still the Drum she had known for most of her career.

'I used to come here a lot in the old days,' she said to the waiter, who had probably been in short trousers the last time she'd had a team meeting here.

'Oh, did you?' replied the boy.

He had that professional waiter's tone to his voice which was meant to suggest that he was frightfully interested in what she had to say, and would, under any other circumstances, have been more than willing to listen to her all day, Sadly, however, on this particular day he had a great deal to do.

'I was expecting it to look different,' she said, not willing to be abandoned quite yet. 'I thought that by now the brewery would have converted it into a theme pub – something like a mock coaching house or a Wild West saloon.'

'They don't want to spend any money on the place,' the waiter told her. 'There's not much point if it's going to be demolished.'

'Demolished!' she repeated, surprised at how shocked she was. '*When* is it going to be demolished?'

The waiter shrugged. 'This year? Next year? Five years from now? It all depends when the fat cats who own the brewery get a big enough offer from the fat cats who want to build expensive flats. But whatever happens, its fate has been decided, and sooner or later, it's coming down.'

The news depressed Paniatowski, though she couldn't say exactly why, and it was with some relief that she saw Jack Crane walk into the bar.

Crane looked around him. 'That was quite a Machiavellian move, boss,' he said, not without some admiration.

'What was?' wondered Paniatowski, genuinely mystified.

'Holding the meeting here. I wouldn't call it emotional blackmail exactly, but it's certainly cashing in on our natural desire to relive past triumphs.'

'I hadn't thought of it like that,' Paniatowski said.

That wasn't quite true, she now realized. But Jack, for all his brain power and emotional intelligence, had still got the whole thing backwards. She hadn't done any of this to motivate them – she'd done it in an effort to convince *herself* that it could still be done.

It was a little awkward at first, and as Meadows told her story, Paniatowski started to think this had all been a mistake. Then, as they began discussing what lines of investigation the police would probably follow, and how their own lines could run in parallel – thus avoiding the two getting tangled up – she realized that they had started to find their old rhythm, and a little over an hour after the meeting started, they all knew what they had to do.

'Is there anything else before we call it a day?' Paniatowski asked.

'Yes,' Meadows said. 'There are two things that keep nagging away in my brain.'

'And what are they?'

'The first is that someone told Andrew Lofthouse where to find his wife, and I don't know who that someone is.'

'Lots of people must have known,' Beresford said.

'That's where you're wrong. None of the staff or clients knew her real name, and since she never left Overcroft House, there was no chance of anybody seeing her on the street.'

'Didn't the police know where she was?' Crane asked.

'Yes, they did. I have to register it with them. It's part of our licensing conditions.'

'Well there you are then,' Beresford said. 'We don't like to think there are bent bobbies, but there always have been and there always will be. It doesn't even have to be a police officer. A civilian clerk could have got hold of the information.'

'But if he was going to risk his job by telling Lofthouse, he'd expect some kind of reward, wouldn't he?' Meadows asked.

'Well, yes.'

'That didn't happen in this case. Lofthouse told me he found out through an anonymous letter. So we really have two questions in one. Firstly, who found out? And secondly, why did he want Lofthouse to know?'

They sat in silence for a while, then Paniatowski said, 'Beats the hell out of me. What's your other worry, Kate?'

'It's Lofthouse himself. I just can't work him out.'

'Is there something in particular that's bothering you?'

'The whole S&M-wife-beater thing. Some men are into S&M, and some men get off on beating up their wives, but the two simply don't mix.'

In the old days, Colin would unthinkingly have jumped in with both feet at this point, Paniatowski thought, and hopefully marriage and fatherhood have made him a little more sensitive.

Alas, they hadn't!

'I don't see what your problem is,' Beresford said. 'It seems to me that a man who would get pleasure from kicking the shit out of his wife would also enjoy whipping her.'

'They're two entirely different things, sir,' replied Meadows, showing uncharacteristic patience with him. 'The wife beater doesn't usually get any pleasure out of the fact – he hits his wife because he's angry with life. He has to take his frustration out on something, and his wife is both handy and complication-free. Wouldn't you say that's true?'

Beresford thought back to the wife beaters he had come across during his time with the police.

'I suppose so,' he admitted.

'The sadist is different. He takes pleasure from inflicting pain, but he's not a psychopath, and it's usually his intention to bring pleasure to his partner, too. In that way, it's an act of intimacy –

often, even, of love. That's why it's incompatible with being a wife beater.'

'Then maybe he's a fake sadist,' Beresford suggested. 'Maybe he only pretended to be, so he could follow you into that club.'

Meadows shook her head. 'He's the genuine article. He's into both sadism and masochism – as many of us are.'

'How can you be so sure?' Beresford persisted.

'I just know,' Meadows said cagily.

'If you were the one asking the questions, you wouldn't take that as a satisfactory answer,' Beresford pointed out.

'Look, this is the world I live in, so you'll just have to take my word for it,' Meadows said.

She sounded angry, Paniatowski thought. But it seemed like the sort of anger that people sometimes used as camouflage or diversion.

'Tell me again what happened when you went back to his house,' she said.

Meadows sighed, as if she suddenly tired of the whole situation. 'He said that if I didn't do the things he wanted me to do, he would tell my board of governors he'd seen me in the club,' she said.

'What kind of things are we talking about here?'

'The sort of things Colin would regard as being perverted,' Meadows said, and the anger had, if anything, gone up a notch. 'But it really doesn't matter what they were, does it? The important thing is that I refused to do them.'

'Even if it meant you losing your job?'

'Yes.'

'And then . . .?'

'And then I left.'

'And he was alive when you left him,' Beresford said.

'What are you saying?' Meadows hissed. 'Are you implying that I killed him?'

'Of course not,' Beresford said hastily. 'We know you would never do anything like that.'

But did they?

Paniatowski was beginning to wonder. Kate Meadows was their colleague and their friend, but they hadn't seen much of each other during the previous few years, and people changed over time.

Colin Beresford had changed, for example. He kept his trousers firmly zipped in the presence of any woman but his wife. And he drank nettle beer, for God's sake! She would never have believed it if she hadn't seen it with her own eyes.

So what if Kate had changed too? What if her job had become more important to her than another person's life? What if she had killed Andrew Lofthouse to silence him?

But if that were the case, why had she asked for help?

Because what better way to throw a spanner in the works – to lay down a smokescreen – than to alter the equation by bringing the old team into play?

TWELVE

When discussing the merits of St Mary's Roman Catholic Church as opposed to the protestant cathedral, it was often pointed out that while St Mary's, perched atop Woodstock Hill, was closer to God, the cathedral, located in the centre of town, was much more convenient for the bus station.

Many people assumed that St Mary's was part of the nineteenth-century gothic revival, but in this they were wrong. It had been built four hundred years earlier, and it had an energy and spirit about it which later imitations somehow failed to capture. It seemed to be striving to touch the heavens, at the same time as it was attempting to entice the heavens down to its level, and it had been Monika Paniatowski's parish church since the day she'd been told she was pregnant and had redis-covered her lost faith.

Monika was standing in front of the altar. A statue of the crucified Christ was in her direct line of vision, but she had turned to the left, and was offering her devotions to the long-suffering Virgin Mary.

She was the only one in the church at that moment, but knew that in around about five minutes, Father Brendon would appear, and head to the vestry, where he kept his late afternoon tipple of Irish whiskey. When he did, she would ask him if they could pop into the interrogation box for a few minutes, and since he was not a man to be enslaved by routine, she was sure he would have no objection.

She heard the door clank open, and turned around expectantly, but the man walking towards her was not red-headed and middle-aged, with his well-rounded figure shrouded by a cassock. Instead, he was still in his twenties, tall, well-built, and blessed with jet black hair and deep soulful eyes. He was wearing a dark suit, and the only thing that identified him as a priest was the dog collar round his neck.

He was a very handsome boy – a very handsome *man* – Paniatowski told herself for perhaps the thousandth time, and she could think of half a dozen girls whose hearts – and hopes for the future – had been shattered when he'd weighed the pull of God against the pull of the world, and decided it was really no contest.

He walked briskly down the aisle to the place where she was standing, and smiled warmly at her.

'What are you doing here at this time of day?'

She shrugged, awkwardly. 'I was just passing by, and I thought I'd drop in,' she said.

The priest's smile broadened. 'Bollocks!' he said. 'You were hoping to catch Father Brendan on his Bush Mills run, and talk him into going into the magic box.'

He called it the magic box, she called it the interrogation box, she thought. Both terms would be frowned on by the church authorities, and yet each, in its own way, described the essence of the confessional.

'Yes, I was going to ask him if he would hear my confession,' she said, embarrassedly.

'Would you like *me* to hear your confession?' he asked.

'Jesus Christ, no!' she said, before she could stop herself. 'I'm sorry about that,' she mumbled. 'I shouldn't have . . .'

'No, you shouldn't,' he said sternly. 'As a properly brought up Whitebridge lass, what you should have said, "Eee, by 'ecky thump, I couldn't go in there with thee, lad".'

He was laughing at her, as he always had done, but she didn't mind that.

Didn't mind it! She positively revelled in it, because that was how most people communicated in Central Lancs, and it was important that he should still want to communicate with her, because it showed he still cared.

'Seriously, why don't you want me to hear your confession?' he asked.

'Isn't that obvious?' she asked. 'It's because you're my bloody son!'

'I may be your son out there, but once in here, I'm the father and you're the child,' he said. 'Besides, since I'm only really a conduit between you and God – since what I say to you will be the words He's putting in my mouth – it shouldn't matter what relation I was to you. I could be your father, or your uncle, or your husband . . .' He paused, and grinned again. 'No, that last one wouldn't work, would it?'

'Everything you've just said makes perfect sense, but it still seems rather incestuous to me.'

'How about this, then?' he suggested. 'We nip round the corner to the café, and over a cup of tea, you tell me what's worrying you so much that you want to see a priest at this time of day.'

'Fair enough,' Paniatowski agreed.

The sign over the door said: *Sand Witch.*

It was a pleasant, conventional café, with a bell which jangled when you opened the door. The curtains and tablecloths were made of gingham, and sitting under glass on the counter were cakes which ranged from coconut tarts to macaroons.

There were no other customers, and they chose a table next to the window. In response to the bell, a waitress appeared from the back room. She was a well-groomed woman in her early thirties, and when she saw who her customer was, a wide smile came to her face.

'What can I get you, Father Tom?' she asked.

'Just a cup of tea for me, thanks, Sylvia,' Thomas said. 'What about you, Mum?'

There was a sharp intake of breath as the waitress realized that Father Tom had a mother, just like any ordinary mortal.

'I'll have tea as well,' Paniatowski said.

Once the waitress had retreated into the darker recesses of the café, Thomas said, 'So what was it you wanted to talk about, Mum?'

Paniatowski had been intending to talk about Kate and Louisa, and the whole mess, but now she found she simply couldn't.

'I can't tell you what's on my mind,' she said.

He looked hurt. 'Is that because you don't trust me – or because you still can't accept that I'm actually a priest?'

'It's neither of those things,' Paniatowski said, reaching across the table and grasping his hand. 'Of course I trust you, and of course I accept that you're a priest.'

'But . . .?' Thomas asked.

'But you're too close personally to the people I wanted to talk about.'

'I see,' Thomas said. Then he shrugged his shoulders, and added, 'Well, if I want you to respect my choices, I suppose I have to respect yours.'

Sylvia returned with the pot of tea. 'Would you like a selection of cakes?' she asked. 'I've got a lovely Jamaican ginger.'

Thomas looked questioningly at his mother, but even the thought of anything spicy made Paniatowski's stomach churn, so she shook her head.

'We'll skip the cakes, thanks,' Thomas said.

'Well, I certainly won't get rich off you, will I?' Sylvia asked.

'Your kindness is earning you riches in heaven,' Thomas said.

Sylvia laughed. 'Well, that is a comfort, Father,' she said. 'I must tell that to the landlord, next time he comes round for his rent.'

Once she'd gone, Thomas reached into his pocket and produced a tin of tobacco and a packet of cigarette papers.

'Have one of these,' Paniatowski suggested, offering him her packet of Silk Cut. 'It'll save all that messing about.'

Thomas shook his head. 'I find the act of rolling cigarettes very relaxing,' he said, though his hands were telling quite a different story as they struggled to make the roll-up look anything like cylindrical. 'Besides, I don't want to get used to shop-bought cigarettes, because I couldn't afford them.'

'There's really no need for you to go short of your little luxuries,' Paniatowski admonished her son. 'A senior police officer's pension is surprisingly generous, and these days I've no one to spend it on but myself.'

Another shake of the head. 'I'd feel obliged to put any money you gave me straight into the poor box,' he said. 'And do you know what I'd feel as I was slipping the notes through the slot?'

'No, what?'

'I'd feel mild annoyance at you for putting temptation in my way, and real anger at myself for somehow finding the strength to deny myself some proper ciggies.'

Paniatowski examined her son's face for some sign that he was making a joke, but he appeared to be very serious. It was so difficult to know when she was connecting with him, because they seemed to exist on two different planes.

'You're a complicated person, Thomas,' she told him, taking a deep drag from her Silk Cut, and thinking that his attempt at making a cigarette looked like a deflated zeppelin.

'Yes, I am complicated,' her son agreed. 'So are you. So is everyone, which is hardly surprising, since God made us in His own image, and He's very complicated indeed. Anyway, what are you doing still smoking?' he asked. 'After your last health scare the doctor told you to stop smoking, and you swore to me that you would.'

'It's true, I did say I'd give it up,' she admitted. 'But what I never realized was that having nothing to do can be almost as stressful as having too much. I smoke because I'm bored, Thomas, and since none of my children has chosen to fill up my life with their grubby little offspring . . .' She clapped her hand to her mouth, but it was already too late. 'Oh my God,' she said, only making matters worse. 'I didn't mean you. Of course I didn't. I respect the path you've chosen.'

'It's all right,' Thomas said soothingly. 'And you can't have meant Philip, either, because you haven't so much as spoken to him for years.'

'Don't blame me for that!' Paniatowski protested. 'He refuses to see me.'

'That's because he's ashamed,' Thomas said softly. 'But that is very convenient for you, isn't it? Because the simple truth is, *you* don't want to see *him.*'

'I love him, but I also despise him, and I can't look him in the face after all he's done,' Paniatowski said.

'Have you ever thought about forgiving him?' Thomas asked.

'I've forgiven him again and again,' Paniatowski replied. 'It made no difference. And this last time – well that was impossible to forgive.'

'Forgiving is never impossible,' Thomas said.

'Do you know what he did?' Paniatowski demanded angrily.

'Yes, I know what he did.'

'Well, maybe you need reminding of the details. He attacked a man in a pub. A man he didn't know. A man he hadn't even had an argument with. He knocked him to the ground, and while he was lying there defenceless, he deliberately broke both his legs. That was pure viciousness – pure evil. How can you even begin to defend him for that?'

'Let me tell you a story about this café, Mum,' Thomas said. 'Did you happen to notice as we came in that it was called the Sand Witch?'

'Yes, I did, as a matter of fact,' Paniatowski replied.

'Didn't it strike you as an odd name?'

'It did, a little,' Paniatowski admitted.

'I'll tell you how it came about,' Thomas said. 'Sylvia wanted to give her café a distinctive name, so she hired the art teacher from a local school to paint her a sign to hang over the front door – just like the signs that pubs have. The one he painted had a woman with a black pointed hat and a big nose in the foreground, and some palm trees in the background. In her hands, the woman was holding an old-fashioned broom. Do you get it?'

'She's a witch, standing on the sand, so that makes her a sand witch,' Paniatowski said.

'Spot on. Anyway, it had only been hanging there for a couple of days when someone stole it. Sylvia said it must have been an art lover, and most of her customers agreed with her – but not the reasons she might imagine.'

'They thought it was stolen by someone who loved art so much he couldn't bear to see it hanging there,' Paniatowski guessed.

Thomas grinned. 'It was pretty horrible. It looked as if the witch was more likely to sweep the beach with her broomstick than fly away on it. So Sylvia asked the artist to paint another one. His second attempt was a little better, but this time somebody thought it would be hilarious to spray paint a prick and balls on the witch. And that was the point at which Sylvia gave up.'

'You told me that story for a purpose, didn't you?' Paniatowski asked.

'Yes,' Thomas agreed.

'And may I enquire what that purpose was?'

'The sign was removed, but the name stayed over the door, so now, when people see the name Sand Witch, they simply assume that Sylvia doesn't know how to spell "sandwich". The point is that people often draw the wrong conclusions when they don't know the full story, and that's why it's sometimes best not to draw any conclusions at all.'

'We're back to talking about Philip, aren't we?'

'We never stopped talking about Philip.'

'I said something about him viciously beating up someone for no reason, and you launched into your sandwich story.'

'That's right.'

'So you're saying there are important details of the case that I'm missing.'

'I hope I'm not saying that,' Thomas responded. 'I certainly never meant to.'

'Ah!' Paniatowski said, suddenly getting it. 'Philip told you something in confession, and you're being very careful not to reveal even a hint of what that something might be.'

'He wants to see you,' Thomas said. 'Go and see him in the remand centre. You really need to talk to him – you both need to talk to each other.'

Paniatowski sighed. 'It's complicated being a priest, isn't it?'

'Yes,' Thomas agreed. He smiled again. 'Everybody joins the priesthood for the hair shirts and the fasting, but you soon learn that it can't be fun all the time.'

Just a glimpse of the Lofthouse's kitchen would have been enough to drive his wife into a fit of envy and rage, Paul Mason thought. The envy part was obvious – she would have sold her soul to have a kitchen like this one. The rage would stem from the fact that the people who were lucky enough to call it their own had done so little in there that most of the expensive equipment looked as if it had never been used.

And the chances were, it actually *had* never been used, if the number of fingerprints Mason was able to lift were anything to go by. Maybe things had been different when Mrs Lofthouse lived there, but Lofthouse himself seemed to regard the fridge as little more than a chilled cupboard in which to stow his booze.

It was not until he had been working in the kitchen for around half an hour that it occurred to him that he had no idea where his partner was, and he was just about to call O'Casey on his mobile phone when the man himself walked in, carrying a stepladder.

'Did you get that from the garage?' Mason asked.

O'Casey clicked his tongue disapprovingly. 'No, not from the garage. We haven't checked the garage out yet. I borrowed it from a neighbour.'

'That was very obliging of him,' Mason said.

'Not really,' O'Casey said. 'I gave him something in return.'

'And what might that "something" have been?'

'I gave him the gory details of what had gone on in here.'

'Christ, you didn't tell him about the decapitation, did you?' Mason asked. 'Sergeant Boyd will have your balls if you did.'

'Of course I didn't tell him that,' O'Casey said. 'My gory details came from *Taste the Blood of Dracula*, as anyone who's seen that fine film will quickly realize.'

'One of these days, you'll get us both in trouble,' Mason warned him.

'Well, that's something to look forward to,' O'Casey said.

'What's the ladder for, anyway?' Mason asked.

'I've been thinking about that hook in the bedroom you spotted . . .' O'Casey began.

'Oh, for God's sake, there's enough for us to do without worrying about the bloody hook,' Mason said.

'This is an orderly house,' O'Casey said. 'All the fitments are there for a purpose. So what's the purpose of the hook?'

'I don't know, and I don't care,' Mason said.

'And that's where we differ, because I do,' O'Casey responded.

O'Casey placed the ladder slightly to the side of the chandelier.

'I'm going up, Captain, wish me luck,' he said.

'Make us all proud of you, you young whippersnapper,' Mason said – but his heart was not really in it.

O'Casey began to climb, and soon the upper half of his body had been engulfed by the hanging crystal.

'This is weird,' he said.

'That's one word for it,' Mason replied. 'Me, I'm going outside for a quiet smoke.'

He opened the French windows and stepped onto the balcony. From where he was standing, he could see all the way to the moors. This view was another thing his wife would sell her soul for, he thought, or rather, since she'd already have given away her own soul for the kitchen, she'd barter his.

He finished his cigarette, extinguished the last of the burning embers with his thumb nail, and put the stub in an envelope he had taken out of his pocket. When he re-entered the bedroom, he saw that the ladder had been moved slightly away from the chandelier, and that O'Casey, still standing at the top of it, was looking very pleased with himself.

Mason sighed, knowing that for a few minutes at least, O'Casey was going to be completely insufferable.

'All right,' he said, having decided to get it over with as soon as possible, 'tell me what you've found.'

'There's a trackway here,' O'Casey replied, running his finger along the ceiling. 'It's very skilfully disguised, so you have to be on a ladder to see it, but it's here right enough.'

'And what's it for?' Mason asked. 'So you can run your model train upside down across the ceiling?'

'No,' O'Casey said, 'it's for this.'

His hand disappeared under the inverted pyramid of shimmering glass, and when it emerged again, it was pulling the hook. O'Casey guided it until it was two feet clear of the chandelier.

'That's as far as the track goes,' he said. 'But that's not the end of the ingenuity of this little device.'

'Why, what else does it do?' Mason asked. 'Play highlights from *Les Misérables*? Offer advice to the lovelorn?'

But O'Casey was not about to let sarcasm sour his moment of triumph, and so he chose to simply ignore the comment.

'There's a switch in the base of the hook, and when you click it, the hook is locked in place,' he said.

To demonstrate, he threw the switch, and then pulled on the hook. It stayed where it was.

'All right, so it's ingenious,' Mason conceded. 'But what's it for?'

'There's something I can see on the hook itself that might provide the answer to that,' O'Casey said.

And suddenly, the light playful tone was gone from his voice, and his whole stance became more serious.

He reached across to the hook, and appeared to be delicately picking something off it. Satisfied he'd got all he could, he carefully descended the ladder, holding his spoils at some distance from it in the palm of his gloved hand.

When he reached the foot of the ladder, he held out his hand to Mason the opportunity to examine his treasure.

'What do you make of that?' he asked.

'Looks like bits of a few strands of rope to me,' Mason said.

'But it's probably not just any old rope, is it?' O'Casey asked.

Mason thought about it, then a sudden realization hit him with all the force of a bucket of icy water.

'The lab will have to do some tests before we can be sure,' he said cautiously, 'but it looks to me to be the same kind of rope as the one that was used to hang Andrew Lofthouse from the gallery.'

'Yes,' O'Casey agreed. 'It does, doesn't it?'

THIRTEEN

In the five hours since darkness had fallen, the temperature had dropped several degrees, and most of the people out on the street were swathed in overcoats and scarves. Not so the bouncer at the Hellfire Club. He stood in the anonymous entrance to the club with only an open leather waistcoat between his chest and the elements. If he was dressed like that just to make him look hard, it was a waste of effort, Colin Beresford thought. The man *did* look hard in a leather waistcoat, but then again, he would have looked hard in a pink tutu.

Beresford studied him in the dim light cast by the lamp over the door. There was something familiar about him, yet he was having difficulty putting a name to the face.

You're getting old, he told himself. The drawers in your mental filing cabinet are starting to stick.

Bollocks, I'm a just little bit out of practice, said the part of his brain which specialized in living with denial.

'Oy, you, granddad, no hanging about,' the bouncer called to him.

Granddad!

Beresford took a step closer to him.

'I want to ask you some questions,' he said.

'Well, you'll just have to wait,' the bouncer told him. 'I've already done Mastermind and University Challenge this week, and I'm knackered. Look,' he said, softening his tone, 'I don't want to get violent with you, but I can't have you loitering here, because you'll put the punters off.'

The bastard was patronizing him, Beresford thought, and he really hated that. What he hated even more was the idea of having to appeal to the brute's better nature. But he recognized that he had no choice, because time was short, and if the official police investigation wasn't already hot on his heels, it soon would be.

Just how big a lead could he have? he wondered.

Twenty-four hours, he decided – twenty-four hours at best.

He took a deep breath. 'Look,' he said, 'it's really important to me – and quite a lot of other people – that you spare me five minutes of your time.'

'You're going to make me hurt you, aren't you?' the bouncer asked, with what could have been genuine regret. 'I don't want to do it, but you're really leaving me . . .' He stopped, mid-sentence. 'Hang about! Aren't you Police Constable Beresford?'

Police Constable Beresford!

That wasn't so much a blast from the past as a blast from another lifetime.

'Yes, I'm Colin Beresford,' he admitted.

'I heard you were dead,' the bouncer said.

'Reports of my death have been greatly exaggerated,' Beresford replied.

And he thought, Jesus Christ, I'm starting to sound just like young Jack Crane.

Except that Jack wasn't so young any more, either.

'You remember me, don't you, Constable Beresford?' the bouncer asked, and when it became plain that Beresford didn't, he added, with just a hint of hurt in his voice, 'I'm Freddie Bairstow. I used to live in Inkerman Street.'

Freddie Bairstow! *Little* Freddie Bairstow – with his runny nose and fourth-hand shoes with no laces!

'I do remember now you remind me,' Beresford said. 'Looking back, it feels as if I spent half my shift at your house. It was all because of your father, wasn't it?'

'Yeah, well, I know it's wrong to speak ill of the dead, but my dad was the meanest son of a bitch who ever drew breath,' Freddie said.

Yes, that was a pretty fair description of the man, Beresford thought.

Bazza Bairstow had been a big feller – bigger even than his son. When he had worked, he'd been a builder's labourer, but working was a habit he'd done his best to avoid, and he'd spent most of his time either in the pubs or competing in bare-knuckle fights on the nearest convenient patch of waste ground.

He'd had one other hobby, too, which he practised when the

pubs had closed for the night, and that involved beating the crap out of his mouse of a wife.

Wife beating had been quite common on Inkerman Street back in those days – so common, in fact, that most people (including the victims) hardly gave it a second thought. If they'd been asked their opinion – which they never were – they'd probably have said that it had always gone on, and would always go on. The only three things that were inevitable in life were death, taxes and wife beating – and if you were a crafty bastard, you could avoid paying the taxes.

What had made Bazza Bairstow's particular enactment of this ancient rite noteworthy was its viciousness. His attacks on his wife could be so savage that even men who took their belts to their own wives had been moved to call in the police.

'There was this one time you got tired of coming round,' Freddie Bairstow said to Beresford. 'Do you remember?'

It wasn't so much I was tired of it as that I couldn't take the poor woman's suffering any more, Beresford thought.

But aloud, he said, 'Yes, I remember.'

'You told my dad that he'd better stop leathering my mam or else you'd do something about it, and when he asked you what, you told him you'd teach him a lesson by giving him a taste of his own medicine.'

'Oh yeah? And how many other bobbies will you bring with you to teach me this lesson of yours?' Bazza had sneered. *'If I was you, I'd make sure it was five or six, or you could end up being the one that gets leathered.'*

He'd have had no difficulty in getting half a dozen other constables to come with him, Beresford had thought. If anything, there'd have been so many willing volunteers that he'd have had to hold a raffle to decide which lucky bobbies got the opportunity to see how well Bairstow's teeth stood up against their boots. But men like Bazza thrived on pain, and for them there was no shame in getting beaten up by half a dozen boys in blue. If anything, the battered and bloody Bazza would be seen as a hero, even among the men who had formerly despised him for the way he treated his wife.

'I've no need to bring any other officers with me,' Beresford had told the bully. *'I can deal with a bag of piss and wind like you on my own.'*

He'd sounded confident, but that had been mainly bravado, because Bairstow really was a big, hard feller, and even when they'd been squaring up to each other in the back yard, Beresford had only given himself a forty per cent chance of winning.

'I'd never seen anything like that before,' Freddie Bairstow said, wonderingly. 'I've never seen anything like it since, for that matter.'

And you shouldn't have seen it then, Beresford thought, because it was not something a policeman should ever have done – but every time I looked at that poor woman, I felt as if my heart would burst with pity.

'You gave him a really good battering, didn't you?' Freddie Bairstow asked, the admiration in his voice obvious.

Better than good – or maybe worse than it – Beresford thought. If I'd had even half an ounce less of self-discipline, I'd have not stopped until I'd killed the bastard stone dead.

'And while he was lying there by the bin, you told him that if he ever raised his hand to my mam again, you'd come back for an encore – only next time, you'd do it in the open, where the whole street could see it,' Freddie Bairstow said.

'And *did* he raise his hand to her again?' Beresford asked.

'Not as long as you were on that beat,' Freddie told him. 'He did start again once you'd been transferred, but it was never as bad as it had been, because he was frightened of marking her, and you getting to hear about it. And every time he'd given her a belting, he'd buy us all fish and chips, which he'd never done before.'

'So I did make some difference,' Beresford reflected.

'You made a lot of difference, and my mam was grateful to you until the day she died.'

'And how about you?' Beresford wondered. 'Are you grateful enough to answer some of my questions?'

Freddie Bairstow grinned. It wasn't a pretty sight.

'Ask me anything you want to know, Mr Beresford,' he said, 'and if I don't know the answer myself, I'll do my best to beat it out of somebody else.'

'Let's start with Zelda,' Beresford suggested. 'She was here the other night, wasn't she?'

Freddie Bairstow's grin widened. 'Do you know Zelda, Mr Beresford? Well, well, well, I am surprised. I always thought you were a straight in-and-out man.'

Beresford almost blushed. He'd never been as crude as that in his approach to women.

Had he?

'Just answer the questions and keep your wisecracks to yourself,' he said sternly.

'Oh, sorry Mr Beresford,' the bouncer replied. 'Yes, she was here.'

'She came alone, didn't she?'

'Yes, she did.'

'But did she also leave alone?'

'No, she left with a man.'

Well, at least Meadows' story checked out so far.

'Did you recognize this man?' Beresford asked.

For a moment, Freddie seemed confused by the question, then he said, 'Do you mean, had I seen him before? Or do you mean, do I know who he was?'

'I meant both those things.'

'I'd seen him plenty of times before, but I couldn't tell you his name, because like a lot of the punters, he always wore a mask.'

Well, that shot down Meadows' theory that a man couldn't be both a wife beater and a sadomasochist, because Lofthouse was obviously both, Beresford thought, perhaps a little smugly.

'Did he usually come alone?' he asked.

'No, apart from last night, he always brought a woman with him.'

'The same woman?'

'No, some nights it was one woman, and other nights it was the other.'

'But only ever one of two women?'

'Yes.'

'And I suppose you can't tell me who they were, either.'

'I've got no clue about the younger, prettier one . . .'

'So she wasn't wearing a mask?'

'Yes, she was.'

'So how do you know she was pretty?'

'Well, you can somehow always tell, can't you? And she had a nice body, too.'

'So you don't know who she is, but you recognized the other one?'

'Sort of.'

'So *she* wasn't wearing a mask?'

'She was wearing a mask, too, but she had a voice you couldn't miss – it was a bit posh, like she had a plum in her mouth, and a bit screechy, like an angry owl.'

'So what am I supposed to do?' Beresford wondered. 'Stop every woman I meet to find out if she talks with a plum in her mouth and screeches like an angry owl?'

Freddie grinned again. 'Nah, you can't go doing that Mr Beresford! It would take you forever.'

'That's exactly what I was thinking.'

'And as it happens, there's no need for any of that palaver, because, as it happens, I came across the woman somewhere else.'

'Where?'

'In the magistrates' court.'

'So what was she – a shoplifter?'

Freddie's grin broadened. 'No, she's as far from that as she possibly could be.'

'You're surely not trying to tell me she's a bank robber?'

'You're going in the wrong direction, Mr Beresford.'

Beresford sighed. 'This is harder work than pulling teeth,' he said. 'Are you going to tell me what she was doing there or not?'

'My cousin Billy was caught in the act of selling half a dozen microwave ovens he didn't exactly own—'

'You mean, he stole them,' Beresford interrupted.

'Not him,' said Freddie, sounding offended. 'Somebody else stole them – he was just the innocent party who was helping to recirculate them. Anyway, he was hauled up before the beak, and I went along to give him moral support. Well, he told the magistrates that he now realized he'd done wrong, and they went into a huddle – as they do – to decide his fate, and it was just after that I heard the owl woman speak.'

'And what did she say?' Beresford asked.

'She said, "We're prepared to give you another chance. On this occasion, we're fining you one thousand pounds, but if you offend again, you'll almost certainly go to prison."'

'Wait a minute,' Beresford said. 'Are you telling me that the owl woman was one of the magistrates?'

'That's right,' Freddie Bairstow agreed. 'Takes all sorts to make a world, don't it?'

But was it all true? Beresford wondered. In fact was *any* of it true? Well, he could certainly check out the veracity of the first part of the story then and there.

'So you say you don't know the man's name?' he asked.

'That's right, Mr Beresford.'

'His name is – or, more accurately, was – Andrew Lofthouse.'

For a moment, the name seemed to mean nothing to Freddie. Then a look of shock – which Beresford was convinced couldn't have been faked – spread across Freddie's face.

'Andrew . . . Lofthouse . . .' the bouncer spluttered. 'But isn't the man who . . . who . . .'

'Got murdered a few hours after he left the club?' Beresford supplied. 'Yes, he is.'

'And that was the night Zelda left the club with him!'

'That's right.'

'Bloody hell, things aren't looking too rosy for her, are they?' Freddie asked.

No, Beresford admitted gloomily – they weren't.

The longer the evening briefing went on, the more despondent DS Boyd felt. He had worked on other investigations which had not made as much progress as might have been expected, but with them there had always been the hope that tomorrow would bring with it the big break – the vital clue that would crack the case open. At this briefing, no one felt optimistic. The investigation lacked life. It lacked purpose. It was going through the motions, but that was all.

'We have more information about vehicle movement on the night of the murder,' DCI Dawson was telling the team. 'Previously we only knew about two cars. They arrived together, at about ten o'clock, and one of them left again around midnight, at which time, according to the doctor, Lofthouse was still alive. Now we've found a new witness who claims there was a third car.' He turned to Boyd. 'Could you give us the details, sergeant?'

'The witness, a Mrs Crabtree, a widow, lives about three hundred yards from Lofthouse's,' Boyd said. 'She went to bed at eleven o'clock, but had difficulty sleeping. She says she woke up several times during the night. On one of those occasions, she heard a car pull up just along the road. She thinks that was at about twelve thirty. Then at one thirty, she heard a car drive away. All the neighbours say it wasn't them, so the chances are, our killer was in this third car.'

'Of course, it could simply have been the second car returning, in which case it doesn't tell us anything we didn't already know,'

Dawson said. 'Also, I'm not sure how much we can rely on this Mrs Crabtree.' He chuckled. 'My wife often claims not to have had a wink of sleep all night, yet when I've got up to go to the bog, she's been snoring like a pig.'

Why – in God's name – was he doing this? Boyd thought anguishedly. The new information should have been used as a spur to urge the investigation forward, not as an indication of just how hopeless the whole situation was.

'There's one more thing before you go,' Dawson said. 'The SOCOs have found a hook set into the bedroom ceiling, and on that hook were strands of rope which – according to the lab – match the rope that was used on Lofthouse.'

Why wasn't I told about this before? Boyd thought. I'm his bagman. He should have briefed me.

'Now I, for one, have no idea what this means,' Dawson continued. He laughed again. 'I'm assuming that Lofthouse wasn't carrying out executions in his bedroom, so . . .'

'It's got to be auto-erotic strangulation, sir,' Boyd said. 'It's the only possible explanation.'

Dawson looked far from pleased at being interrupted. 'I've noticed that about you, sergeant,' he said.

'Noticed what, sir?'

'That as soon as you've formed an opinion, it automatically becomes the absolute truth as far as you're concerned. The noose could suggest auto-erotic strangulation, but there could be any number of other explanations for its presence. I suggest you sleep on it, and see just how likely your theory looks in the cold light of day.'

'There's obviously more to be found in the house, sir,' Boyd said, choosing to ignore the insult. 'We need more men there.'

'I disagree,' Dawson replied. 'O'Casey and Mason are best left to work alone.'

'With respect, sir, you're wrong,'

'Am I, indeed?' Dawson asked, and though there was a large clock on the wall in front of him, he checked his watch. 'That's all for today, people,' he continued. 'I want you back here at seven thirty sharp in the morning.'

As the team started to head for the door, Dawson said, 'Not, you, DS Boyd. I'd like a word with you.'

Which was just his way of signalling to the rest of the officers that he was about to give his bagman a real bollocking, Boyd thought.

When they had the room to themselves, Dawson said, 'You will *not* contradict me in public, Sergeant Boyd.'

Boyd was well aware of what was expected of him. 'I'm sorry, sir, I know that was wrong of me,' he said, and though he knew he should have left it there, he heard himself continue, 'the problem was that you were in danger of shifting the team's focus in the wrong direction, and once that's happened, it's very hard to get them on track again.'

'Let me be perfectly clear on this,' Dawson said angrily. 'I set the focus of this investigation, not you. And if you can't live with that, you should request a transfer. I have to tell you that I certainly wouldn't oppose such a move. So what's it to be?'

It would be a relief to be taken off the case, Boyd thought, but the big drawback would be that it would leave Dawson in sole charge – and that couldn't be allowed to happen. So if the price of staying on the investigation was to eat some humble pie, he was prepared to do it – a whole bakery full, if necessary.

'It's your case, sir. I fully accept that,' he said.

'And so you're willing to follow my lead without further argument?'

'Yes, sir,' Boyd agreed, but he was thinking, I'll follow it right up to the point at which your stupidity and pig-headedness make it impossible to follow it any longer.

Outside, the weather was doing its best to fulfil the forecaster's prediction of overnight snow, but so far it had only managed a few isolated flakes, which lay on the ground like light dandruff on a dark jacket, and then were gone.

Inside, Monika Paniatowski was sitting at her kitchen table, slowly sipping her first drink of the day. Her intention, when she'd sat down, was to think through what they should know – and what they already *did* know – about the murder of Andrew Lofthouse. Yet somehow, thoughts about homicide kept getting nudged out of her mind by her recollections of the conversation with her eldest son, Thomas, earlier in the day.

Philip hadn't wanted to see her because he was ashamed, Thomas had said.

'*But that is very convenient for you, isn't it?*' he'd asked. '*Because the simple truth is, you don't want to see him, either.*'

He was right, and in acknowledging that, she was also

acknowledging that *she* was ashamed too – ashamed that though she loved Philip, her love did not seem to be deep enough to give her the strength to face him.

'*Have you ever thought about forgiving him*?' Thomas had asked.

And she had answered that she had – time and again – but after the last time, it was impossible.

'*Forgiving is never impossible,*' Thomas had said.

And then he had told the story of the café name, which had really been more of a modern parable.

And what was the moral of that parable?

That you should never draw any conclusions until you knew the full story.

He'd hinted that he *did* know the full story, but he couldn't reveal it, because he'd heard it in confession.

He'd pleaded with her to go and see Philip, and now she decided that she would.

The next day!

First thing in the morning!

She took a sip of her vodka and tried to redirect her thoughts to the murder of Andrew Lofthouse.

Jim Hadley was at home. He was feeling insecure – perhaps even frightened – which was strange, because while his house could not exactly have been called a fortress, it was certainly one of the most secure buildings in Lancashire – if not the whole of the British Isles.

One of his acquaintances once said that nature could be very fair-minded, and that Jim was a perfect illustration of that. Nature had given Hadley a face so lacking in distinction that it was almost as hard to insult it as it was to say something nice about it – a face you could make a real effort to remember, yet forget the moment he was gone.

To compensate for this, he had been given an exceptional brain, which was both original and quirky. He could have used that brain for anything. He might have written surprising and outstanding books on topics which – until those books appeared – most people didn't think were worth writing about at all. He might have speculated on the meaning of the universe, or have finally answered the age-old question of exactly what man was for.

Instead, he had focussed his intellect on home security. He had started out by devising locks that couldn't be picked, windows that couldn't be forced, and alarms that couldn't be tampered with. As technology developed, he had moved into software, and had devised programmes that even Moscow's most dedicated hackers had trouble breaking into.

His business had grown and grown, though he had never been tempted to expand it beyond the north-west. In the process, he had become really rather prosperous. But unlike many tycoons, he had not, along the way, accumulated a wife – or wives – and children. Thus, at forty-five he was still a bachelor, and though he had a number of business associates who he might choose to call friends, business associates were essentially all they were. And so he lived alone, in a large house filled with the latest labour-saving devices, and guarded by a security system which would have cost a fortune if it hadn't been his own.

So why was he so worried, he asked himself, as he gazed at the bank of monitors which were relaying images from the half a dozen cameras he had positioned around his property. His windows were bulletproof, his doors had steel cores. He was as safe as any man on earth.

But he didn't *feel* safe, because he knew that for most of the day, someone had been watching him. He couldn't say how he knew this – he had seen nothing – but he *knew*.

He picked up his phone and dialled a mobile number he knew by heart.

'Yes?' said a voice on the other end of the line.

'It's me.'

'I know who it is. What do you want?'

'I'm afraid,' Hadley said.

'Oh, for God's sake!'

'Could you come round? I'd feel safer if you came round.'

'It's too risky.'

'It isn't. Not if you were careful.'

'Learn to stand on your own two feet,' said the voice – and he could hear the contempt in it. 'Be a man'

And then the line went dead.

He paced up and down his living room. He had nothing to worry about, his very logical mind assured him. In his whole life, there had only been one man who had cause to hate him – and that man was dead.

So relax Jim, he told himself. Pour yourself a drink, put your feet up, and watch some television.

But his hand was already reaching for the phone to ring the number again.

FOURTEEN

Friday, 4 February, 2000

The snow had failed to establish itself in the town, but it had managed to lay a thin white carpet over the moors, which even in the weak early morning sunlight seemed to glisten. Monika Paniatowski moderated her speed for once, which she took as a sign that she was finally developing a mature attitude to road safety, but may have had more to do with her reluctance to reach the end of her journey.

She reached Blackthorn Remand Centre at just after nine. It stood in splendid isolation against the backdrop of an anaemic winter sky. The Centre was a Victorian building, and shared a number of grim and imposing architectural features with other institutions of the period, so that while it was easy to see it as a prison, it would have required no more effort to accept it as a workhouse or fever hospital.

She presented her papers at the guard house, and the big central gates swung slowly and ominously open. Ahead of her was the main prison building. It was made of sturdy Accrington brick, and seemed hardly at all affected by a century of merciless moorland weather.

Many of the windows were small and barred. She wondered whether it was possible for the prisoners to look out of them, and whether looking out of them would be a good idea, given that the view was of those big gates, opening with a promise of freedom and then remorselessly slamming closed.

The warder who was assigned to her at reception led her down a long windowless corridor with acoustics which made the click of Paniatowski's heels bounce off the walls like ricocheting machine-gun bullets, and the dull thud of the warden's boots sound like bodies hitting the ground. The interview room was empty, save for a table in its exact centre, and two chairs, one each side of the table. Paniatowski noted the legs of both the chairs and the table were bolted to the floor. As she sat down, she saw that two sturdy metal rings had been sunk into the tabletop opposite her.

'When the prisoner is admitted, he will be instructed to sit in the other chair,' the warder told her in a voice which managed to sound both bored and menacing. 'Under no circumstances are you to touch him, nor pass anything across the table to him. You must not ask questions about the centre's regime, nor invite the prisoner to comment on it. You will be permitted to talk about family matters, but must not say anything likely to provoke the prisoner to behave in any manner which does not conform to standing orders. If I am not satisfied you are adhering to these strictures – or if I judge that you are failing to conform to any of the other conditions laid down in the handbook – I will terminate this meeting. Do you understand?'

'Yes,' Paniatowski said.

The warder nodded, and pressed a button on the wall. The door opened, and Philip entered the room. He looked somewhat like his brother, but where there was calm and nobility in Thomas's face, there was only danger and uncertainty in his brother's.

Philip was flanked by – and handcuffed to – two large officers. The officers marched him over to the table.

'The prisoner will sit down,' the warder barked.

The escort executed the sideways shuffles necessary to get Philip into the right position, and once he was there they unlocked the handcuffs which had attached him to them, and fastened them to the metal hoops. Once that operation was completed, they left the room.

'Is that really necessary?' Paniatowski asked the warder, looking at her son's manacled hands.

'It's the standard procedure when handling violent inmates,' the warder replied.

'But I'm his mother!' Paniatowski protested.

'That doesn't make any difference,' the warder said. 'Men like him are as likely to attack their own mothers as they are to attack anybody else.'

'How dare you—' Paniatowski began.

'Leave it, Mum,' Philip said urgently. 'Leave it before he takes it as an excuse to stop this meeting.'

'You'd be wise to listen to your son, madam,' the warder said. 'In fact, before we go any further, I'm going to insist you promise to behave.'

'I promise,' Paniatowski said, as she pictured the warder's guillotined head bouncing down the scaffold steps.

'Well, just be careful,' the warder advised.

Boing, boing, boing, Paniatowski thought, as she watched the imaginary head reach the ground.

Philip had his hands on the table, and she saw that since the last time they'd been together, he'd had letters crudely tattooed on the backs of his fingers, so that even when he made his hands into fists, the letters would still be visible.

'My left hand spells out "Hell" and my right hand spells out "Shit",' he said, noticing that she was looking at them.

Paniatowski smiled. 'Well, if you have an "o" tattooed on your right thumb, it will become a much nicer message,' she said. 'I don't know what we can do about your right one, though.'

Philip did not return her smile. 'Why are you here?' he asked.

'Thomas told me you wanted to see me, Philip.'

'And that's the only reason, isn't it?' Philip asked bitterly. 'You're here because your beloved Thomas wanted you to come!'

'No, I'd have come before – but you wouldn't let me,' Paniatowski protested.

'I just couldn't bear the idea of seeing the look of contempt in your eyes,' Philip said.

And can you see it now? Paniatowski wondered.

'I've always loved you, you know,' she said.

'Do you love me as much as you love Thomas and Louisa?' Philip challenged.

'Yes,' Paniatowski said firmly.

'But you don't like me as much, do you?'

'You haven't always made it easy to like you,' Paniatowski admitted.

'If you love me, prove it,' Philip said. 'Do one thing for me.'

'What?' Paniatowski asked, dreading what he might say.

'When I'm sentenced next week, they say I'll get at least twelve years,' Philip said. 'They'll send me to a maximum-security prison like Durham, for at least the first half of my sentence.'

'Yes?' Paniatowski said.

'I need a week's parole before I go.'

Paniatowski gasped. 'But that's impossible, Philip. You're considered dangerous. That's why it took two guards to bring you here. That's why you're chained up now.'

'Look, I got into a fight . . .' Philip began.

'No, you didn't. You attacked a man who was a complete stranger to you in a pub. And you didn't just knock him down, did you? You deliberately broke both his legs.'

'I had to do that,' Philip muttered. 'I had to make sure he'd be out of action for a few months.'

'For God's sake, why?' Paniatowski asked, exasperatedly.

'It doesn't matter,' Philip said.

Thomas knew, Paniatowski thought. Philip had told his brother – but he wouldn't tell his mother.

'Doesn't matter?' she said. 'Of course it matters. If you had what you thought was a good reason for what you'd done, you just might get a lighter sentence. As it stands, it's just mindless violence, and society wants you off the streets for as long as is legally possible.'

'I'd behave while I was out on parole,' Philip said, and he was sounding desperate now. 'I'd wear an ankle bracelet if they wanted me to. I'd live with you, and I'd stay away from pubs and never go out after dark.'

'I don't understand why it's so important to you,' Paniatowski admitted. 'What do you want to do with this week of freedom?'

'You used to be a chief inspector,' Philip said. 'You've got influence with all sorts of people. You could persuade them to let me out – if you really wanted to.'

'It doesn't work like that, love,' Paniatowski said. 'I could be the current chief constable, never mind a retired DCI, and I still couldn't swing it.'

'But if you could swing it, would you do it?' Philip asked.

'Before I did anything, I'd need to know why you're so desperate to get out,' Paniatowski told him.

Philip stood up. 'Get the guards to take me back to my cell,' he told the warden.

The warden pressed the button and the guards appeared in the doorway.

As they were reattaching the handcuffs to their wrists, Philip looked at his mother one more time.

'Do this one thing for me,' he begged. 'Do it – or you're dead to me.'

Kate Meadows never locked her office door. This was a deliberate decision on her part. It was designed to send a message to the other residents of the house, and that message was, 'We're all in this together. Your fight is my fight. But we have to trust each other – because without trust we have nothing.'

And it had worked. Though any member of the household could have entered the office, she believed that no one ever had.

Until now!

Now, the office felt as she had felt on the first night of her honeymoon – violated!

She looked around for evidence with which to back up her gut feeling.

Had that file lying on the desk been positioned at exactly that angle?

Hadn't the cup containing all her pens and markers been moved slightly to the right?

She couldn't know for sure.

She opened the desk drawer. She always had a hundred pounds in there to meet emergencies, and when she counted the notes, she found it added up to exactly that amount.

This was ridiculous, she told herself. The house was a sealed unit, and if anyone had entered the office, that was where they had come from. Yet if she discounted the three small children, there were only five other adults to consider – no, she corrected herself, there were only four other adults now Jane had gone – and she trusted them all absolutely.

She was getting paranoid, she told herself, but after everything that had happened, it was hardly surprising, was it?

The woman leaving the solicitor's office was wearing a navy-blue suit. The skirt part of the suit was slightly too short for her somewhat stumpy legs, but the jacket had been cleverly cut to disguise the fact that those legs were topped by a rather square body. Her hairstyle was elaborate and expensive, her make-up carefully applied. In other words, thought Beresford, she was a woman who tried to show herself off to some advantage – and was almost successful in that aim.

What else did he know about her? He knew her name was
Cecilia Maitland Williams, that she was thirty-eight years old, and
that she was divorced. She was a successful solicitor – a senior
partner in her firm – and a part-time magistrate. And unless he
was very much mistaken, she was one of the two women who
regularly accompanied Andrew Lofthouse to the Hellfire Club.

He followed her down the street, and when she entered the
Copper Kettle Café, he was right behind her.

She ordered an espresso coffee and a croissant, and took her
order over to one of the tables.

Beresford waited until she had sat down, then said, 'Mrs
Williams?'

'Maitland Williams,' the woman said, sounding annoyed. '*Ms*
Maitland Williams.'

'My name's Beresford,' he told her. 'I used to be a policeman
– a detective inspector in the Mid Lancs Constabulary. Do you
mind if I join you?'

'I most certainly do,' Ms Maitland Williams replied. 'I don't
believe, even for one second, you were ever a policeman at
all, and if you don't stop bothering me, I'll summon someone
who is.'

Beresford laughed. 'Nice try,' he said, 'but I can tell from the
look in your eyes that I've got you worried.'

'I most certainly am not w—'

'And you've got a lot to be worried about – dead lover, nocturnal
visits to places part-time magistrates really shouldn't go to—'

'Is it money you want?' the woman demanded.

'No. All I need is five minutes of your time.'

For a moment, Maitland Williams hesitated, then she said, 'All
right, sit down.' Her voice was trying to create the impression that
she knew she was granting him a privilege he was not really worthy
of, and once he had sat down she looked at her watch and added,
'Five minutes and no more.'

'All right,' Beresford agreed. 'Firstly, do you admit that Andrew
Lofthouse was your lover?'

'No, I do not. He was just a friend.'

'But a very *close* friend?'

'I suppose so.'

'Didn't it bother you that you were going out with a wife
beater?'

'Andrew never beat Jane. She made all that up.'

'She was living in a shelter for battered women, for God's sake.'

'It was all a pretence. Overcroft House was never more than the stage on which she chose to play out her own little melodrama.'

'How do you know she was in Overcroft House?' Beresford asked.

'Andrew told me.'

'And how did he know?'

'He got an anonymous letter.'

'Do you have any idea who sent it?'

'Of course not,' she said scornfully. 'As I've just told you, it was anonymous.'

'Lofthouse took you to the Hellfire Club, didn't he?' Beresford asked.

Ms Maitland Williams began to look uncomfortable again. 'Once or twice,' she admitted.

'It was a lot more than that,' Beresford said confidently. 'So what's your particular kink?'

'I don't have a kink, as you so crudely put it,' the woman said haughtily. 'It amused Andrew to watch the perverts down there, and I went with him, just to keep him company.'

'Yes, he seemed to like company,' Beresford said, whimsically.

'What do you mean?'

'He often took another woman to the club.'

'That's a lie!' Ms Maitland Williams said so loudly that several other customers turned round. 'It's a lie,' she repeated in a hiss. 'He wouldn't have taken anybody else. I was the only one he lo—' She stopped abruptly, and looked as if she would gladly have bitten off her own tongue.

'The only one what?' Beresford asked.

'Nothing.'

'The only one he loved?'

'No, I . . .' the woman glanced down at her watch. 'Your five minutes is almost up. Ask the rest of your questions.'

The question Beresford wanted to ask was, 'What did Andrew Lofthouse see in you?' because Lofthouse had been a good-looking man, and by no stretch of the imagination could Cecilia Maitland Williams be called an attractive woman.

He had considered the possibility that Lofthouse had not been as superficial as he was himself – that the man looked below the surface for an inner beauty – but having spent a few minutes with this woman, he could find no inner beauty to speak of, and dismissed the idea.

He had wondered if perhaps beauty didn't matter because it had no part to play in a sadomasochistic partnership, but he found it impossible to imagine Meadows with an ugly partner, and assumed that Lofthouse had been the same.

All of which brought him right back to the question he wanted to ask, but knew that he couldn't.

He decided to approach the problem from a different angle.

'Were you Andrew Lofthouse's solicitor?'

'I used to be, but as things developed, I turned his business over to another member of my firm.'

For 'things developed' read 'once he seduced me' Beresford thought.

'But you must know a great deal about the business from the time you *did* represent him,' Beresford said.

'It doesn't matter whether I do or do not,' Maitland Williams said primly. 'As a solicitor, it is my duty to keep my client's business confidential.'

'Unless you know he's done something illegal,' Beresford said.

'How dare you! That is an outrageous thing to suggest!' Maitland Williams said.

But the outrage had come too late to hide the shock that Beresford had read in her eyes.

'Did he have any enemies in the business world?' he asked. 'Were there people who might consider themselves – rightly or wrongly – to have been cheated by him?'

'I can see no reason why I should continue to answer your questions,' she said.

'Can't you?' Beresford asked. 'Eventually, you know, you'll be questioned by the police, and it might be a good idea for you to practise your answers on someone else first.'

'Do you think the police will ask me about Andrew's business practices?' Ms Maitland Williams asked, with a hint of panic in her voice.

'Bound to,' Beresford assured her.

'There were other bottlers and distributors who probably envied Andrew's success,' she said carefully.

'Andrew and Jane's success,' Beresford corrected her.

'Andrew was very much the driving force. Jane was lucky to have him.'

''Cos you're looking through the eyes of love,' Beresford sang softly to himself.

'What was that?'

It was time to be brutal.

'Did it never occur to you that the main reason Andrew wanted you around was because he needed a solicitor who was bent – and who better than a solicitor who was *only* bent because she was crazy about him?' Beresford asked.

He was prepared for her to start screaming. He was ready, should she attempt to scratch his eyes out. But she didn't do either of those things. Instead, she burst into tears.

'That's a terrible thing to say,' she sobbed. 'That's really horrible.'

He almost felt sorry for her. Then he remembered that she was almost definitely a crooked magistrate, and that he had to do whatever it took to save the neck of his old mate Kate.

The office of the managing director at the Whitebridge Bottling and Distribution Company had a glass frontage through which it was possible to look down on the factory floor below.

'I once had a shop steward who complained that from this office it was possible for me to spy on my workforce,' Jane Lofthouse said. 'I pointed out to him that it cut both ways, and not only can I see what they're doing, but they can see what I'm doing. That's the way I've always run this company – nobody should have anything to hide, because everybody should be pulling their weight.'

She was dressed all in black, but she wore her clothes with style, so it could have been either a sign of mourning or a fashion statement.

'How are you coping with being on the outside again?' Kate Meadows asked, remembering how hesitant she had been in the doorway of Overcroft House, only a day before.

Jane sighed. 'It's not easy,' she said. 'For a start, after six weeks in Overcroft House, it's hard not to feel agoraphobic. And then there's the way some of the staff look at me.'

'And what way is that?'

'I suppose it's best described as a mixture of pity and reproach. They're very sorry for what's happened to me . . .'

'So they know you've been in Overcroft House?'

'I'm not sure they know anything as specific as that, but they've got a pretty good idea of why I had to disappear for six weeks.'

'So where does the reproach come into it?'

Jane laughed, perhaps a little awkwardly. 'That's human nature for you – they knew I had a good reason to go, but they still felt deserted.'

'They think you abandoned them to the mercies of your husband.'

Another laugh. 'I wouldn't put it as strongly as that. Andrew might not always have been a popular boss, but he was certainly a competent one, and even those people who would admit to being glad to see the back of him, are shocked by the fact he was murdered.'

'Do you still think it was a good idea to discharge yourself from Overcroft House?' Meadows asked.

'Yes,' Jane said decisively. 'I'm badly needed here. Morale has never been as low as it is now, and though it won't be easy, it's my job to build it up again.' She glanced out of the window, then continued, 'So now we've got my situation out of the way, would you like to explain why you're here, and why you've brought your dishy friend with you.'

'Jack and I used to be in the police together, and we're investigating your husband's murder,' Meadows said.

Jane frowned. 'Wouldn't you be better leaving that up to people who are *still* policemen?' she asked.

'Not really,' Jack said, 'because we're trying to keep Kate out of it.'

'But why should Kate . . .' Jane began. 'Ah, I see. You think she might fall under suspicion because she had an argument with Andrew a few hours before he was killed. But surely, that's nothing like enough to make her a suspect.'

It is if you add the fact that having already injured him, she was stupid enough to go back with him to the house in which his body was discovered, Crane thought – but it would only complicate matters to explain that to Jane.

'It's not so much Kate we're trying to protect here as the reputation of Overcroft House,' he lied.

'I can understand that, but I still don't understand what your reason for being here is,' Jane said.

'Jack needs to talk to your staff,' Kate explained. 'He needs to find out if any of them had a motive for killing your husband.'

'None of them did,' Jane said firmly. 'I know them all very well, and I can assure you that killing is simply not in their nature.'

Killing is in everybody's nature if the circumstances are right, Crane thought, but aloud, he said, 'I'm more than willing to accept your judgement on that, but you see, they might know something – without even realizing it – which will lead us to the killer.'

'Won't the police object when they know you've been questioning my people?' Jane asked.

'They would if they found out,' Kate said.

'And how could you possibly avoid that?'

'Jack's a professor at the university,' Kate explained. 'His cover story will be that he's doing the groundwork for a sociological study of the modern workplace.'

'So you're a sociologist?' Jane asked.

'I can produce a letter from the head of the sociology department saying I'm doing the work on her behalf,' Crane said.

'That's not the same thing,' Jane Lofthouse pointed out.

'No, it isn't,' Meadows agreed, 'but if this sociologist will back him even if she's questioned by the police, it's almost as good as. She will back you, won't she, Jack?'

'Yes,' Crane said. 'She's an old friend.'

'An old *girlfriend*?'

'We had our moments,' Crane admitted.

'My employees trust me,' Jane Lofthouse said. 'I don't like lying to them.'

'And I don't like the idea of Kate being arrested and Overcroft House being closed down,' Crane said bluntly.

'I'm still not happy about it,' Jane Lofthouse said, 'but you're right – after all Kate's done for me, I can't let her down now.'

'That's settled then,' Crane said, trying not to look too relieved.

The room that the Lofthouses called the study led off the bedroom, was rectangular in shape, and was dominated by the Edwardian partnership desk which stood in the centre of the room. There were two large bookcases, one along the wall next to the door, the other along the wall opposite the window. The one by the door contained mostly technical books, many of which were about industrial sterilization and hygiene in the bottling industry. The bookcase opposite the window held mainly hardback fiction of the kind that is sold by book clubs, and bought by people who always intend to spend more time reading, yet somehow never do.

O'Casey dusted the fiction shelves for prints, and was unsurprised to find that there weren't any.

'Do you read many books yourself?' Mason asked him, from the other side of the room.

'I'm from Ireland,' O'Casey replied. 'We have a strong oral tradition.'

'Meaning what, exactly?' Mason asked.

'That we talk so much there's very little time left for reading,' O'Casey replied.

Mason grunted with satisfaction. 'That's what I figured.'

O'Casey was just about to walk away from the bookcase when an odd thought struck him.

'Have you ever seen a bookcase in which all the books fitted exactly?' he asked.

'What do you mean by that?' Mason wondered.

'All the books are the same height, and there's absolutely no space between them and the shelf above.' O'Casey took hold of one of the books and pulled. It came out – but not easily. 'Arguably, they're *too* big for the shelf.' He looked at the book. 'The top of the cover's damaged from jamming it in where it wasn't meant to go. And it's probably the same with the other books.' He removed two more. 'It is,' he confirmed.

'Now why would that be?' Mason wondered.

O'Casey reached through the space he had created, and tapped the wall with his knuckles. There was a hollow sound.

'There's your answer,' he said. 'It's not so much a bookcase as a disguised entrance to another room.' He knelt down and examined the base of the bookcase. 'Tiny casters,' he informed Mason. 'There's some kind of a brake on them, but if I can release that, it should be a piece of piss to move the bookcase.'

He could – and it was. The bookcase glided easily out of the way to reveal a door with a recessed handle and a keyhole.

O'Casey tried the handle, and was not surprised to find that the door was locked.

'So what do you think we do now?' O'Casey asked.

'Now we inform Whitebridge Central, somebody there goes to see a magistrate to get a warrant, and we force it open,' Mason told him.

'Yes, that would work,' O'Casey agreed. 'On the other hand,' he reached into his pocket and pulled out a bunch of skeleton keys, 'we could use these.'

'Where the hell did you get them from?' Mason asked.

'They were in the evidence room. They've been there for years. I'm sure whoever used them has probably served his sentence by now and having learned his lesson, is leading a life of perfect respectability. That being the case, it seemed a pity to leave them gathering dust.'

'Do you realize how many regulations you've probably broken already?' Mason wondered.

O'Casey chuckled. 'It's all part of my retirement plan. When I've stopped working for the police, I'm going to supplement my pension by becoming a safe cracker.'

'Well, you seem to have the crackers part covered already,' Mason said, but he knew from experience that there was no point in further argument.

O'Casey tried three of the keys before he found the right one to open the door.

'What happens now?' Mason asked.

'Now I go in,' O'Casey replied. He stepped through the door. 'It's like a big wardrobe in here, but you wouldn't find any of this stuff in your wardrobe. At least, I hope you wouldn't.'

Mason sighed. 'Too flashy, is it?'

'You could say that.'

When he stepped back into the study, O'Casey was holding what could only be described as a full-length leather corset. There were pointed studs on the outside. They looked rather sharp.

'There are studs on the inside, as well,' O'Casey said. 'And this is quite conventional compared to some of things that are hanging in there.'

'What do we do now?' Mason asked.

'Now we ring DCI Dawson and tell him that we've found a pervert's dressing room, which said pervert carelessly left unlocked,' O'Casey said.

Roger Dalton, marketing manager and officially number two in the command chain of Hadley Securities, was eating his lunch at his desk when his phone rang, and a voice he recognized as belonging to Helen Cosgrove, Jim Hadley's secretary, said, 'Is Mr Hadley with you, Mr Dalton?'

Dalton put down the spoon with which he had been unenthusiastically scooping out low-fat yogurt.

'No,' he said, 'I haven't seen him at all today.' He paused. 'You sound worried? Are you?'

'I am a little bit,' Helen confessed. 'You see, he's not been in at all this morning.'

'Maybe he's decided to take a little time off,' Dalton said, eyeing the chocolate cake which his wife must never find out about. 'He can do what he likes, you know. After all, he is the boss.'

'Mr Hadley never takes time off,' Helen said. 'You know that yourself. If he's not in the office he's down at the workshops, and I know he's not down there now, because I've just rung them.'

It was true, Dalton thought. Jim Hadley didn't ever take time off.

'Maybe he's feeling unwell,' he suggested.

'Even if he was, he'd have phoned in, because he's supposed to be meeting some important clients in half an hour.'

'Why don't you ring his home?' Dalton suggested.

'I wonder why I never thought of that,' Helen said.

'Well, you can't think of everything,' Dalton said, because he made it a policy never to speak to people as if they were idiots, even when they clearly were.

'Can't you recognize sarcasm when you hear it?' Helen asked angrily. 'Of course I bloody thought of it, and of course I rang him. I've been ringing him all morning. He doesn't bloody answer.'

'Can I remind you who you're talking to?' asked Dalton, who was touchy by nature and had never felt he was accorded the respect he was due within the company.

'I'm sorry, Mr Dalton,' Helen said. 'I should never have spoken to you like that, but I'm just so upset, you see.'

'Well, if you make sure it doesn't happen again, we'll forget it,' said Dalton.

He was lying. He wouldn't forget it. He had put a black mark against her name, and it was in indelible ink.

He turned his thoughts back to the problem in hand. If Hadley didn't answer the phone it was either because he couldn't answer or because he wasn't there. The first of these possibilities was concerning, the second mystifying.

'I'm sure there's a perfectly reasonable explanation, but just to make certain, I'll go straight round to Jim Hadley's house,' he said.

'Thank you, Mr Dalton,' the secretary gushed. 'Thank you so much.'

Too late, Dalton thought. You'll not get back in my good books now.

He hung up, and looked at the piece of chocolate cake. Should he eat it now? No, he had been looking forward to it as only a guilty sin can be looked forward to, and when he indulged himself, he wanted to take his time over it.

And besides, although there probably *was* a perfectly reasonable explanation for the boss's behaviour, his stomach had tied itself into such a knot in the last couple of minutes that he was not sure he would have been able to hold it down.

FIFTEEN

DCI Dawson and DS Boyd stood in the Lofthouses' bedroom, examining some of the costumes which had hung in the closet of the room next door and were now spread out on the bed.

'Well, this certainly throws a whole new light on the case, doesn't it, sir?' Boyd asked.

'Does it, indeed?' said Dawson, with a marked lack of enthusiasm. 'In what way?'

What the bloody hell was the matter with the man, Boyd wondered. The further the case progressed, the more stupid and obtuse Dawson seemed to grow, until he had finally reached the point at which he was about as much use as a spare prick at a wedding.

'What it tells us, sir, is that hanging Lofthouse wasn't something the killer suddenly came up with after he'd caved his victim's head in. What it actually turns out to have been was a pre-determined part of a sadomasochistic ritual.'

'And you draw this rather hasty conclusion from what we've found in the wardrobe?'

'From what we've found in the *hidden* wardrobe? Yes, sir.'

'Hasn't it occurred to you, sergeant, that perhaps Mr Lofthouse just liked collecting costumes, and had nothing at all to do with actual sadomasochism?'

'That's a little unlikely, isn't it?' Boyd asked.

'Not really,' Dawson replied. 'I once knew a man who was an avid beer mat collector – he had samples from all over the world mounted on his living room wall – but he was a lifelong teetotaller, so he never touched a drop of the stuff himself.'

'But what about the hook?' Boyd asked.

'The hook?' Dawson replied, as if he had no idea what his sergeant was talking about.

Yes, that thing in the ceiling, just above our heads, you bloody moron, Boyd thought.

But instead of putting that thought into words, he just pointed to it.

'Ah, yes,' Dawson said.

'It must have been used for auto-erotic asphyxiation,' Boyd said. 'It can have had no other purpose.'

'But this is the bedroom he shared with his wife,' Dawson said. 'How could he do something like that right under her nose?' He paused. 'Unless, of course, she was involved.'

'That's unlikely,' Boyd said. 'She doesn't seem to have been the partner in any of his sex games – she was just the one he beat the crap out of when he was frustrated with life.'

'But she must have known what was going on – if anything was,' Dawson said.

'Not necessarily. All this may have taken place when she was out of the house. And even if she was here, he probably told her to stay away from the bedroom – and she was too scared to do anything else.'

'So are you saying we should shift the focus of this investigation and put all our efforts into the pervert angle?'

Shift the focus. Boyd repeated silently. What focus? As far as he could see, the investigation didn't *have* a focus.

'It's certainly a possibility I think we should explore, sir,' he said cautiously. 'I believe there are a number of clubs in the area that cater for that kind of activity, and I think we could use them as a starting point.'

'Before we go about transferring valuable resources into that

line of enquiry, I'd like to see a little more evidence to back up
your theory,' Dawson said.

And it suddenly occurred to Boyd that perhaps – for his own
twisted reasons – Dawson didn't want to get a result on this case.

With this new perspective in mind, he quickly ran through what
options he was faced with.

It seemed to him to boil down to only two.

One: he could stick with his boss, like the loyal bagman he had
always tried to be, and when blame was being dished out, he could
accept his share of it, even though failure to solve this case was
likely to put back his career advancement by at least two years.

Two: since Dawson had made the decision to fail, he himself
was now free of any obligations, and could do whatever it took
to survive.

It wasn't exactly hard to decide which was the more attractive
of the options.

When Roger Dalton left the office, his plan was to drive straight
to his boss's house in the country and find out exactly why
Hadley had uncharacteristically absented himself from work,
but his resolve was weakened by the sight of a cake shop on
the outskirts of Whitebridge, and once he was inside, it was
difficult to restrain himself from buying up half the shop. In
fact, when he emerged he was feeling quite proud that he had
restricted his purchase to four small cakes – or 'fancies' as they
were known in Lancashire.

The knot of anxiety he had acquired when he first learned about
his boss's erratic behaviour seemed to have quite unravelled, and
once he had driven past the sign announcing that he was leaving
Whitebridge and wishing him luck, he pulled into the first lay-by
that he saw. Opening his cardboard treasure chest, he gazed down
lovingly at the contents. It would be excessive to eat them all in
a single session, he told himself, so he would just have the one
that seemed most appealing.

He frowned. The problem was that he didn't dare let his wife
see any of them, so he would have to dispose of the lot before he
got home. He supposed he could sample a little of each of them,
and throw the rest away, but it seemed a shame to waste good
food.

Very well, a compromise was in order. He would eat two of the cakes in the lay-by, and two after he had seen Hadley.

He bit into the first one – a lemon drizzle cake – and felt his taste buds performing somersaults.

The week before, when his wife had banished cakes from his diet, she had given her reason as a fear that he was diabetic. Sweet things always made him go to sleep, she claimed, and one day they would send him into a coma from which there would be no return.

She was exaggerating as usual. Though he refused to be tested for it, he was sure he was not diabetic, and if he did fall asleep after eating cake, well, that only showed that he was well-contented.

He polished off the fancy in a little over a minute.

Too fast! he told himself. You shouldn't just gobble it down – it was a work of art, and deserved to be savoured.

He would have a short pause before he attacked the next one, he decided. Then he closed his eyes and fell asleep.

Ruby Watkins would have preferred to supervise the birth of Lizzie Grimshaw's baby under hospital conditions, but her room was clean, light and airy, and it would serve well enough. Lizzie herself was a perhaps little underweight, but otherwise in excellent health, and Ruby was not expecting any trouble delivering her baby.

The only problem was the wardrobe.

When Kate Meadows had promised Lizzie she could have it in her room, Ruby had gone along with it, because it seemed the only way to avoid a scene. Now, however, she was beginning to have her doubts about that decision. The wardrobe had been scrubbed down and sterilized, true, but it still felt slightly unhygienic. Besides, its very bulk was an impediment to good birthing practice.

It would simply have to go, she decided, and rather than come straight out with it, she would lead into the subject gently.

'The baby should be born any day now,' she said to Lizzie, who was lying on her bed after the examination. 'Are you ready for it?'

'More than ready,' Lizzie replied. 'Mrs Maybe's made sure I've got all the nappies and dried milk I need, and I've got lots of toys for when the baby's old enough to notice them.'

The midwife smiled. 'I don't have to ask if you're excited,' she said. 'I can tell from your voice that you are.'

'I am,' Lizzie confirmed. 'My baby girl will be the most beautiful baby in the world.'

'You mustn't assume it will be a girl,' Ruby cautioned. 'It could just as easily be a boy.'

'It'll be a girl,' Lizzie said confidently. 'I know it will.'

'You won't be disappointed if it's a boy, will you?' the midwife asked, anxiously.

Lizzie laughed. 'Of course not, I'd love him just as much as if he was a girl – but that isn't going to happen.'

It was moments like this that the midwife cherished – the warmth, the love, the happiness and the anticipation were a glorious, joyful mixture which couldn't be found anywhere else.

'I'm going to have to ask Ms Meadows to have that wardrobe removed,' she said.

Instantly, the joyful mixture was gone, and an arctic chill filled the room.

'What was that you just said?' Lizzie demanded.

'I'll . . . I'll ask Ms Meadows to have that wardrobe removed,' the midwife repeated, and was surprised to discover that she was a little frightened.

'It stays,' Lizzie said coldly.

'But it will be in the way when we're trying to deliver your baby,' the midwife protested.

'Work around it,' Lizzie told her.

'If you're keeping something in it that is very important to you, I'm sure we can move it elsewhere,' the midwife assured her.

'There's nothing in it,' Lizzie said. 'It's empty. Take a look, if you don't believe me.'

'Well, then, if it's empty . . .'

'If you can't work with it in the room, I'll find another midwife who can,' Lizzie said. 'And if I can't find another midwife, then me and Mrs Maybe will deliver it. But the wardrobe stays. Understood?'

'Understood,' Ruby said, wonderingly.

Over the years, she had seen pregnancy affect women in all kinds of ways, sometimes even changing their whole personalities, but never before had she known a patient who changed from a girl frightened of her own shadow into a midwife-eating tiger.

'So what is it you're doing again?' asked the red-headed girl in the tight uniform.

Jack Crane suppressed a sigh. 'We're doing a sociological study of how various businesses react to a traumatic change in their organizational structure,' he explained. 'To put it in terms of this company, we want to study what effect of Mr Lofthouse's death has on the way things are run.'

The three women and one man who worked on the production line exchanged glances.

'It doesn't have any effect on us at all,' said the man, who was in fifties and balding. 'Whoever's in charge, the conveyor belt keeps moving, and we have our job to do.'

'So you're saying things would stay the same if, for example, the Americans took over?' Crane said.

'Are you telling me they've sold the plant to the Yanks?' the man asked, alarmed.

'No, it's a hypothetical question,' Crane said.

'We don't need no hypothermic questions here,' said a buxom brunette, who clearly had no idea what the word meant.

'And we don't want to work for no Yanks,' said the third girl, a bottle blonde. 'It was a Yank who put my great aunt Eunice in the club during the war, and she's seen neither hide nor hair of him since.'

He was pitching this all wrong, Crane realized. It wasn't a mistake he'd have made a few years earlier, when he'd been an active police officer, but now he was so used to talking almost exclusively to undergraduates that he was aiming this way above the heads of the people he was questioning.

'Let me put it another way,' he suggested. 'You'll all miss Mr Lofthouse, won't you?'

Giving the circumstances, it was the kind of question to which there was only one possible answer, and the assembly line workers all agreed that yes, they would miss him, though it seemed to Crane that their enthusiasm was not wholehearted.

'And you must have missed Mrs Lofthouse, while she was away,' he said.

This time, the response was warmer.

'We've all been with Miss Bright – Mrs Lofthouse I should say – since we left school, and she's been a good boss to us,' said the brunette.

'I imagine everybody likes her – even her business rivals – but I can't see Mr Lofthouse being quite so popular,' Crane said, pushing his luck.

'Now how would we know about their business rivals?' asked
the man. 'We don't see any business rivals while we're at work,
and we don't mix in the same circles outside.'

Of course it wasn't reasonable to expect them to be able to
answer that sort of question, Crane thought. So maybe this whole
sociological survey idea was turning out to be a non-starter.

'Is Mr Hadley a business rival?' the bottle blonde asked.

'No,' the man said, not unkindly, but certainly patronizingly.
'Mr Hadley's the feller who set up our security system. He's
nothing to do with bottling.'

'Oh,' the blonde said, somewhat discouraged.

'Why did you ask about him?' Crane said.

'It doesn't matter,' the blonde told him.

'I'd really like to know,' he persisted.

The blonde hesitated. 'A few weeks ago, I was in a pub called
the Ploughman's Arms, over in Stockford . . .' she said finally.

Stockford, Crane noted. That was a small village about ten miles
from Whitebridge.

'What were you doing way out there in the back of beyond,
Ellen Atherton?' the redhead asked.

'I just fancied a change,' the blonde said, evasively.

'Were you on your own?'

'No.'

'So who were you with?' the redhead asked.

'It doesn't matter,' the blonde said.

'I'd like to know,' the redhead insisted. 'We've never had no
secrets from each other before, and we're not going to start now.'

The blonde sighed. 'If you must know, I was with Jerry Miller.'

'He's engaged to Linda Cowgill from packing, isn't he?' the
redhead asked.

Yes,' the blonde admitted, 'but he was thinking of breaking it
off.'

'He didn't though, did he?' the redhead asked challengingly. 'I
know that for a fact, because I saw her yesterday, and she was
still wearing her engagement ring.'

'No,' the blonde admitted, rather sadly, 'as it happened, he
changed his mind.'

'You were telling me about Mr Hadley,' Crane said.

'That's right, I was,' the blonde agreed, gratefully. 'Me and
Jerry went into this pub, and I saw Mr Lofthouse sitting there all

by himself. I almost went across to say hello, because it would have been rude not to, but then this woman came out of the toilets and sat down next to him. Well, I couldn't do it then, could I?'

'Why not?'

'They were acting very friendly – if you know what I mean.'

'Maybe they were friends,' the man suggested.

'Very, *very* friendly,' the blonde countered. 'They kept kissing, and passing a cocktail cherry from her mouth to his and then back again.'

'That's disgusting,' the redhead said.

'And all the time this was going on, Mrs Lofthouse was at the conference in Manchester, drumming up business for us,' the blonde said.

'He ought to be ashamed of himself,' the brunette said.

'It's a bit too late to be ashamed now, isn't it?' the man pointed out. 'He's bloody dead.'

'Yes, well, that doesn't mean he shouldn't be ashamed of himself if he wasn't,' the brunette said.

'Who was this woman?' the redhead asked. 'Do you know?'

'Oh, I know all right,' the blonde said. 'She was that solicitor who you see in the office now and again. I forget her name.'

'Miss Maitland Williams?' suggested the redhead.

'That's her,' the blonde confirmed.

'I'm not normally one to speak ill of the dead, but if that's who it was then he wanted his head seeing to,' said the man, 'because who in his right mind would knock off a piece like her when he had a lovely wife like Mrs Lofthouse?'

'I don't see what any of this has to do with Mr Hadley,' Crane said, in an effort to get the conversation back on the right track.

'Ah well, you see, that's when I noticed Mr Hadley,' the blonde said. 'He was sitting right at the other end of the room, and I don't think Mr Lofthouse had even seen him . . .'

'When a man's trying to get his end away, the very last thing he notices is somebody watching him from the other side of the bar,' the man said.

'Don't judge everybody else by your own standards,' the blonde said cuttingly. 'Anyway, the important thing is that he was watching Mr Lofthouse, and honestly, if looks could kill, they'd have had to carry Mr Lofthouse out of the pub in a box.'

At first, Roger Dalton had no idea where he was, but slowly his half-asleep half-awake brain began to collect up the clues and piece them together.

For a start, he was sitting down rather than lying down, so he wasn't in bed. Next, movement of the lower half of his body was restricted. When he shuffled his feet, they brushed against objects that had some movement in them, but were clearly anchored to some kind of base. When he raised his legs slightly, he knees pressed against a barrier which seemed quite thin and appeared to be curving outwards.

As an experiment, he opened his eyes, and discovered he was looking at a window. But it wasn't the sort of window you find in a house, it was a . . . it was a windscreen!

He was awake now, and the whole situation had become clear to him. He was sitting on his car – somewhat cold and stiff – in a lay-by, with a box of fancies resting in his lap.

He checked his watch.

God, he had been asleep for hours! They would be wondering what had happened to him at the office, except that by now the office would be closed. And he still had no idea what had happened to the boss.

He brushed away the crumbs from around his mouth, put the box of cakes on the passenger seat, and switched on his engine.

Better late than never, he told himself – but it would have been better if he hadn't been late at all.

The lay-by was a little over two miles from Hadley's home – which Dalton thought of as Hadley's 'country pile' – and so it was a matter of minutes before he found himself on the long driveway that led up to the place.

The house was impressive without being ostentatious. On the first floor, there were five bedrooms and two – or was it three? – bathrooms. On the ground floor, there were, as might be expected, a cloakroom, a kitchen, a dining room and two reception rooms.

There was also a magnificent games room which held a full-size snooker table and was totally wasted on Hadley, who much preferred to spend his time in his garage/workshop, trying out his new ideas. Some people, Dalton reflected, just didn't know how to enjoy their money.

As he walked up to the front door – fine, polished Burmese teak – he noticed it was slightly ajar.

There was no point in spending a fortune on a security system and then leaving the front door open so that anybody could just walk in, he thought. Yet he could almost have filled a book with people – normally quite sensible people – who'd done just that. Even so, he was surprised to discover that his own boss, who earned his living from security, should have been guilty of such a cardinal sin.

He pressed the doorbell, and heard the chimes of *Widdecombe Fair* reverberating somewhere in the distance.

He was also conscious of another sound – a buzzing noise. He wondered what it could be.

He waited for about a minute, and when no one had come to the door, he rang again.

The seconds ticked by, and the buzzing persisted.

He had two choices, he decided – he could either turn around and go away, or he could enter the house uninvited. On balance, he favoured the latter, because he had to do something to justify his wasted afternoon, and anyway, someone should inform Hadley that he had neglected to close the door.

He stepped inside the entrance hall.

'Mr Hadley?' he called out – because he didn't work for the kind of firm where you used your boss's first name. 'Mr Hadley! Do you know your front door is open?'

The buzzing noise was even louder now he was inside, and seemed to be coming from somewhere above head level.

Flies?

This was February. There weren't supposed to be any flies about.

Yet the noise seemed to get even louder, as if his arrival had infuriated the creatures.

He looked up, and saw that a sack seemed to be hanging from the rail on the upstairs corridor. This was what was attracting the flies, and there were literally thousands of them.

And then he realized it wasn't a sack at all!

He experienced a sudden, excruciating pain in his stomach, and felt his body jack-knife.

It couldn't be Jim Hadley, he told himself. It simply *couldn't* be.

But he knew that it was.

He opened his mouth and spewed most of the lemon drizzle cake on to the expensively tiled floor.

SIXTEEN

There was a bend in the driveway leading to Jim Hadley's home, and so it was only when Crane rounded it that he could see the caravan of vehicles parked in front of the house. There were four of them – two patrol cars, an ambulance, and a Honda Accord. The Accord didn't actually have the letters CID painted on its doors, but might as well have done.

Crane's first instinct was to slam on the brakes, execute one of those U turns that always featured in American cop movies, and get the hell out of there. Then he checked in his rear-view mirror, and saw that there was another patrol car rounding the bend, and thus blocking his escape.

'Well, shit!' he said.

He wondered what to do next. One alternative was to drive up to the house and try to bluff his way out of the situation he'd found himself in.

Another was to . . .

Actually, he decided, there weren't any others.

He parked close to the ambulance, and waited for someone to approach him. When someone did, it was not a naive rookie, as he'd hoped, but a street-smart-looking sergeant.

Crane wound down his window. 'Good evening, sergeant,' he said.

'Who are you?' asked the sergeant, who had obviously decided the usual social niceties were an unnecessary luxury.

'My name's Crane,' Jack said. 'Dr John Crane.'

'We don't need you,' the sergeant told him. 'We've got our own medics.'

'Well, in that case, I'll be on my way,' Crane said, firing up his engine.

If he could just pull off before it occurred to the sergeant to ask him what he was doing there in the first place, he just might get away with it, he thought.

'Hello, Jack! What the bloody hell are you doing here?' asked a cheery voice from over the sergeant's left shoulder.

The sergeant turned, and Crane saw PC Tony Baker standing there.

Baker was a nice enough feller, Crane thought, but if you put his brain on one end of a seesaw and a field mouse's brain on the other end, it would be Baker's end which stayed in the air.

'Do you know this man, Baker?' the sergeant demanded.

'Yes, sarge, he used to be one of us, but now he has a much cushier life teaching English at the university.'

'I thought you said you were a doctor,' the sergeant said.

'I am,' Crane confirmed, 'but not the medical kind.'

'So what have *you* got to do with our Hanging Man, Jack?' Baker asked, totally oblivious to the tension in the air.

'Yes,' the sergeant said. 'What *have* you got to do with our Hanging Man, Jack?'

So Hadley was not only dead, he'd been hanged.

Excellent, Crane thought. When things were already head-spinningly complicated, an extra complication was just what you bloody needed!

'I did have a reason for visiting Mr Hadley, but it couldn't possibly be connected with the murder,' Crane said.

Although he was already starting to wonder if that was strictly true.

'Murder?' the sergeant repeated. 'Who said anything about a murder?'

'Didn't you?'

'No, I didn't.'

'Then I must have guessed.'

'Well, since you seem to be so good at guessing, guess what I'm going to say next.'

'Are you going to say I should park somewhere out of the way, and stay there until the investigating officer can find the time to deal with me?' Crane asked.

The sergeant smiled. 'Smart lad,' he said.

DS Boyd and DCI Dawson stood at the far end of Jim Hadley's entrance hall. The smell wasn't so bad there, but the ambulance men at the other end of the room, who were currently involved in the process of lowering the corpse to the hall floor, were wearing masks.

'The man was a well-known security expert, and this place is wired up as tight as a duck's arse, so how the hell did the killer get in without tripping the alarm?' Dawson asked.

'There's a small control room under the stairs,' Boyd said. 'It's there that the alarms are activated and deactivated. They're deactivated now, which probably means that they were switched off when the killer came in.'

'There's no chance they could have been turned off from outside the house, is there?' Dawson asked.

'There wouldn't be much point in alarms you could do that to, now would there?' Boyd asked.

'So Hadley deactivated the alarms himself?'

'It's certainly looking that way,' Boyd said. 'There's no doubt it was the same killer in both cases, is there, sir?' he asked, shifting gear.

'None at all,' Dawson agreed reluctantly. 'Unless,' he added, with a sudden hint of hope in his voice, 'you think this was a copycat murder.'

Yes, you'd love it to be a copycat murder, wouldn't you, Boyd thought, because if it was, you could foist this particular investigation off on some other poor bugger.

But aloud, he said, 'There's no chance of that, sir. The modus operandi is exactly the same – kill the victim with a blow to the back of the head, strip him naked, then hang him over the banister. The only difference is that this one wasn't decapitated, and the reason for that is probably that the killer didn't *throw* Hadley over the rail as he threw Lofthouse. Instead, he must have *lowered* him – which would suggest he'd never intended to pull Lofthouse's head off, and wanted to avoid doing the same with Hadley.'

'Still, it *could* have been a copycat,' Dawson said.

'It couldn't,' Boyd contradicted him. 'We released the fact that Lofthouse had been killed before he was strung up, but we never specified how. And we didn't mention that he was naked, or that he'd been washed down with surgical spirit. Well, Hadley is certainly naked, and I'm willing to bet the doc will say he's been washed down. And then there's the rope – I'm convinced it will turn out to be the same sort as the rope used on Lofthouse.'

He was right, Dawson thought despairingly – both men had been killed by the same person. And that changed everything,

because while he might get away with not solving one murder –
especially with Chief Superintendent Towers covering his back
– he wouldn't get away with failing to solve two, even with the
Lord God Almighty as his sponsor.

And where did that leave him? It meant he had no choice but
to try his best to get a result. He could only pray that Chief
Superintendent Towers would see it that way, too.

'We need to find out what connects the two victims, and what
it was that they both did – or both knew – that would make our
killer want to see them dead,' he said. 'Do you agree, sergeant?'

'Yes, sir,' Boyd said, clearly knocked off balance by his boss's
sudden attack of professionalism. 'And since the pattern has been
repeated, I'd like to look into the sadomasochistic angle – if you've
no objections, that is,' he added, taking advantage of Dawson's
change of heart while it lasted.

'No, I have no objections,' Dawson said. 'In fact, sergeant, I
think it's a good idea.'

A uniformed sergeant appeared in the doorway. He stepped to
one side to allow the ambulance men to wheel the stretcher out
of the room, then walked over to the detectives.

'Excuse me interrupting you, sir,' he said to Dawson, 'but we've
got an ex-bobby outside who turned up twenty minutes ago, and
seems unwilling to provide a satisfactory explanation as to why
he's here. Do you want us to take him down to Whitebridge Central,
or will you have a word with him on site?'

'We'll start with having a word with him here – and see where
it goes from there,' said the newly-decisive DCI Dawson.

The two policemen approached Crane's car from the rear, so he
had no idea they were even there until they opened the back doors
and slipped inside.

'They tell me you're an ex-bobby,' DCI Dawson said.

'I am,' Crane confirmed.

'Good, that means we can cut out all the preliminary bullshit
and get right to the heart of the matter,' Dawson said. 'Do you
want to tell us why you're here?'

'I'm doing some work for the university sociology department,'
said Crane, who had decided that if he was going to lie through
his teeth, he should at least make his story consistent with the one
he'd used at Lofthouse's plant. 'The department is conducting a

survey, and I was going to ask Mr Hadley if he would be willing to cooperate with it.'

'Did you know him?'

'No.'

'Not even vaguely?'

'I've never met him. I don't even know what he looked like.'

'The last time *we* saw him, he looked a mess,' Dawson said.

'Was he dead before he was hanged, like the last one was?' Crane asked.

'Who says he'd been hung?' Dawson demanded.

'I'll take that as a yes,' Crane said.

'You seem very interested in him considering that you say you'd never met him and you didn't even know that he was dead until one of our men told you. Have I got that last bit right, by the way?'

'What bit?'

'That you didn't know he was dead until one of my men told you.'

'Yes, you have. After all, I'd never have driven out here if I'd known he was dead, would I?' Crane said.

Idiot! he rebuked himself.

He should have known that you should never say more than is absolutely necessary when talking to the police – because given half a chance, they'd twist your words and use them against you.

Should have known? He *did* bloody know, because he'd been in the game himself.

'You'd never have driven out here if you'd known he was dead,' mused Dawson, proving Crane's point. 'I'm not sure about that. You might have been revisiting the scene of your crime. A lot of killers do.' He chuckled. 'Just taking the piss out of you, son, bobby-to-ex-bobby. You're still quite a long way from becoming our prime suspect. Still,' he shrugged, 'you never know how things might turn out.'

There was nothing Crane could say that would make his position any better, so he said nothing at all.

'Just as a matter of interest, do you happen to have an alibi for last night – say between the hours of eight and two in morning?' Boyd asked.

'Yes, I do,' Crane replied.

There was a silence which lasted for perhaps twenty seconds, then Boyd said, 'Are you going to tell us what it is?'

'Of course – as soon as you can give me a good reason why I should,' Crane replied.

Sally Spencer

There was another silence, but this one lasted no more than ten seconds before Boyd spoke again.

'So you say you're a sociologist.'

'No, I said I was helping out the sociology department,' Crane replied.

'Why would they ask for your help?'

'The professor thought that since I knew this area well, I might have more luck in getting people to cooperate than she would.'

'Than *she* would,' Dawson said. 'So the professor's a woman, is she?'

Yes, lots of women hold important positions now, Crane thought. There's even a woman chief superintendent in Mid Lancs Police, who, once upon a time, called me Uncle Jack.

But this time, he was wise enough not to put his thoughts into words.

'If we check with this professor, she'll confirm what you've just told us, will she?' Boyd asked.

'Yes, she will,' Crane said confidently.

Dawson opened the car door, and stepped out.

'Right, you're free to go,' he said, 'but if you're planning to take any excursions beyond the Lancashire border, you'd be wise to let me know.'

There were three of them in the Drum and Monkey – the vodka, the fruit juice and the pint of best bitter. The other beer drinker should have been there, too, but something seemed to have delayed Jack Crane.

'We'd best get started,' Paniatowski said, glancing at her watch. 'I'll kick off.'

She picked up a couple of pages of notes from the table, stared down at them with a look of surprise on her face, then reached into her pocket for her reading glasses.

'I only used to need specs when my eyes got tired, but it's all the bloody time now,' she complained. She ran her eyes up and down the page. 'I collected most of this information over the phone. It's far from ideal – face-to-face contact is always much better – but we simply haven't got the manpower. I talked to the bosses of several companies that Whitebridge Bottling either dealt with or competed with.' She paused. 'Actually, that's not strictly true. Most of the people I talked to were no longer in charge.'

It was not until she had started making the calls that she'd realized just how much out of the loop she actually was – just how many of the current movers and shakers she either didn't know or had known as very junior members of the organizations they were now heading. So she had found herself having conversations with men whose voices were starting to quaver and whose memories were starting to fade. It was called making the best of the situation, she supposed.

Or maybe it was simply clutching at straws.

'There was pretty much of a consensus among both the customers and the competitors,' she said. 'They all liked Miss Bright – that's what they mostly called Jane Lofthouse – but there wasn't the same warmth of feeling for her husband.'

'Did they think he was a crook?' Beresford asked.

'I wouldn't put it as strongly as that,' Paniatowski replied. 'They didn't like him and they didn't entirely trust him. They certainly thought he was capable of pulling a fast one, but it was likely to be an *unscrupulous* fast one, rather than an *illegal* one. I didn't get the impression that any of them – or any of their successors – would want to see Andrew Lofthouse dead. Of course,' she spread her hands in a gesture of helplessness, 'you miss the nuances over the phone. It's a bit like doing brain surgery, when the only tool you have is a garden spade.'

'I think he *is* a crook,' Beresford said. 'Why else would he be knocking off that solicitor?' He held up a restraining hand to Meadows. 'And please don't give me any of the usual crap about looks only being skin deep, and some women having beautiful souls. I've talked to the woman, and there's nothing beautiful about her soul. I think Lofthouse needed somebody with legal training to break the law, which she did out of gratitude for him slipping her a length now and again.'

'Elegantly phrased,' Meadows said dryly. 'But I'm not saying you're wrong in this case.'

The door opened, and Crane entered the bar. He looked rough.

'What's happened?' Paniatowski said.

Crane told them about how he got his lead on Hadley, and how he had gone to Hadley's house and found the police there.

'Well, it's looking less likely that Hadley killed Lofthouse,' Beresford said.

'And more likely that they were both killed by the same man,' Crane said.

'Talk me through that,' Paniatowski said.

'They were both prosperous middle-class businessmen, and they both lived alone in large houses,' Crane said. 'We don't know all the details of the murders – the police will be holding some of them back – but we do know they were both hanged in their own homes, probably when they were already dead. It has to be more than a coincidence.'

'Could the hangings have been part of a sadomasochistic ritual, Kate?' Paniatowski asked.

'Sadomasochists do hang each other – or rather they assist their partners to hang themselves – but it's all carefully controlled, because no one is supposed to die,' Meadows said. 'I've never heard of hanging people *after* they've died. We're not into necrophilia.'

'Maybe it was done to misdirect the police,' Paniatowski said. 'Maybe the killer wanted the police to think the murders were connected to sadomasochism, even if they weren't.'

'If DCI Dawson does latch on to the S&M angle, you're going to be in deep shit, Sarge,' Crane said to Meadows. 'Because the first thing he'll do is question the people at the Hellfire Club, and that could well lead them to you. In your situation, I think I'd get rid of the Zelda costume.'

'I've already done that,' Meadows said.

The expression which suddenly appeared on Meadows' face both shocked and horrified Paniatowski. She'd seen the same expression – an odd mixture of surprise, guilt and fear – on the faces of many criminals when they realized they'd given too much away – but she'd never seen it on the face of one of her own officers before.

'When did you get rid of the Zelda stuff?' she asked.

'Does it matter?' Meadows replied, defensively.

'Yes, it does,' Paniatowski said firmly. 'You should know as well as anyone sitting around this table that the details are always important.'

Meadows shrugged. 'After I left Lofthouse's place, I drove out to the moors and burned the costume and the wig.'

'But that was before you knew Lofthouse had been killed,' Paniatowski said, worriedly.

'Yes, I suppose it was,' Meadows replied, and her voice had grown unexpectedly apathetic.

'So if you didn't know he was dead, why did you burn it?'

Another shrug. 'I was sick of it. I wanted it gone.'

'Do you have an alibi for last night, Sarge, between the hours of eight and two?' Crane asked.

'What! Are you accusing me of killing Hadley now?'

'No, I'm not – but Dawson might.'

'I was in Overcroft House,' Meadows said wearily. 'I went to bed early.' She looked at each of their faces in turn. 'I didn't kill Lofthouse, and I didn't kill Hadley.'

'We know you didn't,' said Paniatowski, and wished she could sound more certain.

Chief Superintendent Towers was already at the Grapes when Dawson arrived.

This wasn't going to be easy, Dawson thought – it wasn't going to be easy at all.

But surely, Towers wouldn't cause a scene in the pub, with everybody looking.

Would he?

'Sit down,' Towers said. He signalled for the waiter, then turned to Dawson. 'I hear there's been another murder. Is it connected to the first?'

'We think so.'

The waiter arrived. 'My friend's buying tonight,' Towers told him. 'Isn't that right, Eric?'

'Er . . . yes,' Dawson agreed. 'We'll have two glasses of Bell's.'

'He means we'll have two glasses of Glenlivet twelve-year-old malt,' Towers said. 'And you'd better make them doubles.'

The waiter went back to the bar.

'So, you were the one who wanted this meeting,' Towers said. 'Shall I guess why you wanted it?'

'If you like,' Dawson said miserably.

'You wanted to tell me that you can't hold back on your investigation any longer – that you have to pull out all the stops in an effort to catch the murderer?' Towers guessed.

'Look at it from my perspective,' Dawson pleaded. 'The way I conduct this investigation from now on will be examined under a microscope, and if there's anything I can be criticized for, I bloody well will be.'

'Quite right,' Towers said. 'You have to do the best job you can.'

'Bloody hell, you've changed your tune,' Dawson said, amazed at how easy it had been.

'Needs must, old son,' Towers said philosophically. 'If you go down, the chances are that you'll try to drag me with you.'

'I would never . . .'

'Of course you would. There's no point in pretending. I've never had a particularly high opinion of you, and you're certainly not going to improve on it by lying to me.'

'I've never had a particularly high opinion of you, either,' Dawson said sullenly.

'That comes as no surprise to me at all,' Towers replied, 'but there's one huge difference between you and me. Do you know what it is?'

'No,' Dawson said, wishing he was dead.

'The big difference between us is that you're scared of me, and I'm not scared of you,' Towers told him. He patted Dawson on the shoulder. 'No hard feelings. You've done what you could, and it just wasn't good enough, so I'll have to find another way to nobble St Louisa.'

'I want you to do something for me, for a change,' Dawson said, sulkily.

'Do you indeed?' Towers asked. 'And that might that be?'

'There's an ex-bobby called Crane hanging around on the edge of the investigation. He says he's doing work for the university, but I don't believe him. I want you to use your influence to get him off my back.'

Towers looked gobsmacked. 'Crane did you say?' he asked. '*Jack* Crane? Got a patch over one eye?'

'Yes, that's him.'

Towers chuckled. 'Have I said something funny?' Dawson demanded.

'Jack Crane was one of Monika Paniatowski's team back in the day – and they were all joined at the hip, which means that if he's involved in any of this, it's probably on Monika's behalf.'

'I don't get it,' Dawson admitted.

'Of course you don't. That's because as a detective, you'd make a good hatstand. So I'll spell it out for you – slowly. It's beginning to look as if Paniatowski is sticking her big Polish conk into this investigation. Now it's very unlikely that somebody as independently minded as Louisa Rutter would have asked for her mother's help, so that means that Monika's doing it off her own bat. She probably realizes this investigation is important for her daughter's advancement, and she's arrogant enough to think that she can solve a case that nobody else can.'

Towers took a card out of his pocket, wrote some names on it, and handed it to Dawson.

'Monika Paniatowski, Kate Meadows, Colin Beresford, Jack Crane,' Dawson read. 'What am I supposed to do with this?'

'I want to know what they've been doing for the last couple of days, and I want them followed from now on,' Towers said. 'I'll put my own lads on it, but I may need to use a couple of yours, as well.'

'You . . . you want to build up a case against them for obstructing justice,' Dawson gasped.

'Exactly.'

'You do realize it's an offence punishable by imprisonment?'

'Of course I realize it.'

'So are you planning to send DCI Paniatowski to gaol?'

'Not necessarily,' Towers said. 'If Louisa Rutter is prepared to take very early retirement, any evidence we've collected will disappear. But if she resists – well, she'll just have to get used to only seeing her mum on visiting days.'

He had spent the previous few hours hiding in the evergreen bushes in the Corporation Park, but when he heard the town hall clock strike midnight, he broke cover.

The temperature had dropped below freezing, and he was grateful for that, because although his body was aching with the cold, the weather had at least served to keep most people off the streets.

His knee had been damaged in the fall, so he made slow progress and was forced to rest it every couple of hundred yards. He wondered if he had done himself any permanent damage, and decided he probably had.

That didn't matter.

There was only one thing that mattered.

There was too much light from the moon for his liking, but the street lamp across from the target house was out, and that was a lucky break – the first one he'd had all day.

He positioned himself next to the lamp-post.

He was suffering from hunger pains now, and it felt as if he had a rat inside him, gnawing away at his vital organs. He could have prevented this by bringing some food with him, but that would have increased the risk element, and he had taken enough risks already.

'You only have one chance, and this is it,' he said softly to himself.

One chance, and even that was bound to end in failure eventually – but the longer he could put off that failure, the better.

The target house was in darkness, as were all the other houses along the street, but now he saw a tiny speck of light, bobbing about in one of the upper rooms.

A torch!

The light disappeared, and he had to wait what seemed like a lifetime before it reappeared on the ground floor.

And then it was gone from there, too.

He counted slowly to twenty, and then started to cross the road. His knee should have been better for the rest, but perhaps that rest had been *too* long, and now it seemed to have locked, and he dragged it behind him like the useless appendage it had become.

He opened the gate and stepped into the garden. He was glad of the moonlight now, because there were a number of large plant pots in the garden, and without it he would undoubtedly have crashed into them.

There were steps down to the basement, and he took them slowly, his good leg holding his weight while he swung the useless leg into the right position. And finally he was outside the basement, looking in.

And there was that small dot of light.

SEVENTEEN

Friday, 4 February, 2000

Arthur Sweeting's first job, when he left school, had been as a library assistant, or, to be more accurate, as the library assistant's assistant. He had never been overly ambitious or dynamic, but like the tortoise in the fable he had been slow and dependable, and when he retired from the library, half a century later, it had been as deputy librarian (popular fiction).

In the five years since his retirement, he had grown chrysanthemums, collected postage stamps from the Pacific Islands, and pottered about in general. His life followed a calm and unruffled path. He had never married, and had never been the kind of man to whom surprising things happened, so when he heard the hammering on his front door at five thirty in the morning, his first thought was that he was having a bad dream.

The knocking persisted.

He wondered who it could be.

It was too late for hooligans, creating a disturbance on their way home from the pub.

It was too early for the postman to be delivering a package. Besides, the postman's knock was always somewhat restrained, and the person at the door now was giving it a real hammering.

Whoever it was, it wasn't just disturbing him, it was also disturbing his neighbours, and since Arthur couldn't have that, he supposed he'd better go and see what the problem was.

He rose reluctantly from his bed, found his slippers and dressing gown, and went over to the window.

He raised the sash, and looked down on to the street. He could see several men standing there. They were all wearing helmets and heavy padded jackets. They also seemed to be carrying rifles, but they couldn't be – not in Arcadia Terrace. 'What do you want?' he asked, noting that there was a slight tremble in his voice.

One of the men looked up.

'Police!' he said. 'Could you open your front door for us, please, Mr Sweeting.'

'I'm not sure I . . .'

'If you don't, we'll have to smash it in – and you wouldn't want that, would you?'

'No, I . . .'

'Then open the door. And be quick – because time is pressing.'

Arthur Sweeting had never done anything quickly in his life, but he did his best to comply with the instruction. Once in the hallway, he opened the door, with the chain still on, and said, 'I'd like to see some kind of identification before I let you in, if you don't mind.'

A gloved hand held a warrant card up in front of him. The card said the man was Sergeant Albert Ingham, and that he was a member of the Central Lancs Police Armed Response Unit.

'Will that do you?' Ingham asked.

'Yes, I suppose so.'

'Then open the bloody door.'

Sweeting slid back the chain and opened the door, and immediately the hall was filled with men.

Big men!

Men wearing body armour!

And yes, it *was* guns they were carrying!

'Sign this,' said Ingham, holding out an official looking piece of paper and a cheap pen.

'What is it?'

'Just bloody sign it.'

Arthur Sweeting knew his rights, and knew he shouldn't sign anything without reading it first, but somehow his hand wasn't listening to his brain, and almost without realizing it, he laid the paper against the wall, and signed it at the bottom.

'You've just agreed to let us use your house as an access route to your back garden,' the man explained.

'But why should you want to go into my back garden?' Sweeting asked. 'There's nothing at all that could be of any possible interest to you out there.'

'I don't give a toss about your garden – it's the garden on the other side of the wall that we need to get to,' the sergeant said.

'But there must be some mistake,' Sweeting protested. 'I know the owner of that house. Her name is Monika Paniatowski. She's a retired lady now, but she used to be a chief inspector. Her daughter is still in the police.'

'Thank you for that information, but we already know whose house it is,' Ingham said.

It was five thirty-three when the alarm buzzer rang in Kate Meadows' bedroom, and when she checked the control panel, she saw that the source of the alarm was Lizzie Grimshaw's room.

'Oh, for God's sake,' she groaned, 'couldn't you have waited a couple more hours, Baby Grimshaw?'

Apparently not!

Lizzie Grimshaw was waiting for her on the upstairs landing.

'I'm not worried,' she said, though the expression on her face told quite a different story.

'Have your waters broken?' Meadows asked.

Lizzie nodded. 'Just before I pressed the buzzer.'

'And are you having contractions?'

'I've had one.'

'I want you to time the gap between them,' Meadows said.

'Will that help?' Lizzie asked.

'It will help the midwife to estimate when the baby might arrive,' Meadows explained.

'The midwife,' Lizzie repeated. She looked around her in panic. 'Where is she? Why isn't she here?'

'I haven't rung her yet,' Meadows said softly, as she guided Lizzie back into her room, and navigated her around the wardrobe which had been nothing but a bloody nuisance from the start.

'What if she doesn't get here in time?' Lizzie asked, as Meadows guided her into her armchair.

'She will,' Meadows promised. 'You've only just started your contractions, so there's lots of time yet.'

'But what if she doesn't?' Lizzie persisted.

'Then I'll deliver the baby myself – I've done it dozens of times.'

'Really?'

'Really,' Meadows assured the girl.

True, her experience was confined to foals and calves on the family estate, but there was no point in explaining that now.

'Try to relax,' she said. 'I'll be back in a few minutes.'

She stepped out into the corridor, and her heart sank as she saw Harriet Hobbes standing there.

Harriet was the house worrier. She was an expert at worrying, and like an athlete who had learned how to master the techniques of both the marathon and the sprint, she was equally at home with minor short-term worries and major long-term ones. Thus, she worried about world peace *and* whether there was enough bread in the bin to last out until morning – and treated them both as a major cause for concern. Meadows believed that there was never any excuse for a man hitting his wife, but suspected that if she had been married to Harriet, she would have been sorely tempted.

'Could I have a word with you?' the bloody woman asked.

'I'm a little busy at the moment, Harriet,' Meadows replied.

'It's very important – and it won't take long.'

Meadows sighed. 'Go on.'

'There's an intruder that wanders around this house late at night,' Harriet said, in a confidential whisper.

'This house has the best security system available,' Meadows said, exasperatedly. 'Nobody could have got in without setting off all the alarms.'

'Well, somebody did,' Harriet said firmly. 'Both last night and the night before.'

Ah, Meadows thought, all is explained.

'I know what's happened,' she said. 'You heard someone the night before last, and that set your imagination galloping, so you thought you heard someone last night, too.'

'So you admit there was someone the night before last?' Harriet said, triumphantly.

'Yes,' Meadows said. 'It was me you heard – either going out or coming back.'

'You?' Harriet asked suspiciously. 'Going out late at night?'

'Yes,' Meadows confirmed. 'I'm a big girl now, and I can go out on my own any time I want to.'

'But why would you want to?'

God, the woman was impossible.

'I felt like a breath of fresh air,' Meadows said, trying to sound her professional best, yet aware that some of her irritation was still managing to get through.

'You want to be careful,' said Harriet, who was always too

wrapped up in her own concerns to read the signals other people were sending out. 'It's dangerous after dark. The night before last – the very night you were out alone – there was this man called Hadley who got himself killed *in his own home*.'

'In his own home,' Meadows repeated. 'So what you're saying is that being at home is risky, and leaving the house was the best thing I could have done.'

'No . . . I—' Harriet said helplessly.

'I'd love to stay and chat for longer,' Meadows interrupted, 'but, you see, Lizzie is having her baby, and she's relying on me to make the arrangements. I'd like to thank you for reporting your concerns,' she continued, in her most official voice, 'and rest assured that they've been duly noted.'

And without waiting for a reply, she headed for the stairs.

The man standing on Monika Paniatowski's doorstep was wearing body armour and a combat helmet. Both his hands were occupied. In the left, he had a warrant card which he had raised to Paniatowski's eye level. In the right, he was grasping a Heckler and Koch HK416 assault rifle.

'Commander J C Moore,' Paniatowski read from the warrant card. 'So what can I do for you and the small army you seem to have brought with you?'

'We're looking for your son, Philip Paniatowski,' Moore said, in a tough gravelly voice that Monika thought he might have been practising.

'Then I suggest you go to the remand centre where he's being held,' Paniatowski told him.

'Very funny,' Moore said, though he didn't sound amused. 'He *was* in the remand centre until last night, then he escaped.'

Paniatowski knew she should feel disturbed at the news that a violent criminal, who deserved to be locked up, was out on the loose. Yet her first reaction wasn't alarm at all – it was pride.

Her son had shown spirit. Her son had shown ingenuity. For the moment, at least, he had beaten the system.

The feeling did not last long, and what replaced it was a gut-churning fear, because these men who were searching for him were heavily armed and meant business, and if Philip resisted – and being Philip, he might well – they would take him down as if he were no more than a mad dog.

She became aware that someone – probably Moore – was speaking to her, but through her mental turmoil it sounded like an echo in some distant cave.

'I asked you if you were hiding him,' Moore said, speaking very slowly and distinctly in case she was having trouble following him, 'and I must warn you, madam, that if that is what you are in fact doing, there will be serious consequences for you.'

She looked him the eye. She could tell he thought he was a hard man, and probably he was, but then she was a hard woman.

'Are you threatening me, sunshine?' she asked.

'No, madam, I am merely making you aware of the harsh realities of life. And I don't like being called "sunshine".'

'So what should I call you?'

'I would prefer to be addressed as "commander".'

'I'm sure you would,' Paniatowski said. 'And as a retired senior police officer, calling me madam doesn't quite cut it for me – so give me the respect I'm entitled to, and call me "ma'am".'

'I—' the commander began.

'I haven't finished yet,' Paniatowski snapped. 'Thank you for making me aware of the harsh realities of life, but it really wasn't necessary, because I was dealing with harsh realities when you were a gurgling, puking baby, lying in your cot and wondering when the great milk tit in the sky was going to pay you another visit.'

'I'm just doing my job, ma'am,' the commander said stiffly.

'Then learn to do it with a bit of humanity, because that's what makes you a good bobby, rather than just a competent one,' Paniatowski said. 'You're going to search my house from top to bottom. That's your job. But you won't find my son, because wherever he is, he isn't here. So there's no need for smoke cylinders or stun grenades or whatever else you might be thinking of using. I want my house leaving as you found it. Is that clear?'

It was too much to expect the commander to say yes, but he did give a slight nod which she could interpret as agreement if she chose to.

'I'd like you to step outside now, ma'am,' he said. 'And I'd appreciate it if you'd stay out of the house until we've finished in there.'

Paniatowski did as she'd been instructed, and was shocked to discover that her legs had turned to jelly.

She wanted to help Kate, she thought – she really did – but the only really important thing at that moment was to find Philip before the police did.

Lizzie Grimshaw sat in her armchair, hugging herself and moaning softly.

'You've got nothing to worry about,' the midwife cooed. 'Everything's fine.'

'I'm frightened,' Lizzie told her.

'You shouldn't be. Everything's right on schedule, and in a few hours you'll be lying in your bed, cuddling your little baby.'

'I don't want to lose her,' Lizzie sobbed. 'I don't want it to be like last time.'

The midwife gave Kate Meadows a worried look, but when she turned back to Lizzie, she had forced a gentle smile to replace it.

'Are you saying that you had a miscarriage?' she asked.

'Yes.'

'When was this?'

'Last year.'

'Did you see a doctor after it had happened?'

'Yes.'

'And did he suggest that you might have a specific problem?'

'I don't know what you mean.'

'Did he say there might be a reason you lost the baby?'

'Yes. When I told him I fell down the stairs, he said that explained it.'

There was something in Lizzie's tone which alerted Meadows' old bobby instinct.

'And did you fall down the stairs?' she asked.

Lizzie looked down at her knees.

'No,' she said in a voice so quiet the other two barely heard it.

'So what did happen?'

'When I told Gary I was going to have a baby, he *threw* me down the stairs.'

'So why did you lie about it?' the midwife asked, in a voice that lay somewhere between amazed and outraged.

'Leave it,' Meadows said.

But there was no stopping the angry midwife now.

'Why didn't you tell the doctor exactly what had happened?' she demanded.

'Because . . . because he'd have told the police,' Lizzie said.

'Quite rightly, too! And they would have arrested this so-called boyfriend of yours, wouldn't they?'

'Yes, but they'd have let him go – they always let him go.'

The midwife looked at Meadows for confirmation.

'Unless things have changed dramatically since my day, it's very likely that's exactly what would have happened,' Kate said. 'Only a small percentage of wife beaters ever end up in gaol, because without witnesses, it's very difficult to put a case together.'

'That's disgraceful,' the midwife said.

'It's the way of the world,' Meadows told her.

'They would have let him out, and . . . and this time, he would have killed me,' Lizzie said.

'Where is he now?' the midwife asked. 'Is he still a danger to you?'

Lizzie looked across at her wardrobe, as if she hoped to find her answer in its old-fashioned fake hardwood doors.

'No,' she said finally. 'He had a nasty accident, and I don't think he's properly recovered yet.'

'It's a pity this nasty accident of his didn't kill him,' the midwife said, with some venom. 'But if you know you're safe, you should stop thinking about him and concentrate on having happy thoughts. That's what your baby needs – to be born to someone with happy thoughts. Can you do that for me?'

Lizzie smiled.

'I'll try,' she promised.

'Good girl,' the midwife said.

It was just after noon, and Jack Crane was sitting at a table under the window in the Prince Albert bar of the Royal Victoria Hotel. It was here that the crème de la crème of Whitebridge society met to swap stock market (and racing) tips, hold business meetings, and exchange salacious gossip about their friends. The place was plush and expensive and guaranteed to impress people not used to such opulence, which was precisely why Crane had chosen it for his encounter with the woman.

The woman in question appeared in the doorway. She was wearing a blue and white check business suit. It probably hadn't been that expensive, but it was doing its best to look as if it came from a pricy range.

The woman's gaze swept the room, then settled quickly on him.

He would have liked to think that was because he exuded the air of being a high-powered academic, but he knew that the more likely explanation was that he'd told her over the phone that he wore an eye patch.

She walked over to him.

'Professor Crane?'

'Yes. And you are Miss Helen Cosgrove, PA to late Mr Hadley, of Hadley Security Systems?'

'I am.'

'Then please sit down, Miss Cosgrove, and I'll order you a drink.'

She chose a vodka martini, which she probably thought showed how sophisticated she was. Crane put her age at around thirty. She was not unattractive, though she probably wouldn't turn heads in the street.

'Now, as I explained over the phone, I'm writing a book,' he said.

Miss Cosgrove's drink had arrived, and she took a dainty sip. 'I've already told the police all I know.'

'They probably weren't interested in the same things I'm interested in,' Crane lied. 'The idea behind the book is to compare and contrast real murders with murders in literature. For instance, we might take the case of Alyona Ivanovna – who, as I'm sure you know, is the pawnbroker in *Crime and Punishment* – and Margaret Grayland, the sub-post mistress who was the first victim of the post office bandit known as the Black Panther. In what ways were they different, and in what ways were they similar? Was there anything about them that marked them as victims? How did the people around them react to their deaths?'

She had very quickly become bored with this monologue, which had been just what he intended to happen, because the last thing he wanted was for her to have any interest in him.

He droned on for another couple of minutes, then, estimating she was just this side of being comatose, he said, 'Are there any questions you'd like to ask me?'

'Yes,' she replied. 'Over the phone, you said something about a fee.'

'That's right,' he agreed. 'I'm willing to pay fifty pounds,' he caught the look of disappointment in her eyes, and added quickly, 'but that, of course, is only an advance. Once the book is published and starts to sell, you'll get a share of the royalties.'

'Will they be much?' she asked.

He shrugged. 'Who can tell? It all depends on the great book-buying public. But books like this do have a tendency to become bestsellers, and if we also sell the film rights . . .' He left it there, gave her imagination a little time to fill in the gaps, then said, 'Shall we begin?'

'What about the contract?' Helen Cosgrove asked.

'It's being drawn up even as we speak. But, of course, if you'd like the advance now . . .'

'I would.'

Crane took five ten-pound notes out of his wallet, and laid them on the table. Helen Cosgrove swept them up in much the same way as an eagle might sweep up an unsuspecting lamb.

'There's one thing I'd like to make clear before we start,' she said. 'I'd never be doing this if I'd been treated better.'

'You've been treated badly?' Crane asked, because he was expected to.

'You could say that. Mr Hadley had promised me that next month he'd upgrade my job to executive assistant, which, apart from anything else, would have meant I had a key to the executive toilet. Now Mr Hadley's dead, and Mr Dalton – who, I, personally, wouldn't put in charge of a fish and chip van – is the boss,' Helen Cosgrove moaned.

'And he's blocked your promotion,' Crane guessed.

'This morning he informed me by memo – *by memo!* – that I'd been reassigned, and was now PA to some spotty youth who has only just been made up to under-manager. Yesterday I was reaching for the top of the ladder, and now I'm back down at the lowest rung – so why shouldn't I make a bit of money on the side, when it's offered to me?'

'Yes, why shouldn't you?' Crane agreed. 'So how long have you worked for Mr Hadley?'

'Five years.'

'So you must know him well.'

Miss Cosgrove frowned. 'I wouldn't say that, exactly.'

'I mean, of course, as well as an employee can be expected to know an employer.'

'I suppose so.'

'What kind of man was he?'

Her frown deepened.

'Did you ever see any of those films about inventors?' she asked.

'You know the sort of thing – they've got brilliant minds, but they're forever forgetting where they've left the car, or accidently eating the dog's biscuits, because their thoughts are somewhere else?'

'Yes, I do know what you mean,' Crane replied. 'So are you saying Mr Hadley was absent-minded?'

'Well, not exactly *absent-minded*, but he tended not to notice things that didn't concern work. He was a bit of a scruffy dresser, and he didn't really know how to talk to people – especially women – unless it was about security systems. I suppose you could say he just wasn't sociable.'

'Wasn't he a member of the golf club?' Crane said. 'I would have thought that was sociable enough.'

Miss Cosgrove giggled. 'A member of the golf club? Whatever makes you think that?'

Yes, whatever *did* make him think that? Crane wondered. Somebody must have told him, but the only person he had discussed Hadley with had been Kate Meadows.

'I take it from your response that he wasn't a member,' he said aloud.

'He wasn't. If he had been, I'd have known about it, because I paid all his bills. He really wouldn't have fitted in, you know. He could have afforded a flashy car, but he always drove around in one of the company's vans. They wouldn't have liked that up there.'

Crane grinned. 'Yes, I can see how that might offend "our betters".'

'Mind you, considering how much he'd changed over the last couple of months, I suppose it's just possible he might have ended up at the golf club eventually,' Miss Cosgrove said.

Like soldiers noticing the sudden unexpected presence of an officer, the hairs on the back of Crane's neck sprang to attention.

'How had he changed?' Crane asked.

'He started dressing better for one thing – sometimes he'd come to work looking quite smart – but I'm sure he didn't buy his new clothes himself.'

'What makes you say that?'

'He had absolutely no sense of style – and at his age, style isn't something you just pick up on your own.'

'I'll take your word for that,' Crane said.

'And there was more of a spring in his step.' Miss Cosgrove giggled again. 'It's always seemed a bit of a cliché to me – a spring in his step – but there really was one in his case.'

'And how do you explain that?'

'Well, it's obvious, isn't it? He'd got himself a girlfriend – or maybe a boyfriend. I couldn't say which, because I find it impossible to imagine him in bed with a woman, but equally impossible to picture him with a man.'

'So maybe you're wrong about him having found somebody.'

'I'm not wrong. I can tell when a man's besotted – and he was.'

'You didn't see anybody who could have been this mysterious partner, did you?' Crane asked.

'No.'

'Because somebody killed him, didn't they, and I'm thinking that maybe it was his lover's ex-partner who did it.'

'That's possible,' Miss Cosgrove conceded. 'Or maybe it was an accident – just a game that went . . .' An expression of sheer horror came to her face. 'I mean . . . I didn't . . . I don't know what I mean,' she garbled.

'Maybe it was just a game that went wrong,' Crane mused. 'What could have led you to that particular conclusion?'

'I don't know. I was just being stupid.'

'You are aware, aren't you, Miss Cosgrove, that your future royalties are conditional on your being completely open and frank with us,' Crane said severely. 'If we find out you've been holding back anything, the whole contract is null and void.'

Helen Cosgrove hesitated for perhaps half a minute, then she said, 'Look, I'm not exactly proud of this, so you must promise never to tell anyone else what I'm telling you now.'

'I promise,' said Crane, and as the author of the book that would never be written he meant it sincerely – it was only the ex-policeman, out to help his friend, who held such promises worthless.

'Well, Mr Hadley had a drawer in his desk that he kept locked, you see, but what he didn't know was that I had a key,' Miss Cosgrove said.

'And you used to look at what he put in there?'

'I did check on it now and again, yes. I considered it part of my job as his PA to know what he was thinking. It helped me to prepare in advance to meet his needs.'

'I'm sure any good PA would have done the same,' Crane said. 'So what was it that you found?'

'Once, there was this glossy magazine . . .' Helen Cosgrove lowered her voice, 'and it wasn't the kind of magazine you see in newsagents, if you know what I mean.'

'Are you saying it was a pornographic magazine?'

'In a manner of speaking, yes, but I've always thought porn was meant to turn you on, and this definitely didn't turn *me* on.'

'Tell me more.'

'Well, it was pictures of people being hurt, and hurting other people. It was . . . what do you call it?'

'Sadomasochism?'

'That's right. And there was one particular section – it makes me shudder just to think about it – of people hanging. Well, that's what Mr Hadley died from, isn't it – hanging? So like I said, I just wondered if it was part of a game gone wrong.'

'Did you tell the police this?' Crane asked.

Miss Cosgrove looked down at the table. 'No, I didn't,' she admitted.

'*Why* didn't you tell them?'

'Because I didn't want them thinking that I was the kind of person who snooped into things that didn't concern them.'

The police would know dozens of things that the team didn't know, Crane thought, but in this matter at least, the team had the advantage.

When Paniatowski found Thomas, he was on his hands and knees in the vestry, scrubbing the floor.

'What in God's name are you doing?' she asked, before she could stop herself.

'In God's name, I'm cleaning His house,' Thomas said.

'Yes, but what I meant was, why are *you* doing it?' Paniatowski said. 'I thought the church employed a cleaner.'

'And so it does, but I gave her the morning off.'

'And if you must do this instead of parochial work – which I think you'll have to agree would be a much more valuable use of your time – then why must you use a hand scrubbing brush? Haven't you got a brush with a long handle, so you could do the job standing up?'

Thomas climbed to his feet and put a hand on his mother's shoulder. 'This is different to parochial work, but it, too, is worthy

of my effort,' he said. 'And using the hand brush reminds me of
what a humble, insignificant person I am, which, I hope, serves
to make me a much better priest.'

Paniatowski felt a wave of shame wash over her. 'I'm sorry,
Thomas,' she said. 'I shouldn't have spoken to you like that. But
I'm very nervous today – very worried.'

'Of course you're worried – Philip is your beloved son,'
Thomas said.

'So you know about Philip?'

'Yes.'

'Then how can you be so calm yourself? There are groups of
men armed with guns out hunting him.'

'I know there are,' Thomas said. 'They have been to this
church. They wanted to search it, to make sure I hadn't hidden
my brother here.'

'And what did you say?'

'I said the only way they could defile the sanctity of the church
was by killing me first.'

'So they just went away?'

'Yes, I think they didn't see any point in making a scene when
it was obvious that I was telling the truth.'

'So I repeat what I said before – how can you be so calm?'

'The police won't find him, and when he is ready to give himself
up, he will ring me, and I will collect him myself.'

'You think he'll do that? Give himself up?'

'I know he will. He's on a mission, and when that mission is
completed, he will surrender to the police and take his punishment
like a man.'

'You know where he is, don't you?' Paniatowski said, with
sudden realization.

'Ask me something else,' Thomas said.

'How did he get from the remand centre to wherever he is now?
Did you drive him there?'

Thomas smiled. 'No comment.'

'I'm not a bobby, and you're not a suspect,' Paniatowski said
angrily. 'I'm your bloody mother. I'm his mother, too, and I
demand to know where he is.'

'Philip asked you to do something for him, and you refused,'
Thomas said. 'He feels you have let him down, and he doesn't
want to have anything more to do with you.'

'Do you know what it was he asked me to do?'

'Yes, he asked you to get him out on parole.'

'That was an impossibility – it would never have happened, however hard I'd tried.'

'I know that,' Thomas said. 'And I have explained it to him. But that is not how he sees it.'

It wasn't fair, she told herself. She could have aborted these seeds of lust – these seeds of mindless, uncaring violence – which had been planted in her womb. No one beyond the church would have blamed her if she had – and even within the church there would have been those who tacitly agreed it was for the best. But she hadn't had an abortion – she had borne the twins, brought them up as best she could, and given them all the love there was within her.

And what was the result? Thomas didn't need her, and Philip didn't want her. It really wasn't fair. And though it was wrong to ever think that God got great pleasure from playing malicious practical jokes on the faithful, that was what this felt like – a cruel joke that had the name of the omnipotent trickster all over it.

'Are you sure you're doing the right thing?' she asked her son.

'I'm sure I'm doing what I have to do,' Thomas replied.

And he sounded almost as broken-hearted as she was.

There were some bouncers who did very little exercise, but relied on their sheer size and weight when it came to dealing with violent situations. Freddie Bairstow was not one of them. He put in five solid sessions at his local gym every week, as regular as clockwork, and it was as he was leaving the gym that late afternoon that he saw the tall, gangly man loitering near the entrance.

'They said I'd find you here,' the man said.

'And they were right,' Bairstow replied. 'Do I know you?'

'Not yet, you don't,' the man said, producing his warrant card. 'DS Boyd. I'd like a few words with you down at the station.'

'What if I say no,' Bairstow asked.

Boyd shook his head, wonderingly. 'A man with your record should know the drill by now,' he said. 'If you won't come in voluntarily, we'll arrest you on some trumped-up charge or other, like walking on the cracks in the pavement, or being a dickhead in a built-up area. We won't be able to make it stick, of course,

and we'll have to release you again, but not before you've spent
a night in the cells.'

Bairstow glanced down at his watch. 'Look, I've got to report
for work in about three hours,' he said.

'Ah yes, your job as doorman to the deviants,' Boyd said. 'Don't
worry, if you cooperate with us, we'll be finished with you long
before that.'

EIGHTEEN

It hadn't been a particularly easy birth, the midwife thought,
but it would have been an exaggeration to call it a difficult one.
Lizzie had been in some pain, but had borne it with unexpected
fortitude, and now, half an hour after the birth, the new baby lay
cradled in the arms of her triumphant mother.

'Isn't she beautiful?' Lizzie asked, bursting with pride and love.

'All new babies are beautiful,' the midwife said, in a voice
which was warm and yet professional.

'What do you think, Mrs Maybe?' Lizzie asked Meadows.

What did she think? She thought what she did about all
newborn babies, which was that they had bodies that looked
like dolls' bodies, and heads like oranges that had passed their
sell-by date.

'She's gorgeous, Lizzie,' Meadows said.

'If you don't mind, I'd like to call her after you,' Lizzie said.

'I don't mind at all.'

And Meadows was surprised to discover that she was, in fact,
rather touched by the gesture.

'What a good idea,' the midwife said approvingly. 'Katherine's
such a nice name for a baby.'

'Is it?' Lizzie asked, sounding puzzled. 'Well, I've already made
up my mind what I'm going to call her, and you like your name,
don't you, baby May.'

'But surely—' the midwife began.

'Is there anything we can get you, Lizzie?' Meadows
interrupted.

'There's no chance of a bottle of beer, is there?' Lizzie asked.

'Certainly not,' replied the midwife, outraged. 'I've never heard of such a thing.'

'You don't even drink beer,' Meadows said.

'I know, but I thought I might try it,' Lizzie replied.

'Not while you're breastfeeding Baby,' the midwife said. 'That would never do.'

'I suppose not,' Lizzie agreed. She paused for a moment. 'If you don't mind, we'd like to be alone now.'

'That's out of the question so soon after you've given birth,' the midwife said briskly. 'You don't have to talk, if you don't want to, but there should be someone sitting quietly in the corner, just to make sure that you – and, of course, Baby – are all right.'

'We want to be alone,' Lizzie said, and though she was not shouting – she was too aware of her baby to do that – it was clear she wished she could.

'It really would be most irregular to abandon you like that,' the midwife said. 'What would other people think, when they found out what we'd done?'

'I don't give a bugger what other people would think!' Lizzie said fiercely. 'We want some time alone.' She turned to Meadows. 'Please, Mrs Maybe, just give me half an hour. If anything goes wrong, the emergency button is right there for me to press.'

Meadows and the midwife exchanged looks, and the midwife gave Meadows a reluctant nod.

'All right, Lizzie, you win,' Meadows said.

'It's not me that wins,' Lizzie told her. 'It's little May.'

Meadows and the midwife went down to the office to complete the necessary paperwork.

'Have you got anything to drink?' the midwife asked. 'I know I shouldn't, but I really need one – something strong, I mean.'

Meadows smiled. 'Yes, I know what you mean.' She reached into her drawer and produced a glass and a bottle of Remy Martin brandy. 'Will this do you, Ruby?'

'It'll more than do me,' the midwife said, with some enthusiasm. 'Won't you be joining me?'

'I'll have one later,' Meadows said, because she had learned from experience that people were uncomfortable drinking in the presence of other people who didn't drink at all.

The midwife poured herself a generous shot, and took a sip.

'Beautiful,' she said. 'Do you think Lizzie really believes your name is Mrs Maybe?'

'Who knows?' Meadows replied. 'But if that's what she wants to call me, I'm perfectly happy with it.'

'She took me by surprise when she insisted we should leave her room,' the midwife said.

'It surprised me, too,' Meadows admitted.

In fact, Lizzie had been full of surprises recently – insisting on having her baby in the refuge rather than a hospital, demanding that the old wardrobe be brought up from the basement, telling the pair of them they had to leave the room . . . None of these were actions she would have expected from timid little Lizzie.

Maybe it was the advancing pregnancy that had changed her. Perhaps, realizing she was going to be responsible for a tiny life, she had also realized that she would have to be more self-assertive.

Yes, that would certainly make sense – but Meadows had a nagging feeling that it was something else entirely.

DS Boyd and DC James sat in the interrogation room, facing Freddie Bairstow. The tape recorder was already running, and the caution had been duly delivered. It was time to start digging.

'I'd like to start by reminding you of your situation, Freddie,' Boyd said. 'You've got a criminal record that's long enough to wrap twice round the cathedral and once around the boulevard, and you've reached that unenviable stage in your career when, even if you come up before the judge on a minor offence, you're going down for a long time. Have I made myself plain?'

'Yes, sir,' Freddie said.

He sounded frightened – and he was. But it wasn't Boyd who was frightening him, because as far as he was concerned, Boyd was soft as shit. No, what *was* scaring him was the person sitting the other side of the two-way mirror. True, he couldn't see the man, and he couldn't actually prove there was anybody there at all, yet he knew there was. He could sense the dark presence – the brooding malevolence. And he understood that whoever the man was, he had the power to crush a bouncer with a criminal record like a beetle – and would take pleasure in doing it.

'Was Andrew Lofthouse a member of the so-called Hellfire

Club?' Boyd asked. 'And before you answer, Freddie, I should tell you that we already *know* he was.'

'You're wrong,' Freddie said. 'He was a regular, but he wasn't a member. We don't have members.'

'Are you taking the piss?' Boyd demanded, in what he probably saw as his tough cop voice. 'You must have members.'

'I swear to you, Mr Boyd, we don't.'

'Isn't there a book somewhere that has all the members' names written in it?'

'No.'

'Don't they have cards that they show to you, when they want to get in?'

'No.'

'So who decides who gets in and who doesn't?'

'I do.'

'On what basis?'

Freddie sighed. There was an art to what he did that required both experience and judgement, but he couldn't expect this bobby to recognize that.

'If you're a regular like Mr Lofthouse, I automatically let you in,' he said. 'If I don't know you, then I have to work out whether you'll fit in, or whether you'll cause trouble.'

'And you always get that right, do you?' Boyd asked sceptically.

'Most of the time,' Freddie said. 'And if I get it wrong, then I just throw them out, and no harm done.'

'Except, possibly to the people you've thrown out,' Boyd said.

'If they don't want to get hurt, then they shouldn't struggle then, should they?' Freddie asked indifferently. 'And if they've got any complaints, they can always report it to the police.'

'Like that's ever going to happen,' Boyd said. 'Let's get back to Andrew Lofthouse. Did he usually come alone – or with someone else?'

'The night he was killed, he came alone, but usually he was accompanied by a woman.'

'Always the same woman?'

'No, there were two different ones.'

'And could you describe them to me?'

I could do more than that, I could tell you where you could find one of them, Freddie thought. But if you think I'm going to drop a magistrate in the shit, you've got another think coming, because I've got enough enemies already, without having the bench against me.

'I can describe their masks,' he said helpfully.

'What do you mean?'

'Most of the people who come to the club wear masks.'

'What, you mean like the Lone Ranger?'

Freddie shook his head. 'Not like that at all. It's more like a carnival. So Mr Lofthouse always wears a devil mask, and the woman he used to come with quite a lot wore a tiger mask. His newer woman wears a leopard mask.'

'What's the difference?'

'One has stripes and other has spots.'

'Are you trying to be funny?' Boyd growled.

'No sir, I was just answering your question.'

'Is it a rule of the club that members have to wear a mask?' Boyd asked.

If that was an attempt to catch him out, it was a very clumsy one, Freddie thought.

'I've already told you, Mr Boyd, that there are no members – and there are no rules, either. Customers only wear masks if they want to – and most of them do.'

'Why do they wear masks?'

'I don't know. I don't ask, and they don't tell me.'

'Take a guess,' Boyd said – and it wasn't a suggestion.

'Maybe it's to hide who they are, or maybe they just think it's a bit of fun,' Freddie said.

'So you're saying they all wear masks,' Boyd said, setting another clumsy trap.

'No, I said that most of them do. The woman he left with the night he was killed wasn't wearing a mask, for example.'

The room was suddenly several degrees colder and dead silent – and Freddie realized he'd just made a big mistake.

'You never mentioned a third woman,' Boyd said. 'You told us he came alone.'

'He did,' Freddie said, almost babbling now. 'He must have picked Zelda up inside.'

Another mistake – and this time a huge one.

'You know her, do you?' Boyd demanded.

'No, I'd never seen her before. But she's a legend in central Lancashire. They call her the sadomasochist's sadomasochist.'

'If you'd never seen her before, how did you know she was this Zelda?'

'She told me she was.'

'And you believed her? Just like that?'

'I could tell she was the real thing. I could feel the power coming from her.'

'And she left with Lofthouse?'

'Yes.'

'Describe her to me.'

'She's about five feet seven with a slim build. She was wearing a purple wig. And a lot of make-up – especially round the eyes.'

'How old is she?'

'Difficult to say with all that make-up, but she's been knocking around the clubs for at least twenty years.'

'Does she have a reputation for violence?' Boyd asked.

The moment he'd spoken, he realized what a stupid question it was, and that was only underlined by the bouncer's involuntary chuckle.

'They've all got a reputation for violence, Mr Boyd,' Freddie said.

The door opened. Chief Superintendent Towers entered the room, and it was clear from the expression on Boyd's face that this was totally unexpected.

Towers mimed to Boyd that he should switch off the tape recorder.

'Interview suspended at six thirty-seven,' Boyd said, clicking the switch.

'Right, I want you, Sergeant Boyd, and you, DC James, out of here,' Towers said. 'And don't come back for at least half an hour.'

'But sir,' Boyd protested, 'we were just getting somewhere. We may even have a possible suspect for Lofthouse's murder.'

'Did I actually issue an order, or am I just imagining it?' Towers said.

'Sir . . .' Boyd began.

'Out!' Towers bellowed.

Boyd, accepting he had no choice in the matter, walked towards the door, trying not to look too much like a dog that had just been given a beating. The constable followed him.

Towers sat down opposite Freddie. 'Now listen to me, you festering toe-rag,' he said, 'I want some information, and you're going to bloody give it to me.'

NINETEEN

There were only three of them at the table in the Drum and Monkey.

'The boss won't be coming tonight,' Beresford said.

Neither Meadows nor Crane asked why, because the answer was obvious – Paniatowski would be visiting her son's old haunts in the desperate hope that she could find him before the armed police did.

'That being the case, would either of you object if I took the chair?' Beresford asked.

'No, you're the obvious choice,' Crane said.

But he was thinking that while Beresford was a good solid bobby, he didn't have Paniatowski's flair.

They talked over their day's discoveries – it didn't take too long – and then it was time to sum up.

'The overall impression I get is that Andrew Lofthouse wasn't a nice man,' Crane said, 'so although he could be charming when he wanted to be, he got up a lot of people's noses. Jim Hadley, on the other hand, lived almost like a hermit until he got himself a girlfriend.'

'Or a boyfriend,' Beresford said. 'The two men were about as different to each other as it's possible to be – so what was it about both of them that made the killer select them as his victims?'

'We don't know for certain they were killed by the same man,' Meadows said. 'There may be significant differences which the police have held back which suggest two killers with very different signatures.'

Beresford frowned. 'Isn't that a bit of a negative attitude to take, Kate?' he asked.

'I prefer to think of it as a realistic one,' Meadows said, almost snottily.

There was something going on that he didn't quite understand, Crane thought.

'We have to have some theory to work from – we always do

– and the best one available is that there were two victims and one killer,' Beresford said.

'I'm not sure the boss would agree with you,' Meadows replied.

'Before we go any further, can we clear something up that's been bothering me?' Crane said.

'Are you trying to change the subject, Jack?' Meadows asked.

Yes, I am, Crane thought, because if somebody doesn't, this meeting's going to end in chaos.

'No, of course I'm not trying to change the subject,' he said. 'It's just that I've got a question I'd like answering, and it slipped my mind before.'

'Go ahead,' Beresford said

'What did Jim Hadley say about his relationship with Jane Lofthouse, Kate?' Crane asked.

'He said he didn't know her very well, but he'd run into her at his golf club's dinner and his lodge's ladies' night.'

'Yet when I was talking to Helen Cosgrove, Jim Hadley's PA, she was willing to swear he never joined the golf club, and being the man he seems to have been, I'd be surprised if the Masons ever even considered him for admission. So why did he lie to you?'

'I don't know,' Meadows said, unhelpfully.

'Perhaps he was working for Andrew Lofthouse,' Beresford suggested. 'And here's a thought – perhaps the girlfriend that suddenly appeared in Hadley's life was none other Miss Maitland Williams, who was actually Lofthouse's mistress?'

'It's possible,' Crane agreed. 'After all, we already knew that Lofthouse and Maitland Williams were into S&M, and now we've learned that Hadley was, too.'

'You've just constructed a conspiracy out of fresh air – a conspiracy of three people which has now been whittled down to one – a magistrate, for God's sake – because the other two have been murdered,' Meadows said. 'Brilliant!'

Beresford and Crane looked at her in stunned silence. They had worked with her for a long time, and if they'd been asked to describe her in five words, the first word they'd both have come up with would have been 'controlled'.

But she was far from controlled now. She seemed on the verge of hysteria.

'You need to calm down, Kate,' Beresford said.

'Calm down?' Meadows repeated.

'If the police happen to pull you in for questioning when you're in this state, you're sunk.'

'I thought the whole point of this little investigation was to ensure I *wasn't* pulled in for questioning,' Meadows said.

'We've done our best to avoid that happening, but our best may not have been good enough,' Beresford said heavily. 'I think one of the things we should be working on now is damage control.'

'I agree,' Crane said. 'So what *will* you tell the police if they want to question you, Sarge?'

'Tell them about what?' Meadows asked, obtusely.

'About the time you spent in Lofthouse's home.'

'I'll tell them exactly what I've told you at least ten times – that I changed my mind and left.'

'That isn't going to be good enough – and you know it,' Beresford said.

'Well, it will have to be,' Meadows answered, defiantly.

'Cast your mind back a few years, Sarge,' Crane said. 'If you'd been in charge of the interview and the suspect had told you what you've just told us, would you have left it at that – or would you have wanted more?'

'I'd probably have wanted more,' Meadows admitted, 'but there isn't any more to tell. I changed my mind, and I left.'

'Did you tell him you were leaving?' Beresford asked.

'Yes . . . no . . . I don't remember.'

She's lying, Beresford thought. There's something she doesn't want to tell us about, and I hope to Christ it isn't that . . .

'It's probably not as bad as it looks,' Crane said, with mock-optimism. 'If the police believe – as Colin and I are convinced they do – that both killings were carried out by the same man, then any case they've been building up against you will fall apart when they realize you've got an alibi for the time Hadley was being murdered.'

'You do *have* an alibi, don't you?' Beresford asked. 'You were at home when Hadley was killed?'

'Yes,' Meadows said, looking away.

'You're lying,' Beresford told her.

'All right, I wasn't at home,' Meadows confessed angrily. 'I was feeling very nervous that night, so I went for a long drive. But I never went anywhere near Hadley's house.'

'How do you know where Hadley's house was?' Beresford asked.

'I read it in the papers, like everybody else.' Meadows stood up. 'I can't take any more of this. Carry on with the investigation or don't carry on with the investigation. I really don't care – because I'm out of it.'

Beresford and Crane made no attempt to stop her. They watched her walk to the door and disappear into the night.

Then Beresford turned to Crane and said, 'Do you think she killed Lofthouse?'

'She's certainly got the nerve and the skill – but so have a lot of other people,' Crane replied.

'Answer the question,' Beresford said sharply.

'No, of course I don't think she killed him,' Crane said.

'I don't, either,' Beresford said.

Neither of them sounded convinced.

'You'll have noticed I've not switched the tape recorder back on, won't you?' Chief Superintendent Towers asked Freddie Bairstow.

'Yes, sir.'

'That's because we're going to play a game, and I don't want any record kept of it.' Towers paused, perhaps to allow his message to sink in. 'Now, here's how we play this particular game,' he continued. 'I ask you a question I really want to know the answer to, you give me that answer, and I let you go. Have you got that?'

'Yes, sir,' Freddie Bairstow said.

And he was thinking, this is one big scary bastard.

'Now here's the question – how did you know that the man who left the club with Zelda was called Lofthouse?'

Freddie shrugged. 'I don't know. I just did.'

Towers moved incredibly quickly. One second he was sitting down, seemingly perfectly relaxed, the next he was on his feet, delivering a back-handed slap that knocked Freddie off his chair and sent him sprawling on to the floor.

It had been a while since Freddie had been knocked down, but his reflexes were still there, and he was back on his feet, his hands bunched into fists, in a couple of heartbeats.

A lesser man would have instinctively cowered in the face of an imminent fight-back, but Towers held his ground.

'If I was you, I'd think twice before I punched a senior police officer,' he said, 'because if you do, I'll make sure you never see the light of day again.'

Freddie unclenched his hands, and sank back into his chair.

'Now that's the first intelligent thing you've done since you got here,' Towers said. He held out a handkerchief. 'Your mouth's bleeding. However did you do that, lad?'

Freddie took the handkerchief and gently dabbed his mouth. 'I must have walked into a door, Mr Towers,' he said.

'It's easily done, but you really should be more careful,' Towers said, in a friendly voice. 'Now, to get back to my question. The reason I'm intrigued, you see, is that I just can't work out how you could possibly have known Lofthouse's name. Let's look at the evidence. He was wearing a mask, so you couldn't have recognized him. Am I right?'

'Yes, Mr Towers.'

'And as you told Sergeant Dickhead Boyd, there was no register of members and no membership cards. You weren't lying about that, were you?'

'No, Mr Towers, I swear I wasn't.'

'The whole point of the Hellfire Club was that people could do dirty, disgusting things to each other anonymously. Isn't that true?'

'Yes, Mr Towers.'

'So given that premise, it's unlikely, isn't it, that Lofthouse would have revealed his name to a piece of shit like you? So I'm still asking myself where you got the name from, and I think I've come up with an answer. Would you like to know what it is?'

'Yes, Mr Towers.'

'You have to say "please" first.'

'Please.'

'Sir?'

'Please, sir.'

'I think that after Lofthouse was murdered, someone came to the club trying to track his movements – and he was the one who told you. Now he couldn't have been from the force, because we've only just discovered what a dirty pervert the man was. So I'm guessing it was an ex-bobby, and I'd like you to give me his name.'

He hadn't done much in my life he could be proud of, Freddie thought, but he wouldn't betray the man who helped him when he was a kid.

'No comment,' he said.

Towers looked pained. 'Don't be difficult, Freddie,' he said. 'You don't want me to knock you to the floor again, do you?'

'Wouldn't make any difference if you did,' Freddie told him. 'It'd still be no comment.'

'It's a question of loyalty, is it?'

'If you like.'

'Then let's just test how strong that loyalty is,' Towers suggested. He reached into his pocket, and produced a small bag. 'Do you know what this is?'

No, but I can guess, Freddie thought.

'I don't want to play this game,' he said.

'That's a pity, because I'm quite enjoying it,' Towers said. 'This, my friend, is a bag of heroin. I should, by rights, have booked it in as evidence, but it slipped my mind, so there's no record of it anywhere in the system. Now, anyone caught with this amount of skag is classified as a dealer, so if we were to find it on you . . .'

'I've never used it,' Freddie protested. 'Not once.'

'That makes your position even worse,' Towers said. 'The judge might just possibly show a little mercy to a man who is an addict himself, but a man who deals in human misery purely for his profit . . .'

'Colin Beresford,' Freddie gasped. 'The man who came to see me was called Colin Beresford. He used to be a bobby himself.'

Towers reached across the table, and patted him on the cheek.

'Good boy,' he said.

Louisa Rutter's body was screaming to her that what it needed most in the world was to go home and get horizontal.

But she couldn't go home, not while her half-brother was some-where out there, being hunted by men with guns. And so she sat in her office – her back aching, her eyes stinging – looking at her computer screen and hoping that one of the reports being fed into it might give her some clue as to where Philip was, so she could get there before the armed police, and persuade him to surrender.

When she heard a tentative knock on the door, she looked up and saw a blond-haired gangly-looking man standing there.

She recognized him, though he had never worked directly with her. He was a sergeant in the CID. And his name was . . .?

Boyd! Daniel Boyd. And if she remembered correctly, his nick-name was Dogged Dan.

She gestured he should enter the office.

'What can I do for you, sergeant?' she asked.

He seemed very ill at ease, shifting his weight from one foot to the other, and then back again.

'This is very difficult for me, ma'am,' he said.

'I can see that,' she told him. 'But it's rather like getting into an outdoor swimming pool in winter.'

'Sorry, ma'am?'

'My advice to you would be to just close your eyes and jump in.'

Boyd closed his eyes, swallowed, and opened his eyes again.

'Chief Superintendent Towers has been investigating your mother, ma'am,' he said in a rush.

'He's been doing *what*?'

'At least, he's been investigating members of your mother's old team, which suggests she might be involved.'

Oh, she will be, Louisa thought. If the old team are involved, Monika won't be far behind.

'What is it they're supposed to have done?' she asked.

'They're conducting their own investigation into the murder of Andrew Lofthouse.'

Oh God, was it as bad as that?

'Does he have any proof of this, or is it no more than a vague suspicion?' she asked hopefully.

'He knows that Dr Crane has been questioning some of the witnesses, and that Colin Beresford has been talking to the bouncer at the Hellfire Club. I don't think he's gone so far as to get sworn statements yet, but that shouldn't present him with any problems.'

'No, it won't,' Louisa said, gloomily.

'You know why he's doing it, don't you?' Boyd asked.

'Oh yes, I know exactly why he's doing it. What I don't understand is why *you* are doing it.'

'I don't know what you mean, ma'am,' Boyd said.

'Office politics is a dangerous game to play, and the lower down the food chain you are, the more dangerous it is,' Louisa said. 'And you, sergeant, are very low down indeed.'

'With respect, ma'am, I don't need you to remind me of that,' Boyd said.

'So what I have to ask myself is why you brought this to me. You can't have taken the risk through personal loyalty, because we've never worked together.'

'You're right,' Boyd said. 'It is a sort of loyalty though – maybe I should call it loyalty to the job, or loyalty to myself.'

'I'd like you to explain that to me,' Louisa said.

'I was questioning Freddie Bairstow, the bouncer at the Hellfire Club, and I was developing this very promising lead when Mr Towers burst in. He ordered me out of the room, and questioned Bairstow himself – with the tape recorder turned off, and no other witnesses.'

'That's bad,' Louisa said.

'There's more,' Boyd said. 'Mr Towers had Freddie released, and when I asked him what else Freddie had said concerning the lead I'd been following, he said the matter had never come up. You see what this means, ma'am?'

'Yes, but I'd prefer you to spell it out for me,' Louisa told him.

'Mr Towers didn't follow through on the one good lead we have. He doesn't care who killed Lofthouse and Hadley. All he's concerned about is nobbling you. Well, I do care, and I want him out of the way, so the investigation can be conducted properly.'

'What was this lead you were following that you think was so promising,' Louisa asked.

'When Andrew Lofthouse left the Hellfire Club on the night he died, he was accompanied by a sadomasochist in a purple wig, who said her name was Zelda. Now if we could track her down . . .'

That purple wig! It was years since Louisa had given it so much as a thought.

Boyd was still talking earnestly about the investigation, but she had stopped listening, and all he had become to her was an unwelcome buzz in the background.

Could it get any worse than this, she moaned, under her breath. Could it possibly get any bloody worse?

TWENTY

Monika Paniatowski had just opened her front door and stepped into the hallway when she heard the phone in the living room start to ring.

'Sod off!' she said wearily.

She took off her coat, and hung it up. She had spent the entire day visiting Philip's known haunts. She had talked to dozens of members of Whitebridge's shadowland – many of them her old snitches. She had reminded them of past favours, and offered them future rewards, and still got nothing. No one, it seemed, had any idea where Philip might be. The phone in the living room was still making its incessant demand.

'Get stuffed!' she said.

She sat down on the chair next to the coat rack and took off her boots. Despite the fact they were fur-lined, her toes felt frozen. She was getting too old for this kind of work, she told herself.

She padded into the living room and glared at the phone, which was still screaming for her attention. On the outside chance it might be someone who had information about Philip, she picked it up.

'Yes?' she said.

'It's me,' replied a voice that was almost as familiar to her as her own.

She let out a gasp which was a mixture of fear and excitement. 'Have you found him, Louisa?' she asked. 'Do you know where your brother is?'

'I'm not ringing about Philip,' Louisa said, and there was an edge to her voice that would have frozen milk. 'How could you do it to me, Mum?'

'How could I do what to you?' Paniatowski asked, but the second the words were out of her mouth, she understood. 'You're talking about my investigation.'

'Your investigation!' Louisa repeated with contempt. 'The police investigate. What an old woman like you does is snoop.'

'You have to understand the circumstances—' Paniatowski implored.

'Is Kate still calling herself Zelda?' Louisa interrupted.

'How . . . how did you know that?' Paniatowski asked.

'For God's sake, Mum, I lived in the same house as you for nearly twenty years. Do you really think you have any secrets from me?'

'No, I suppose not,' Paniatowski confessed.

'I'm expecting a call from Chief Superintendent Towers sometime in the near future,' Louisa said. 'He's not my biggest fan.'

'No, he wouldn't be,' Paniatowski agreed. 'I remember him when he was a sergeant, and even back then . . .'

'He's been putting together a dossier on you,' Louisa said. 'I don't know exactly what he's got yet, but it's bound to be pretty damning. You deliberately withheld information from the police, and you interfered with witnesses.'

'We never—'

'You talked to witnesses before they'd been questioned officially. Did that serve to modify the evidence they'd eventually give? I don't know. But it could have – and under the law, that's enough. You perverted the course of justice, and in a murder case that will definitely get you a prison sentence. The maximum sentence that can be imposed is *life* imprisonment. Do you realize that?'

'Of course I realize that,' said Paniatowski. 'I was a bobby myself – and a good one.' She paused, then said whimsically, 'If I do go to prison, it will at least give me something in common with my son, which I suppose is a sort of silver lining.'

'You can't treat this as a joke, Mum,' Louisa said angrily.

'Can't I?' Paniatowski mused. 'What else is there left for me to do? But I'm sorry for the rest of the team. Do you think they might get off if I took sole responsibility?'

'You still don't get it, do you?' Louisa asked.

'Get what?'

'This whole thing isn't about you at all – it's about me!'

'I still don't understand.'

'Towers wants me gone. He's not even approached me yet, but when he does, he'll offer me his dossier on you in return for my resignation.'

'But that's blackmail!' Paniatowski said.

'Very good,' Louisa said. 'You should be a detective!'

'Now who's making a joke out of it?' Paniatowski asked accusingly.

'Like you said, what else can we do?' Louisa replied.

'I'd like to be there when he offers you that deal,' Paniatowski said. 'I'd just love to see his face when you turn him down.'

'I won't be turning him down,' Louisa told her.

'I can't let you destroy your career for me,' Paniatowski said.

'Maybe you should have thought of that before you embarked on this madcap adventure of yours,' Louisa said cuttingly. 'But it's not open for discussion. Whatever it costs me personally, I can't see my mother going to gaol.'

'Louisa . . .' Paniatowski pleaded.

'Well, now that's out of the way, let's get down to business,'

Louisa said crisply. 'The woman who Lofthouse left the Hellfire Club with was Kate, wasn't it?'

'Yes.'

'So as far as we know, that makes her the last person to see him alive. Would you agree?'

'Well, we have to take into account—'

'*Would you agree?*'

'Yes.'

'And that, as I'm sure you appreciate, makes her our prime suspect. So what I should do right now is send some of my lads round there to haul her in. But against my better judgement, I'm not going to do that. Out of respect for our friendship over the years, I'll give her the chance to surrender herself. She's got until noon tomorrow, after which I *will* let my lads loose.'

'Who's going to tell her that?' Paniatowski asked, fearing what the answer might be.

'You are,' said Louisa, confirming her worst fears.

'You want me to tell my old friend and bagman that she has to give herself up?'

'Yes.'

'Couldn't someone else do it?'

'No.'

'It'll make me feel like Judas, kissing Jesus on the cheek in the Garden of Gethsemane.'

'I'm sorry if that *is* how it makes you feel, but there's nothing I can do about that.'

'You're punishing me, aren't you?' Paniatowski asked.

'After what's happened, don't you think I'm entitled to dish out a little punishment?' Louisa countered.

'Yes, I do,' Paniatowski admitted. 'More than a little.'

'There's one more thing I need to ask you,' Louisa said. 'Do you think that Kate killed Andrew Lofthouse?'

'I think she's clever enough and resourceful enough to have found a way to deal with her problems that didn't involve murder,' Paniatowski said.

'You just can't bring yourself to give me a straight "no", can you?' Louisa asked.

'You're right!' Paniatowski gasped. 'I can't.'

'That's what I suspected all along,' Louisa said, and hung up.

*   *   *

It was after midnight, and Kate Meadows lay stiffly in her bed.

She was dreaming.

Or perhaps it was not a dream.

Perhaps it was simply a memory being played through her dozing mind.

But it didn't really matter which of the two it was, because she knew in her mind that what she was seeing had actually happened, just as it was happening now.

And that scared the hell out of her.

They have each driven their own cars from the Hellfire Club to Lofthouse's home, and once inside, Lofthouse gestures that she should follow him into a reception room which leads off the entrance hall.

'Welcome to my humble home,' he says.

She cannot tell whether he is being genuine or ironic, and thus does not know whether he expects her to respond or to keep silent.

She keeps silent.

'There's a drinks' cabinet over by the window,' he says. 'While I'm making all the arrangements, you can mix us a couple of cocktails. Mine's a pink gin.'

The phrase 'making all the arrangements' chills her.

'I don't drink,' she forces herself to say, 'so if you want me to prepare your drink, you'll have to tell me how to do it.'

'Well, you are a useless little battered hostel warden, aren't you?' he says teasingly. 'Never mind the drink then – just find something to amuse you while I'm gone.'

Coming back to this house was not a wise thing to agree to, she tells herself once she is alone, not a wise thing at all. She should never have put herself in the power of this dangerous man.

It's not too late to change things. She only has to leave this room to be no more than a few steps from the front door. Then there is nothing to stop her leaving this house, getting in her car, and driving away.

Except there is!

She cannot let Lofthouse ruin her life, and she will do anything and everything she can to prevent that happening.

Lofthouse re-enters the room.

'Follow me,' he says.

He leads her up the wide staircase to his bedroom.

And there, hanging from the ceiling, is a noose.

'It's used for auto-erotic strangulation,' he says.

'*I know what it's for,*' she says.

'*My wife loves it. Sometimes I have to tell her to stop, before she does herself permanent damage.*'

He's lying, of course – he's dragging Jane's name into this to make it seem as if what he's asking her to do is perfectly normal.

He produces a set of steps and a piece of black cloth that looks as if it is velvet.

'*The cloth is to prevent rope burns,*' he explains. '*Go on – try it out.*'

'*What happens once I've put the noose around my neck?*' she asks.

'*I take the steps away.*'

'*For how long?*'

'*Not long at all. Just enough time to give you the greatest sexual experience you've ever had.*'

'*How do I know you'll put the steps back? How do I know you won't leave me hanging there until I die?*'

He laughs. 'Why should I want to kill you? And even if I did, can you imagine me committing the crime in my own house?'

He's right. It's not her death he wants – it's her humiliation. And she's willing to humiliate herself to protect what she values most in the world.

He holds out his hand to her.

'*I'll steady you.*'

His grip is firm, but surprisingly gentle.

She reaches the top step. She is not far from the floor, possibly as little as eighteen inches, but that is quite enough to render her entirely helpless once the knot tightens.

'*Put the cloth inside the noose, and slip your head in,*' he says.

She does as she has been instructed. This is the most horrendous moment of her entire life, she thinks.

But she is wrong.

Worse is to come.

She closes her eyes and waits for the steps to be withdrawn.

'*You were really willing to do it, weren't you?*' he jeers. '*You have no pride – no self-respect.*'

She opens her eyes and looks at him. His face is human – but only just. She had never imagined that anyone could look so ugly.

'*Get down,*' he says. '*Get down and get out. I'm sick of looking at you.*'

She descends the steps.

'We had a deal,' she says, and is shocked at how pathetic she sounds.

'I don't make deals with vermin like you,' he says. 'Tomorrow morning I'll ring your board of directors, and by lunchtime you'll be out on the street.'

She had already sunk to the depths of shame and self-loathing when she agreed to climb the steps. It shouldn't make things any worse that it has all been for nothing.

But it does!

It bloody does!

He turns his back on her, as a matador will sometimes do to the bull – to show his contempt!

He is the most loathsome human being she has ever met, yet he can still feel contempt for her – and she can't blame him for that.

Earlier, she noticed a bronze statue of two people engaged in robust sex sitting on one of the occasional tables. Now her mind returns to it.

It would make a formidable weapon, she thinks.

TWENTY-ONE

Saturday, 5 February, 2000

I t had not snowed overnight – as the weatherman had speculated it might – but the heavy grey clouds hanging mournfully over Whitebridge held out the possibility that snow would arrive before noon. In the meantime, it was cold enough to freeze the balls off a brass monkey. People hurried along the streets, eager to be indoors again, and dogs and their owners, out for their habitual morning walks, looked as if they would gladly have forgone the pleasure for once.

Monika Paniatowski parked her car in front of Overcroft House. She had barely slept during the night, but, in a way, her insomnia had been a mercy, because the dreams she had when she did drop off were drenched with guilt and horror.

When Kate Meadows opened the door, and saw the expression on Paniatowski's face, she said, 'It's all come apart, hasn't it?'

Paniatowski nodded. 'Yes, it has.'

'So what happens now?'

'I'm to tell you that you have to present yourself at Whitebridge Central.'

'I didn't do it, you know,' Meadows said. 'I swear I didn't.'

'There's no point in telling me,' Paniatowski said. 'You'd be better saving your protests for the interview.'

'Will you be coming with me?' Meadows asked.

'Of course I will. I'm your friend. I'll always be your friend.'

'Even if it turns out I'm the killer?'

'Even then.'

Meadows smiled weakly. 'I asked Mary, my deputy, to come in early – I must have known this was going to happen, mustn't I? – so there's no problem in me leaving the building. But I would like to do my rounds before I go. After all, this may be the last time I can. Is there any problem with that?'

'No problem at all,' Paniatowski said. 'You've been given until noon to surrender yourself.'

'You just said "surrender" yourself,' Meadows pointed out. 'Not "present" myself, but "surrender" myself.'

'A slip of the tongue,' Paniatowski said.

But they both knew it wasn't.

'It's cold out here. Would you like to wait in my office?' Meadows said.

'That's very kind of you,' Paniatowski replied.

And suddenly it's like they were two polite strangers, talking to each other purely through necessity, she thought.

Meadows knocked on Lizzie's door.

'It's me,' she said. 'Can I come in?'

There was no answer, but that didn't worry her, because having a baby could be a tiring business, and Lizzie could well be sleeping.

She knocked again.

'I have to come in and look at you and little May, Lizzie,' she said. 'I've got what they call "a duty of care".'

There was still silence on the other side of the door, and now she started getting worried.

Had the baby died in the night, and was Lizzie now huddled

in a corner, her thumb stuck in her mouth, barely aware of where she was?

Had Lizzie died in the night, and was the baby now lying there alone and helpless?

She took out her keys. 'I'm coming in,' she said.

And suddenly there was activity on the other side of the door – a degree of banging and thumping that it was hard to believe was being created by one person.

Meadows opened the door. Lizzie was lying in bed, trying to look innocent. May was in her cot, gurgling away happily.

'Hello, Mrs Maybe,' Lizzie said.

'What was all that noise?' Meadows asked.

'What noise?' Lizzie replied. Meadows sniffed. There was definitely the scent of a male presence in the air.

'Where is he?' she asked.

But even as she was framing the question, she realized how stupid it was, because there was only one place he *could* be.

She walked over to the big old-fashioned wardrobe, and opened the doors. There was a big man inside, and he was naked. That he didn't look the least bit threatening was down to the fact that he had his hands held protectively over his genitals, and there was an awkward, embarrassed look on his face.

'Hello, Auntie Kate,' he said.

The four of them sat in Lizzie Grimshaw's room – the mother, her friend, her son and his girlfriend. In the cot by the bed, the baby lay contentedly asleep. Paniatowski and Meadows were sitting on the room's two chairs, Lizzie and Philip perched on the edge of the bed, and they were all drinking cocoa. It was a charming domestic scene, but it perhaps lost a little of its warm glow when you remembered that one of the four was a criminal on the run, and another the prime suspect in a murder investigation.

'We weren't doing anything sexy in bed – not so soon after the baby was born,' Lizzie said. 'But we knew that Philip would be going back to prison soon, and we just wanted to be together for a little while.'

'And then we fell asleep in each other's arms,' Philip said. He chuckled, 'And it wasn't until Auntie Kate started banging on the door that we woke up.'

'I never meant to get pregnant with Philip's baby, you know,'

Lizzie said. 'It was just that right from the moment we met, I knew I loved him, and I wanted to go to bed with him.'

'It was the same for me,' Philip said. 'I think it must have been meant to happen.' He looked into his mother's eyes. 'I've never been a good person, Mum. I know that. But Lizzie is so very, very good, and since I've known her, I think I might have got a little bit better.'

'I think so too,' Paniatowski said.

'I was scared of what Gary would do when he found out I was having another baby,' Lizzie continued. 'This time, he might have killed me – especially if he managed to work out the baby wasn't his. So I came here, but somebody must have told him where I was, because one day, when I looked out of the window, I saw him standing in the street, looking up at the bedrooms, and I was terrified.'

'I asked her to come away with me, but she wouldn't,' Philip said.

'I went to Blackpool on a day trip once or twice, but apart from that, I've never been anywhere. I was as frightened of leaving Whitebridge as I was of Gary. Anyway, even though I loved Philip, I wasn't sure I trusted him.' Lizzie turned to him. 'I'm so sorry, Philip.'

'It's not your fault,' he said softly. 'Every man you've ever trusted has let you down, so why should I be any different?'

Lizzie grasped his hand. 'But I do trust you now. I'll never stop trusting you – and I'll never stop loving you.'

'When did you decide to attack her boyfriend, Philip?' Paniatowski asked.

'Not until the very last minute,' Philip admitted. 'I knew I had to do something to protect Lizzie, but I had no idea what. Then I was in this pub I'd never been to before, and so was he. I heard him talking to his mates, telling them all the terrible things he was going to do to Lizzie once he found a way to get in here. You could see his mates were horrified, but they were too frightened of him to say anything. I realized then that I had to stop him, and that I couldn't put it off any longer.'

'You broke both his legs – in several places.'

'I had to make sure he was out of action until after the baby was born. I . . . I couldn't let him be a threat to my baby.'

'Did you know anybody in the pub?' Meadows asked.

'No, like I said, I'd never been in there before.'

'So if you'd left right away, you might have got away with it.'

'Maybe.'

'But you didn't.'

'No.'

'Why not?'

Philip shrugged. 'If I'd run away, it would have been like saying I was ashamed of what I'd done – and I wasn't.'

Her father had led a cavalry charge against German tanks in the Second World War, Paniatowski thought. He must have known it would be suicide, but he did it anyway – because he felt that was what he had to do.

And now there was her son, knowing he would get a long prison sentence for breaking a vicious bully's legs, but doing it anyway – for much the same reason.

'Why haven't you said any of this before?' she asked. 'Surely you realize that if people know why you did it . . .'

'Can we step out into the corridor, Mum?' Philip asked urgently.

'Of course,' Paniatowski agreed, 'but I don't see why . . .'

'Then let's do it.'

Philip moved awkwardly and stiffly, and when he noticed his mother looking at him anxiously, he said, 'That's nothing to worry about.'

'I'm your mother,' Paniatowski reminded him. 'I'm supposed to worry.'

Philip grinned, and she could see he was in pain. 'It's just a slight injury,' he promised. 'It's the sort of thing you should expect during a prison break.'

In a different situation, she would have said something similar, she thought.

Once they were in the corridor, Philip closed Lizzie's bedroom door firmly behind them.

'You're going to ask me to tell this story at my trial, aren't you?' Philip asked.

'Well, of course I am. If the judge and jury can be made to understand that there are extenuating circumstances . . .'

'I'm not going to do it.'

'Why, in God's name, not?'

'Lizzie would have to appear as a witness, wouldn't she?'

'Yes, she would.'

'I'm not putting her through that.'

'Philip . . .'

'Lizzie is the best person I've ever met. She's so kind and loving. But the people in the court wouldn't see that. What they'd see would be some little scrubber who lived with one brute and probably slept with dozens of other brutes before she found one who was foolish enough to get her pregnant. I'm not putting her through that.'

'If you don't say anything, you could be adding years to your sentence,' Paniatowski warned.

'I know,' Philip said, 'and it makes no difference.'

He would never change his mind. She could see that.

'You're a bloody fool, Philip – and I'm so proud of you,' she said, with a catch in her throat.

There was the sound of a car horn being blown in the street, and Meadows opened the bedroom door.

'Thomas is here,' she said, 'Are you ready, Philip?'

Philip nodded, 'As soon as I've said goodbye to Lizzie and my daughter.'

Paniatowski and Meadows stayed in the corridor.

'I'll wait for you,' they heard Lizzie say. 'It doesn't matter how long you're in prison, I'll wait for you. And I'll talk to our baby about you every day, so that she'll learn to love you like I do.'

Philip appeared in the corridor again. He didn't look back – though it was obviously taking him a huge effort of will not to.

'Can I ask you one question before you go, Philip?' Meadows asked, gently closing the door.

'Of course, Auntie Kate.'

'This building is wired up like Fort Knox. How did you manage to get in without setting off the alarm?'

'Lizzie let me in through the basement door,' Philip said.

Meadows and Paniatowski stepped out into the street, and checked the area around Overcroft House. They were looking for vans which seemed innocent enough, but had no real reason for being in that particular street. They were looking for parked cars in which the drivers and passengers seemed so unaware of their presence that they gazed right through them. And they were looking for any unusual movements on the rooftops which might indicate there was a sniper in place.

Only when they had decided that the area was free of armed police did they return to Overcroft House, and quickly bundle Philip into Thomas's car.

'Go to one of the smaller police stations. They're less likely to have immediate access to firearms,' Paniatowski said urgently. 'Drive straight there, and as you're entering the building, make sure they can see you're a Catholic priest.'

'Relax, Mum, everything will go beautifully,' Thomas assured her.

'I'll come and see you as soon as they let me,' she told Philip. 'And I meant what I said – I really am proud of you.'

As they watched the car disappear round the corner, Paniatowski wiped a tear from her eye.

'Given their origin, it's quite remarkable both your sons have turned out so well,' Kate Meadows said. 'Do you think that might possibly be because you've done something right?'

Paniatowski forced a grin to her face. 'I doubt it,' she said. 'Shall we go and talk to Lizzie now?'

'Oh yes,' Meadows agreed. 'Oh yes indeed.'

Lizzie was still sitting on her bed, and when they entered her room, she looked up guiltily.

'You know what I'm going to ask you, don't you, Lizzie?' Meadows asked sternly.

'No, I . . .' Lizzie replied.

'Yes, you do,' Meadows told her. 'I want to know how you managed to let Philip into the house without setting the alarms off.'

'I . . . er . . . pressed the switch.'

'What switch?'

'The one behind the furnace.'

Meadows and Paniatowski exchanged glances, and Meadows' glance said, 'It's news to me that there's any such switch.'

'And that switched off the alarms?' she asked.

'I think it just stopped the bells going off,' Lizzie said.

'And who showed you how to do this?'

'Nobody.'

'So you just found the switch yourself, and pressed it to see what would happen?'

'Yes.'

'I want you to tell me the truth, Lizzie,' Meadows said.

The girl began to cry. 'I can't, Mrs Maybe. It wouldn't be fair to . . .'

'Fair to who?' Meadows pressed.

'Fair to nobody,' Lizzie said, with sullen defiance.

The switch had been carefully installed behind the boiler. It was not too difficult to access, but unless you were looking for it, you wouldn't even be aware it was there.

'It wasn't here last week,' Meadows said.

'How can you be so sure?'

'I had the boiler serviced. The technician would have noticed. And if you need any more confirmation, the plaster around it still hasn't properly dried out.'

A wire ran from the switch to the ceiling, and followed the wall around until it reached the control box. When Meadows hit the switch, the green light in the control box went out.

'Open the door,' Meadows said.

The door led to the basement steps, and when Paniatowski opened it, nothing happened.

'Close it again,' Meadows said.

When Paniatowski had done that, Meadows flicked the switch again, and the green lights came back on.

'I'm going up to my office,' Meadows said. 'Give me time to get there, then throw the switch again. Count to twenty, switch it back on, and come and join me.'

'Will do,' Paniatowski agreed.

Meadows was sitting at her desk. There was a deep frown on her face.

'The monitors all went off for twenty seconds,' she said. 'Whoever controls that switch can cut out the security system any time.'

'And I know why it's there!' Paniatowski said.

The switch was the hidden factor – the element that knit together all the other, seemingly unconnected, pieces of the puzzle into one coherent unit.

She was not alone in receiving this revelation, Paniatowski saw, because it was plain from the look on Meadows' face that she was thinking exactly the same thing.

'So what's our next move?' Meadows asked.

'We look at the security tape from the day you had your encounter with Andrew Lofthouse,' Paniatowski said, 'and I think I already know what we'll find.'

'So do I,' Meadows told her.

TWENTY-TWO

The first thing Louisa Rutter noticed when her mother appeared at her office door was that Monika was holding her old leather briefcase, which she had carried with her on all her investigations, and which Louisa had assumed she'd thrown out years ago.

Then, before she had time to question her mother about the bag, the guilt hit her.

'I'm so sorry, Mum,' she said.

She threw her arms around Monika and was shocked to realize something she had known, objectively, all along – that she was now much taller and more substantial than her mother.

How did this happen, she wondered – and felt her guilt intensify.

'I should never have done it,' she continued, and she was almost in tears. 'I should never have made you responsible for bringing Kate in. But I was so angry with you.'

'It's all right, don't worry about it,' Monika said soothingly. She gently disengaged from Louisa's grasp, then held out the briefcase. 'I want you to take a look at what's inside this.'

Louisa glanced up at the clock. It was ten minutes to twelve.

'Where's Kate?' she asked. 'Down in Booking?'

'No,' Monika replied. 'She's in the Drum and Monkey, which is where I'll be soon.'

She couldn't allow herself to be angry with her mother again, Louisa thought – not five minutes since she'd apologized for the last time.

'I gave her until twelve noon,' she said levelly. 'I think I was being very reasonable.'

'Kate's not coming in,' Monika said. 'She has no reason to,

because she didn't kill either Andrew Lofthouse or James Hadley.'

Oh God, please don't let her be going soft in the head, Louisa thought.

'I know that Kate's an old friend, Mum, and I'm very fond of her, too,' she said softly. 'But the evidence makes her the prime suspect, and the fact that you don't want her to be the killer doesn't mean she isn't.'

'You're right, of course,' Monika said. 'But the thing is, love, I know who the killer actually is.' She patted the briefcase. 'It's all in here.'

'Mum . . .' Louisa began.

'Read it for yourself, and you'll see I'm right,' Monika said confidently. 'You can close the case by teatime, Louisa. It won't be easy, because a lot of the evidence is circumstantial, but I've got confidence in you.' She turned towards the door. 'If you want me, I'll be in the Drum. We'll be having an inquest, just like we did in the old days, but it's likely to evolve into the mother and father of all piss-ups.'

When the Drum had opened its doors at eleven, Crane and Beresford were already waiting. Meadows had joined them half an hour later, and now the three of them were sitting round a table located approximately where their old table had been.

'So why didn't you tell us from the beginning what happened when you went back to Andrew Lofthouse's home?' Beresford asked Meadows.

'I did tell you,' Meadows said defensively. 'I told you that I was disgusted with the whole business, and so I left.'

'But you didn't give us the details,' Beresford pressed. 'And because you refused to do that, it seemed to us as if you were lying.'

'Leave it, sir,' Crane said.

But Beresford was not in a mood to 'leave it'.

'Don't you see you only brought suspicion down on yourself?' he asked.

'Of course I see,' Meadows said impatiently. 'I see it now, and I saw it at the time.'

'In which case . . .'

'In order to protect my secret identity, I was willing to

participate in auto-erotic strangulation. If you were in my shoes, don't you think you'd find that humiliating?'

'I wouldn't be in your shoes,' Beresford said. 'Besides, I thought that was what you did. I thought you thrived on humiliation.'

'That humiliation is ritualistic and agreed on. What happened to the sarge was more like rape,' Crane said. 'And if you persist in this line of questioning, sir, I shall be obliged to clock you one.'

Beresford stiffened. 'Do you think you could?' he demanded. But he almost immediately relaxed again, and a grin came to his face. 'Yes, you probably could,' he conceded. 'Time catches up with all of us in the end.' He turned to Meadows. 'I'm sorry, Kate. I'm about as subtle as a rhino with a hangover, but I do care about you, you know.'

'I know you do,' Meadows said. She sighed. 'But now I've started, so I might as well tell you the rest. I went out to the moors, when I left Lofthouse's house. I'm not sure why. I think it was maybe because I had half a mind to kill myself, and the moors seemed like a perfect spot to end the Tragedy of Kate Meadows.' She smiled. 'I didn't kill myself.'

Beresford smiled back. 'We noticed,' he said. 'We're good at spotting things like that.'

'But I did kill Zelda,' Meadows said.

'You did *what*?' Beresford exploded.

'I burned Zelda's costume. It was painful for me, but one of us had to die, and she drew the short straw.'

The bar door opened, and Paniatowski walked in.

'How did it go, boss?' Crane asked, when she'd sat down.

Paniatowski shrugged. 'I gave her the file, and left her to read it. There was nothing else I could do.'

'Do you think she'll follow through with it?' Beresford asked.

'We put together a good case, so she'd be a fool not to,' Paniatowski said. 'And none of my children are fools.'

'So where do you think she'll begin?' Meadows asked.

'I don't know,' Paniatowski admitted. 'But in her shoes, I'd start with the solicitor.'

Louisa smiled across her desk at the stumpy woman in the smart suit.

'It was very good of you to spare me the time, Ms Maitland Williams,' she said.

The solicitor shrugged awkwardly. 'I'm an officer of the court,' she said. 'It's my duty to assist the police in any way I can.'

She was nervous, Louisa thought, but that was only to be expected. Anyone – even a solicitor and part-time magistrate – would feel apprehensive when asked to put in an appearance at the local nick.

Louisa was nervous too, because Maitland Williams was the corner stone of the case she was trying to build, and if the theory that Monika had come up with was wrong – or it was right, but she couldn't get the solicitor to admit it – then the whole structure was doomed to collapse.

'You should note that no record – either written or taped – is being made of this conversation,' she said. 'In addition, you should know that the conversation is not being held under caution.'

Maitland Williams laughed uneasily. 'How formal that sounds, Louisa,' she said. 'Anyone would think we'd only just met, whereas, in fact, we're certainly close acquaintances, although I'd prefer to think of you as a friend.'

'I have no friends when I'm in this office,' Louisa said. 'For that reason, I will call you Ms Maitland Williams, and I would like you to call me chief superintendent.'

'Oh,' the solicitor said. 'All right, if that's the way you want it.'

It was a promising response, Louisa thought, trying not to get too expectant. If the solicitor had laughed her comment off and told her she sounded so stiff she must have a broom handle stuck up her arse – or if she had taken umbrage and left – it would probably have shown a clear conscience, whereas her submissiveness would strongly suggest she had something to hide.

'You had a relationship with Andrew Lofthouse, didn't you?' she asked.

'Yes, I was his company's solicitor,' Maitland Williams said.

Louisa clicked her tongue in disapproval. 'You, more than most people, should appreciate how important it is to be honest with the police.'

'All right, we had an affair,' Maitland Williams admitted.

'An affair that involved numerous visits to the Hellfire Club?'

Maitland Williams looked down at her feet. 'Yes.'

'Did you enjoy it there, Cecilia?' Louisa asked softly.

'No, I didn't,' the other woman confessed. 'But it was what Andrew wanted to do, and afterwards . . .'

'Yes?'

'Afterwards, he could be so tender.'

It was so pathetic that it was hard not to feel sorry for her, Louisa thought.

'Let's move on,' she said, briskly. 'I called Companies House about an hour ago, and it seems that Whitebridge Bottling and Distribution is no longer registered in the UK. Why is that?'

'It's registered in the Isle of Man now.'

'Ah, I get it – they've made it an offshore company!' Louisa said. 'But what I still don't see is why a company based solely in Whitebridge should need to register offshore.'

'For a favourable tax position.'

'In other words, tax evasion,' Louisa said.

'No, tax avoidance,' Maitland Williams said. 'Talk evasion is illegal, tax avoidance isn't.'

'I should imagine changing the registration was a job for the accountants, rather than the solicitor,' Louisa said. 'Is that right?'

'There was a little legal work involved,' Maitland Williams said cautiously.

'We've questioned the bouncer at the Hellfire Club, and it seems that Andrew stopped taking you there about eight weeks ago. Is that so?'

'Yes,' Maitland Williams said, sounding miserable again.

'And about two weeks later, Jane Lofthouse booked herself into the battered women's home,' Louisa mused. 'So tell me, why did Andrew dump you?'

'I never said he'd dumped me.'

'But he did, didn't he? And you must have been dreading it all along, because you knew he was out of your league. You'd have done anything to hold on to him. So you went to the Hellfire Club to please him, even though you hated it yourself, and when he asked you to do something illegal, you agreed. But it was all a waste of time, wasn't it, because after you'd done what he wanted – the only thing you had to offer that he was even vaguely interested in – he dropped you.'

This was it, she thought – crunch time. Monika's theory was that if Lofthouse was prepared to go through the whole courtship ritual, he must have really needed Maitland Williams' help with something significant – and the most significant thing to have happened in the Whitebridge Bottling and Distribution Company was the transfer of its assets to offshore status.

And that theory had better be right, because if it wasn't . . . .

Louisa took a deep breath. 'Well?' she said.

'I never did anything illegal,' Maitland Williams said, and she was almost in tears.

She was telling the truth, Louisa thought, with a sinking feeling – or if not the truth, something close enough to it to make no bloody difference.

And yet for an innocent woman, Maitland Williams was acting remarkably like a guilty one.

'Maybe you didn't do anything illegal, but you certainly did do something that was *unethical* – and I want to know what it was,' Louisa said, taking a last, desperate shot in the dark.

'I didn't . . .' Maitland Williams began.

But the look of panic in her eyes told Louisa that she was finally on the right track. 'What will the forensic solicitor find when he reviews your work?' she demanded. 'What will strike him as unusual?'

'Nothing. I . . .'

'Tell me now, and you may just get away with it – hold out on me and I'll ruin you,' Louisa said.

'The ownership of the company was transferred. Andrew got everything,' Maitland Williams said, in a rush.

Bingo!

'And did Jane agree to this?'

'She . . . she signed the documents.'

'But did she know what was in them?'

'If she wasn't sure about them, she should have got her solicitor to check them.'

'She thought you were her solicitor,' Louisa said angrily.

'What . . . what will happen to me?' Maitland Williams mumbled.

'Very little,' Louisa said. 'I'd like to charge you for the part you played in two murders – because you did play a part, have no doubt about that – but I can't do it. I'd like to charge you for your part in cheating Jane Lofthouse out of the business she worked so hard to build up, but I can't do that, either. But I promise you I'll do whatever I can to see you ostracized from Whitebridge society. Now get the hell out of my office.'

*   *   *

Paniatowski switched off her phone and laid it back on the pub table.

'Cecilia Maitland Williams has just admitted that she helped Lofthouse grab control of the company,' she said.

'The moment I laid eyes on her, I knew that something was wrong,' Colin Beresford said. 'As I may have pointed out before, she simply wasn't attractive enough to be of interest to a man like Andrew Lofthouse. I know you still don't like it, Kate, but it's human nature – or male nature, at least. You almost never see a handsome man with a plain woman. And Lofthouse was a *very* handsome man, wasn't he, Jack?'

'Yes, he was,' Crane agreed. He winked at Meadows. 'I'd go so far as to say that if he'd been around in your bachelor days, sir, he'd have been real competition for you.'

'Oh, I don't know about that,' Beresford said. 'I don't know about that at all.' Then he realized the rest of the team were laughing at him. 'Whitebridge was only big enough for one Shagger at a time,' he continued, doing his best to make it sound as if he had been joking all along, 'and back then, if you'd polled the young women of the town, they'd all have agreed it was me.'

'We can assume Jane found out about all this, can't we?' Paniatowski asked.

'Yes,' Crane agreed. 'It's the only thing that would explain her subsequent behaviour.'

'She realized that since the transfer was legal – she had, however inadvertently, signed the documents herself – the only way she was going to get the company back was to inherit it from her dead husband,' Beresford said.

'She decided to kill him,' Crane continued. 'She also decided that the first thing she needed was a rock-solid alibi for when he was murdered, which also enabled her to do the actual killing herself. And that's when she came up with the idea of using Kate's hostel.'

'You're sure she wasn't a battered wife, are you?' asked Beresford, who was reluctant to give up something which had been part of his working theory for most of the investigation.

'Absolutely certain,' Paniatowski said. 'For a start, there's Jim Hadley's claim that she *was* a battered wife.

'He'd said, "I'd run into her at the golf club dinner or my lodge's ladies night . . . I wasn't that close to her – but I was close enough to guess what was going on . . . I wasn't the only one. Everybody could see what was happening, and nobody did anything about it."

'He had two reasons for saying that,' Paniatowski explained. 'The first was that it helped to explain why he was so willing to drop everything and rush over to Overcroft House the moment she called. The second was that it reinforced her story. But we know it was a lie, because we know he never belonged to the golf club or the Freemasons.'

'Andrew Lofthouse was on the point of telling us it was a lie while he was demanding I let him in to Overcroft House,' Meadows said.

'I've seen the bruises,' Meadows had said.

'Oh, I see! You've seen the bruises! And do you know how she got those bruises?'

'No, so why don't you tell me?'

'They . . . they were self-inflicted.'

'He wanted to tell me that she'd got the bruises at the Hellfire Club, and . . .' Meadows began.

'Hang on,' Beresford interrupted. 'If she got the bruises during some perv . . . during some sadomasochistic ritual, why didn't you, of all people, recognize them as such?'

Meadows sighed. 'There are an infinite number of encounters possible. I've never been in one that leaves that particular pattern of bruising, so I didn't recognize it, but . . .'

'And another thing,' Beresford interrupted, 'were you about to say that the reason he didn't tell you how she got the bruising was because that might expose him as a fellow . . . a fellow whatever.'

'Exactly,' Meadows agreed.

'So by the same argument, he would never have exposed you, either. It was all a bluff.'

'That's right,' Meadows admitted. 'The reason he wore a mask in the Hellfire Club was so he wouldn't be recognized – he must have thought it would be bad for business and might ruin his chances of eventually becoming lord mayor. So he would never have exposed me. It was all a bluff, and I fell for it. I humiliated myself for nothing. What an idiot.'

'I'm sorry, I never meant . . .' Beresford said.

'Given the size of your feet, it's almost impossible to imagine one of them would fit in your mouth, but you seem to manage that easily enough, sir,' Meadows said.

'I deserve that,' Beresford admitted.

'Bloody right you do,' Paniatowski agreed. 'What else is there, Kate?'

'I've had dozens of women pass through Overcroft House, and when they eventually decide to step outside they take slow, tentative steps. They're scared, even if the man they're afraid of has been locked up, because that's the nature of terror – it's just not rational. But Jane wasn't like that – at least, not for long. She seemed very confident, and that just doesn't square up with the woman who was so terrified just twenty-four hours earlier that she crawled into a cupboard under the stairs. I should have spotted that, and I didn't.'

'Don't be so hard on yourself,' Beresford said. 'After all you'd been through the day before, it's a wonder you were functioning at all.'

'Why, thank you, Colin, that was really nice of you,' Meadows said.

Beresford shrugged. 'Well, you know . . .'

Paniatowski looked at her watch.

'I wonder how Louisa's getting on,' she said.

They *all* wondered how Louisa was getting on.

TWENTY-THREE

Louisa Rutter had interviewed Cecilia Maitland Williams in her own office. There had been no one else present, and the meeting had not been recorded.

The interview with Jane Lofthouse was somewhat different. This was held in Interview Room A, there was a tape recording machine in operation, and Rutter was accompanied by DS Boyd.

Jane Lofthouse was alone on the other side of the table. She had been offered a solicitor, but had disdainfully turned the offer down.

'The thing I'd like to make plain before we begin is that whatever else happens, I will be charging you with the murders of Andrew Lofthouse and James Hadley,' Louisa said.

Jane Lofthouse smirked. 'Good luck with that.'

'Thank you,' Louisa replied.

It wasn't going to be easy, she thought. True, Jane Lofthouse was arrogant, but then she had much to be arrogant about. Her plan had been bold, the execution of it had been pretty near perfect, and if Philip hadn't broken out of the remand centre, there was an excellent chance that she would never even have been arrested.

'Contrary to what you seem to believe, we have – or will shortly have – all the evidence we need for a conviction,' she continued, with much more confidence than she actually felt, 'but it will make things easier for us if you agree to cooperate, and that might be to your advantage, too.'

'How might it be to my advantage?' Jane wondered.

'I have a lot of sympathy for you,' Louisa said. 'You learned that your husband had stolen your life's work, and you decided to strike back. There's certainly quite a while between the theft and the murder, but if your barrister were to argue extenuating circumstances, the prosecution might well agree to go along with it if you'd already shown willing to cooperate with us.'

'And what about Jim Hadley's murder?' Jane Lofthouse asked. 'Would they accept that as part of the extenuating circumstances package?'

Yes, what *about* Hadley's murder, Louisa asked herself. The question was a logical comeback, and she should have been expecting it – but she bloody well hadn't been.

'Well, you were having an affair with him,' she said, improvising wildly, 'but the jury will probably be able work out for themselves that it was less an act of passion, and more a case of you needing a dupe. So on reflection, you might be better going for diminished responsibility – after all, you've been put under a lot of strain – and it wouldn't do you any harm to have the prosecution behind you on that, either.'

'I'll make a deal with you,' Jane said. 'You tell me what you think you've got on me, and I'll tell you if I'm prepared to confess.'

She was a very experienced police officer, and she should be making a better job of this, Louisa thought.

Maybe it was that she was nervous, because her mother and Kate were relying on her.

Or maybe, she thought miserably, it was because she'd never been very good at this aspect of the work.

'Well, do we have a deal?' Jane asked.

And Louisa realized that she must have been silent for some time.

'All right, we have a deal,' she agreed. 'Shall we talk about this plan of yours? It really was a very good plan, you know, but the time element let you down.'

'What do you mean?' Jane asked.

For the first time in the entire interview, she sounded a little unsure of herself.

'Once the papers had been signed, your husband could have kicked you out of the business any time he wanted to, so you had to make your own move quickly,' Louisa said. 'Seducing poor, lonely Jim Hadley took no time at all. What should have taken longer was developing the role of the battered wife, but you simply couldn't afford the luxury of doing it properly. And that's why, when we get around to questioning all your friends, they'll deny you were ever a victim.'

'Them!' Jane said contemptuously. 'They're so insensitive they wouldn't notice if I stood there bleeding all over the carpet. Unless it was their carpet of course – they'd notice then.'

'I could talk to half a dozen experts right now who'd be prepared to swear under oath that friends – and even casual acquaintances – always notice when a woman is being abused,' Louisa said.

'And I could talk to half a dozen barristers right now who would tear your "experts" apart on the witness stand,' Jane said.

She had an answer for everything, and the problem was they were usually the *right* answers.

'You hadn't really been beaten up at all,' Louisa said. 'The bruises you showed to Kate Meadows and the Overcroft House were injuries you sustained in the Hellfire Club.'

'No, they weren't – and you can't prove they were.'

'Do you deny you went to the Hellfire Club?' Louisa asked.

For a few happy seconds it looked as if Jane would do just that.

Then she said, 'Yes, I did go, as a matter of fact. But I'm a dominatrix. No man there laid a hand on me.'

'I don't believe you,' Louisa said.

'Prove me wrong,' Jane said. 'Talk to members of the club. Call them as witnesses.'

She was really starting to enjoy herself now, Louisa thought. And why wouldn't she – she was winning!

'So, you're in a house you can't possibly get out of without setting off the alarm, so if you can find a way round that, you'll have the perfect alibi. Your lover can circumvent the system – that's the only reason you've made him your lover – but he needs an excuse to get into the building. So what do you do? You've previously prepared an anonymous letter saying where you'll be, and you get Hadley to deliver it to your husband. Andrew rushes round to Overcroft House, and you pretend to be in a panic and demand the right to call in your expert to check the alarms. And while he's doing that, he fits the interrupter switch.'

'It's a good story,' Jane said.

'The only problem is, you can't do it alone. You need someone to switch the alarm back on once you've gone, and switch it off again once you want to get back in. And that's why you've spent the last few weeks making friends with Lizzie Grimshaw. Unfortunately for you, she uses the switch again, to let her boyfriend in, and that's how we discover it.'

'Did Lizzie tell you this?' Jane asked.

'No, for some strange reason, she has a strong sense of loyalty towards you. But she will tell us in the end.'

'I doubt it,' Jane said. 'But what if she does? Who'd believe her – the woman's a bloody halfwit.'

'We haven't traced the interrupter back to Hadley yet, but that's only a matter of time,' Louisa said.

'Again, so what? I never said he didn't do it – but it has nothing to do with me.'

'Why *would* he do it, if not for you?'

'I don't know – and I don't really care.'

'You left the building, and no doubt your lovesick lackey, Jim Hadley, was waiting for you round the corner. He drove you to your house. When you got there, I suspect you told him to stay in the car. Am I right?'

'Yes, he . . .' Jane began. She checked herself and took a deep breath. 'Yes, he would have stayed in the car if that was what happened,' she continued, 'but, you see, it didn't.'

'You went inside. I don't know what you said to your husband, but you got him to turn his back, and when he did, you hit him over the head with a statue. Where was the noose, by the way?'

'The noose?'

'You're not going to deny knowing about the noose, are you?'

'No, of course not. Andrew was very fond of a little auto-erotic strangulation, but I don't know where it was that night – because I wasn't there.'

'It was either hanging from the hook in the bedroom or back in the cupboard,' Louisa said. 'You took it, and tied it to the banister on the minstrels' gallery. Then you stripped him, washed him down, dragged him out to the corridor, put the noose around his neck, and threw him over the rail. And that was where he was hanging when the police arrived.'

Jane laughed. 'I don't think so,' she said.

'Why don't you think so?'

'Simple laws of physics. Once he'd lost his head, there was nothing to keep him up there.'

'How do you know he was decapitated?' Louisa asked, pouncing on what just might be her breakthrough.

'I must have read it in the papers.'

'It wasn't in any of the papers. We held that detail back.'

Jane laughed again. 'You've got me then, because only the murderer could have known Andrew was decapitated. Except that that's not true. Dozens of people knew – policemen, ambulance men, mortuary officials – and, as my barrister would point out, one of them could easily have told me.'

She was right, of course, Louisa thought.

'The reason for all the theatricals was to throw us off the trail,' she ploughed on. 'Purely domestic murders simply aren't that elaborate.'

'I'll take your word for that. After all, you do claim to be the expert.'

'The investigating officers speculated that the murderer could be a policeman or an ex-policeman, because he was smart enough to wipe down the body with a chemical which the lab hasn't precisely identified yet.'

'It could just be someone who watches a lot of American cop shows. Their murderers are always doing things like that,' Jane said helpfully.

'Or it could be someone who's been on mandatory courses on sterilization – someone, for example, in the bottling industry. And I'm guessing that's what the chemical is – something used in the bottling industry.'

'All the chemicals used in the industry are widely available,' Jane said.

'Aside from getting Lizzie to let you in and out, you also wanted her to steal the security tape for you,' Louisa said, shifting ground again.

'Why would I want her to do that? If things had gone as you describe them, I wouldn't have been on the tape, because the system would have been switched off when I was making my entrances and exits.'

'That's true, but when the system is deactivated or reactivated, it registers the fact. So we know that it was switched off at midnight for five minutes, and again at three o'clock for the same amount of time. Three hours was easily long enough for you to drive to your house, kill your husband and get back here, and five minutes was plenty of time to get in or out. You didn't want us to have those timings. That's why you tried to persuade Kate to destroy the tape – for her own protection, of course – and when that didn't work, you talked Lizzie into trying to steal it. Unfortunately for you, Kate had already locked it away somewhere safe.'

'Oh, with rock-solid evidence like that, I suppose I'd better confess now,' Jane said. She laughed. 'I'm joking, of course.'

'Poor Jim Hadley! He couldn't believe that a loner like him would ever interest a beautiful woman like you, and he was willing to do anything he could to keep you. Up to a point! I suspect the reason that you killed Jim Hadley was that he was horrified by what you'd done, and wanted to go to the police. And you killed him in exactly the same way you killed your husband, so that the police would know they were killed by the same person.'

'And that couldn't be me, because when Andrew was killed, I was safely locked up in Overcroft House.' Jane Lofthouse smiled again. 'Is that it? Is that all you've got?'

Yes, that was all she'd got – and she'd failed.

'Interview paused at one-fifteen,' Louisa said, and pressed the stop button on the recorder. 'I think I could use a breath of fresh air,' she said to DS Boyd.

She walked down the corridor, then took out her mobile phone and dialled a familiar number.

'Yes, Louisa?' said an anxious voice on the other end. 'How's it gone?'

'I need help, Mum,' Louisa said. 'I really need help.'

TWENTY-FOUR

Paniatowski stood up and walked away from the table, stopping only when she judged she was out of earshot of the rest of the team. She had been mentally preparing herself for a call just like this one, but now that it had actually happened she felt as if she'd been smashed in the stomach with a sledgehammer.

'Are you there?' Louisa asked, sounding desperate.

'Yes, I'm here,' Monika replied. '*How* can I help?'

'It's ironic,' Louisa said. 'I joined the police because I wanted to be just like you, but I've *never* been like you. I never could do interrogations, and I'm making a real bloody mess of this one. Jane Lofthouse was better prepared for this than I am. Every question I ask, she's got an answer ready. I'm getting nowhere – and she's laughing at me. What do I do, Mum?'

'You could hand the interrogation over to somebody else,' Paniatowski suggested.

'No, I couldn't. It has to be me, because anybody else would drag you and Kate into it, and that would be a disaster.'

It sounds like a disaster already, Paniatowski thought.

'What I always used to do, especially with the confident ones, was look for a weakness – a chink in their armour,' she said. 'What do you think Jane Lofthouse's weakness is?'

'Maybe her arrogance – she thinks she's so much smarter than I am. The problem is, she may be right,' Louisa said miserably.

'Play on that,' Paniatowski said. 'Give her the impression that you don't consider her to be half as smart as she thinks she is . . .'

At the table, the other members of the team tried not to look at their ex-boss, but it soon proved to be an impossible task.

'She looks worried,' Beresford said.

'Well, of course she's worried,' Meadows said. 'She always was a bit nervy at this stage of an investigation.'

'Not like this,' Beresford said. 'The last time I saw her looking this worried was the night Louisa went missing, when she was fifteen.'

'And now she's worried about Louisa again – worried she'll have to resign the job she obviously loves to save us from going to gaol,' Meadows said. 'And it's all my fault.'

'You can't blame yourself,' Beresford told her.

'Can't I? If I hadn't gone to the Hellfire Club, we wouldn't be in this mess. And even if I had gone, but not allowed myself to be intimidated by Andrew Lofthouse's threats, we'd all be in the clear.'

'We've all made mistakes in our time,' Beresford said. 'And look at it this way – if we hadn't become involved, there's a good chance Jane Lofthouse would have got away with murder.'

'If the expression on the boss's face is anything to go by, there's a good chance Jane will *still* get away with murder,' Meadows countered. She turned to Crane. 'Could you possibly go up to the bar and buy me a drink, Jack?'

'Sure,' Crane said. 'Orange juice?'

'No, I'll have a Sidecar.'

'What the bloody hell is a Sidecar?' Beresford wondered.

'A cocktail – brandy, Cointreau and lemon juice. The barman will know how to mix it. And tell him to make it a strong one.'

'I've never seen you drink before,' Beresford said.

'I haven't had a drink since I came to Whitebridge,' Meadows told him. 'That's because I thought I didn't need one – because I thought my days of screwing everything up were behind me. But today I'm right back on form – and that deserves a drink.'

Paniatowski switched off her phone, and walked back to the table. 'That was Louisa,' she said unnecessarily. 'She needed a little advice on how to continue with the interrogation, but she's expecting a breakthrough soon.'

It was a brave attempt at cheering the others up, but sadly none of the others believed her.

In the front parlour of the Grapes, Chief Superintendent Towers held his double whisky up to the light, as if examining it for flaws, then took a generous sip.

'Is it true that Rutter is currently interrogating a suspect in the Lofthouse murder?' he asked DCI Dawson, who was sitting opposite him, and nursing a half of bitter.

'Yes, it is,' Dawson confirmed.

'You should never have allowed that to happen,' Towers said.

'How could I have stopped it?' Dawson wondered.

'You're the chief investigating officer.'

'And Ms Rutter not only outranks me, she's the temporary boss of the whole shebang,' Dawson said. Though he was trying not to show it, he was happier – and more relaxed – than he'd been for days. He couldn't play Towers' games anymore, because there was no arena in which to play them, not now Louisa Rutter had taken the case out of his hands. All he had to do was keep silent, and he was free and clear.

He couldn't do it – couldn't resist the opportunity to have a crafty dig at Towers, even though the man scared him half to death.

'Well, that's certainly pissed on your chips, sir,' he said.

'What do you mean?'

'You can't stop Ms Rutter solving the case anymore.'

Towers took a sip of his whisky. 'And why shouldn't I want her to solve the case?' he asked.

'Well, I . . . I thought that you thought that if the case wasn't solved . . .' Dawson began.

'You really are a fool, aren't you?' Towers asked, contemptuously.

'No, I—'

'As I thought I'd already explained to you, whether or not the case is solved became irrelevant the moment I learned that Rutter's mother had been conducting her own little *illegal* investigation. That gives me all the power over Saint Louisa I need.'

You really are a bastard, aren't you? Dawson thought.

But aloud, he said, 'You seem to have it all worked out, sir.'

'Oh, I do,' Towers agreed complacently. 'If Rutter solves the case, it allows her to go out in a blaze of glory. If she doesn't solve the case, she leaves with her tail between her legs. But either way, she goes.' He took another sip of his whisky. 'There's just one more thing I'd like to make clear now I don't need you anymore.'

'What is it?'

'When I promised I'd make you my deputy, I was lying. You're weak and incompetent and easily bullied – and I'd rather have Donald Duck as my number two.'

When Louisa entered the interview room, Jane Lofthouse glanced at the clock, then said, 'That was a long breath of fresh air. Where've you been? Having a quiet weep to yourself in the ladies' loo?'

No she hadn't, but even so, the comment was a little too close for comfort, Louisa thought.

She sat down again, and switched on the recorder. 'Interview resumes at one forty-five,' she said. She cleared her throat. 'Jane Lofthouse, I am charging you as an accessory before and after the fact in the murders of Andrew Lofthouse and James Hadley. You do not have to say anything, but it may harm your defence if you do not mention when questioned something which you later rely on in court.'

'Accessory before and after the fact?' Jane Lofthouse repeated. 'What is this? A demotion? Half an hour ago, you were threatening to charge me with murder, pure and simple.'

'Ah, but you see, that was before I asked Kate Meadows' advice,' Louisa said.

'You asked Kate Meadows' advice? Why, in God's name, would you do that?'

'Because she's a trained police officer, and while you were in Overcroft House . . . Which is how long, sergeant?'

'Six weeks,' Boyd said.

'While you were in Overcroft House, she had ample opportunity to observe and assess you.'

'So what?'

'The conclusion she's reached is you have neither the personality nor the brain power to devise an intricate murder plot.'

'Well, if that is her conclusion, it just goes to show what a stupid bitch she is,' Jane said. 'No personality or brain power! That's not me she's talking about – it's poor little Jane Lofthouse, the beaten wife. That's just the role I was playing.'

'In her opinion, it was Jim Hadley who came up with the plan, and Jim Hadley who actually killed your husband.'

'Jim Hadley?' Jane repeated, disbelievingly. 'He didn't even have the balls to go back to Overcroft House and remove the interrupter switch from the basement, once it was all over. Do you seriously think he'd be brave enough to murder Andrew? And if he was the one who planned and executed the killing, why was it necessary for me to leave Overcroft House that night?'

'So you do admit leaving it?' Louisa asked.

'No, of course I don't. I'm merely taking your flawed logic and following it to its natural conclusion.'

'I'm merely taking your flawed logic and following it to its natural conclusion,' Louisa repeated. 'You see, sergeant, it helps to be able to use phrases like that. You can use them to camouflage the fact that you're a bit thick.'

'Don't talk to him – talk to me!' Jane Lofthouse said angrily.

'Why did you have to leave Overcroft House that night, you ask,' Louisa mused. 'Well, Kate thinks – and I agree with her – that it wasn't really your choice. Hadley insisted you come along, because he thought he was rescuing you from a brute, and like the knight errant in the story books, he wanted his lady there when he slew the dragon, so that she could admire him.'

'I see. And after he killed Andrew, he killed himself, did he? He hit himself over the back of the head, stripped, washed himself, and hung himself? Is that what happened?'

'Obviously not,' Louisa said awkwardly.

'You haven't thought it through, have you?' Jane Lofthouse demanded gleefully. 'You were so busy worrying over the first murder that you didn't even consider the second.'

It was ridiculous to assume that the police could be so stupid, but it didn't seem ridiculous to Jane. She was now clearly in such a state of arrogant anger that it was easy for her to believe that not only was Louisa not as intelligent as she was, but the woman was a positive moron.

'You . . . you must have had another lover who did that job for you,' Louisa said, playing the part that Jane had assigned to her.

'If I had another lover who was prepared to kill for me, then why did I need to seduce poor useless Jim Hadley?' Jane asked.

'To . . . to deal with the alarm system.'

'But why would I need the alarm system dealing with? Couldn't my other lover have made Jim superfluous by killing Andrew himself?'

'I suppose so.'

'You suppose so! But let's assume, for the sake of argument, that Jim did kill Andrew. Was this other lover of mine a friend of his?'

'What makes you ask that?'

Jane sighed theatrically. 'I really do have to spell it all out for you, don't I?' she asked. 'Don't you think that Jim might just have been a little bit nervous after killing Andrew?'

'I suppose so.'

'Yet again, you suppose so. So we have Jim, who's as nervous as only Jim can be, yet he turns off his alarm system, and lets his murderer into his house. Doesn't that suggest he knew and trusted whoever it was?'

'I never said the alarm system was immobilized,' Louisa said. 'How did you know it was?'

'I . . .'

'Let's just summarize some of the things you've just told us,' Louisa suggested. 'You've told us that you were only pretending to be a victim of domestic abuse. You've told us that you knew all about the interrupter in the basement, and wanted Hadley to go back later and remove it. You've told us that Hadley didn't have the balls to carry out a killing himself. And you've told us that, despite the fact that he was frightened on the night he died, he switched off all his alarms – a detail that was not in the newspapers – because he knew and trusted his killer. Have I got that right?'

For a moment, Jane looked shocked. Then her expression went through a series of minor contortions.

She was starting to realize that she'd made a big mistake, Louisa thought. And now she was faced with a choice. She could admit to being a complete fool – or she could persuade herself it was all part of the plan.

'So you're finally there,' Jane said. 'Thank God for that. Frankly I was wondering just how many *more* hints I was going to have to drop before you got the picture.'

'So you admit to killing your husband, Andrew Lofthouse?'

'He deserved to die. He'd never achieved anything himself, and he was cheating me out of my life's work.'

'I need a "yes" or "no",' Louisa said.

'Yes, I killed him.'

'And did you also kill James Hadley?'

'He was so weak. He wanted to go crawling to the police. He wanted to tell them he had no idea I was going to kill Andrew.'

'And is that true?'

'Not that it matters one way or the other, but yes, it's true.'

'So you admit killing him, too?'

'Putting him out of his misery would be a better way to phrase it.'

'I suppose I'd better change the charge from "accessory to murder" to straightforward murder,' Louisa said.

'Well, I should think you would,' Jane said. 'And let's have no more sloppiness in this investigation, please.'

*   *   *

When Chief Superintendent Towers arrived at Chief Superintendent Rutter's office, the latter was on the phone, and gestured to him that he should take a seat.

Towers lowered himself into a chair in front of the desk. This was going to be fun, he thought – but only for one of them.

'Yes,' Louisa was saying into the phone. 'Yes . . . thank you . . . I'll get back to you as soon as I can.' She replaced the phone on its cradle, turned to Towers, and smiled. 'What can I do for you, Ben?'

'I just dropped by to congratulate you over the Lofthouse case,' he lied. 'It was a good result.'

'It was for me, certainly,' Louisa said, 'but according to what Sergeant Boyd has told me, you must be far from happy with it.'

'So Boyd's been shooting off his mouth, has he?' Towers asked. 'There's a man who likes to play with fire.'

'Or he could just be a man who puts the quest for justice above office politics,' Louisa replied. 'And just so you know, he's under my protection now, so I wouldn't try to exact any petty revenge if I was you.'

And a lot of good her protection was going to be, Towers thought.

'Since you refuse to believe I'm here to congratulate you, you probably wonder why I *am* here,' he said.

'Not at all,' Louisa replied. 'You're here to suggest that I take early retirement, in order to be able to look after my mother. If, however, I refuse to follow your advice and stay on, you'll kindly arrange for my mother to be cared for by HM's prison service. Have I got that about right?'

Towers frowned. 'Impeding a criminal investigation and/or perverting the course of justice are very serious matters,' he said. 'You're being very unwise to treat the matter so flippantly.'

'And I'm not only flippant, I'm very relaxed,' Louisa said.

Towers laughed. 'I've just realized what you're doing,' he said. 'You're putting up a front – it's all pure bloody bravado.'

'Most of the detective work that led to Jane Lofthouse's arrest was carried out by my mother and her team. Did you know that?'

No, he didn't, and the news came as bit of shock, but then he realized it didn't matter.

'Even if *all* the detective work was done by them, it makes absolutely no difference,' he said. 'The law is the law, and there's never any excuse – in the eyes of our system of justice – for breaking it.'

Louisa bowed her head and sighed. 'You're right,' she said. 'Mum's done wrong and she'll have to be punished. But I'd like to ask you one small favour – could I just take her out for afternoon tea before you arrest her?'

'You should be worried – and you're not,' Towers said, sounding worried himself.

'Maybe it's just more bravado,' Louisa suggested.

But it wasn't – he could see that now.

'Just what is the trump card you imagine you're holding?' he demanded.

'I'm just picturing my mother's trial,' Louisa said reflectively. 'Some of the jurors will be old enough to remember her in her heyday, when she was something of a local hero. As for the younger ones – what they'll see is this sweet old lady who could be their granny.'

'Your mother looks less like a granny than any pensioner I've ever met,' Towers said.

'She may not look like a granny now, but I'll make sure she does when she's in the dock,' Louisa said. 'Anyway, her barrister won't discuss whether or not she's guilty, because she obviously is. Do you know what he'll say instead?'

'No, I don't. Why don't you tell me?' Towers said.

Louisa grasped the lapels of her jacket between her thumbs and first fingers – a typical barrister's posture. 'Jane Lofthouse had already murdered two people, and she wouldn't have stopped there,' she said, in a plummy voice. 'Once a woman like her gets a taste for killing, there's no holding her. She'd have killed again, and again, and again. And who might her next victim have been? It could have been a relative of yours – your partner, say, or one of your children. And who stopped her from doing these terrible things? Monika Paniatowski stopped her.'

'But that's rubbish,' Towers protested. 'Jane Lofthouse isn't a mindless psychopath. She only killed for a specific purpose – to achieve a certain aim. It's highly unlikely she'd ever have killed again.'

Louisa slowly shook her head from side to side.

'Ben, Ben, Ben,' she said, her tone larded with regret, 'you should have learned by now that it's the side with the best story that wins any court case – and our story is bloody good. Our barrister's underlying message to the jury – never said explicitly but writ large in capital letters for all of them to see – is that they'll hate themselves if they send my mum to gaol, and the only way to avoid that is to find her "not guilty." And a "not guilty" verdict is what they'll deliver.'

'The judge might set the verdict aside, purely as a matter of law,' Towers said.

'He could – but we both know he won't, because he won't want his family and friends shunning him, and members of his exclusive golf club turning their backs on him. And let's not forget how the tabloid press would react.' Louisa smiled. 'Not that the scenario I've just outlined is actually going to happen, because Horatio Bascombe QC, our esteemed local crown prosecutor, is perfectly capable of picturing what a disaster such a prosecution would be, and in order to avoid the humiliation of losing, he won't even allow it to get to court. But it wouldn't be an easy decision for him to take, and I don't think he would look kindly on the man responsible for him having to make it.'

'This is all a bluff,' Towers blustered.

'It isn't a bluff. There's a part of you that already knows that, and it won't be long – probably only the time it takes you to get back to your own office – for the rest of you to realize you've been backing the wrong horse.'

'I'm not finished with you yet,' Towers snarled.

'I didn't think you would be,' Louisa replied. 'By the way, about that phone call I was taking when you arrived . . .'

'Yes.'

'It was someone from the Police Authority with some very interesting news. The chief con has been offered a cushy job in the Caribbean, and he's decided to accept it.'

'Well, that will mean—'

'That's not the really interesting part,' Louisa said, and turned her attention to a document on her desk.

'What *is* the interesting part?' Towers asked, when perhaps ten seconds had ticked by.

Louisa looked up. 'The interesting part? Oh yes, I've been invited to apply for the post. That's as good as saying I've got the job in the bag, if I want it. It's not the career move that I was planning, but there are certain advantages that might prove virtually irresistible.'

He waited for her to say more, and when it became plain that she wasn't going to, he said, 'Advantages? What kind of advantages?'

'As chief constable, I'd play a major part in deciding who headed the new regional crime squad – and I'd make certain that someone unsuitable didn't manage to talk his way into the post.'

She returned her gaze to the document, and when she looked up again, he was still sitting there, as if frozen into his chair.

'You're making my office look untidy, and I'd be grateful if you'd withdraw,' she said. 'Or to put it another way, bugger off, you devious bastard.'

As she heard Towers' footsteps recede down the corridor, Louisa smiled to herself.

'You may be a much better mean streets bobby than I am, Mum,' she said, 'but when it comes to office politics, I think I could teach you a trick or two.'

'We did it!' Colin Beresford said, after Louisa had phoned the Drum for a third time. 'We cracked another case. And did we manage it through having the boffins tracking mobile phone calls and analysing DNA? No, we did not. We did it the old-fashioned way – pounding the streets and questioning witnesses.' He raised his pint glass in the air. 'So I give you a toast, my friends and colleagues – to old-fashioned detective work.'

The rest of the team clinked their glasses against his. 'To old-fashioned detective work.'

'And now, boss, I'll give you a thrashing at darts,' Beresford said.

Paniatowski shook her head. 'My dart playing days are over.'

'All right then, you can come and watch me,' Beresford said. 'I used to be able to hit nine bull's eyes with twelve darts. Think I still can?'

Paniatowski laughed. 'I very much doubt it.'

'You'll see,' Beresford said, taking her arm and lifting her to her feet. 'You'll see – and then you'll eat your words.'

Left alone at the table, Crane looked down at Meadows' glass. 'I see you're back on the orange juice,' he said.

'That's right,' Meadows agreed.

'And you haven't even touched that Sidecar I bought for you.'

'True.'

'Is that all you want to say on the subject?'

'Yes.'

'Then I'd better shut up about it myself.'

'I think that would be a good idea,' Meadows said.

At the dart board, Beresford was finding it hard to live up to his boast, since of the six darts he had thrown so far, only two of them had even hit the board.

'I'm not drunk, you know,' he said to Paniatowski.

'Aren't you?'

'I can't be. What have I had – seven or eight pints?'

'Something like that.'

'Back in the old days, when we were working a case together, I used to be able to knock that amount back every night. Do you remember?'

Paniatowski laughed. 'I remember – but we're all getting older.'

'Bollocks to that,' Beresford said.

Meadows and Crane walked over to the board. 'We're off,' Crane said.

'Don't . . . don't you want to stop for another one?' Beresford asked.

'I've left my deputy in charge for far too long,' Meadows said.

'And my work has rather fallen behind in the last few days,' Crane said.

'Work?' Beresford repeated. 'You're a university lecturer. You don't do any bloody work.'

'Good old Colin,' Meadows said. 'You'll never change, will you?'

'And is that a bad thing?' Beresford asked.

'Of course not. The world would be very boring without the odd dinosaur rampaging around.'

Once Meadows and Crane had left, Beresford threw another dozen darts at the board before giving up.

'I suppose I'd better be going home myself,' he said. 'My missus will kill me when she sees the state I'm in.'

'No, she won't,' Paniatowski said.

'No, she won't,' Beresford agreed. 'And she'll be ever so chuffed when I tell her we're not going to gaol.' A worried look flashed across his face. 'We're not going to gaol, are we?'

'We're not,' Paniatowski assured him.

'Right, off I go,' Beresford said. 'Are you coming?'

'No, I think I'll stay here a while,' Paniatowski replied. 'And Colin . . .'

'Yes?'

'Take a taxi home.'

'Yes, I will,' Beresford agreed. 'I'm not drunk . . .'

'Of course you're not.'

'. . . but I'll take a taxi anyway.'

Once he'd gone, Paniatowski returned to the table where *their* table had once stood.

It had been good to see the old team again, she thought, and it was wonderful that they all seemed to be having fulfilling lives.

She thought about her children. She wondered what Louisa's next career move would be. She wondered when Philip would be released from gaol, and whether Thomas would ever leave the priesthood.

And she wished she didn't have to go home to an empty house.

PART THREE
A Happy Ending

Friday, 3 June, 2005

There'd been a time when news of a demolition would generate real excitement, and people would come from all over town – and even from the outlying villages – to witness the spectacle. But those days had gone. Now there were films which featured spectacular acts of destruction on a wide screen – and in vivid colours rarely seen in rain-soaked central Lancashire. Even the television was doing its best to make real life seem boring and, in some ways, scarcely real at all. Thus it was on that June morning, it was a very small crowd indeed which had gathered behind the metal barriers to watch the annihilation of a hundred and fifty years of industrial urban history.

Monika Paniatowski placed her hands on the barrier, and looked across the street at the Victorian facade. She had not been near the Drum and Monkey since the Lofthouse investigation, but she felt a stab of regret at the thought that it was soon to be no more than a pile of unidentifiable rubble. She wondered how many hours she had spent in that pub over the years, and decided that it was probably such a staggering amount that it was better not to even try to calculate it.

'I thought I'd find you here,' said a voice behind her, and she turned to see Kate Meadows standing there.

'I was in the area. I thought I might as well take a look,' Paniatowski said, but her words sounded awkward, as if she'd been caught out doing something slightly naughty, and felt the need to justify it.

'I wanted to see it too,' Kate Meadows said, 'and I'm glad you're here to share it with me.'

Paniatowski reached in her pocket for her cigarettes, then remembered she didn't smoke any more.

'So how are things, Kate?' she asked.

'Busy,' Meadows replied. 'The foundation's bought the house

next to Overcroft House to give us room to expand. I'll have to take on two full-time assistants. And how's Louisa?'

'Great!' Paniatowski said. 'Whoever would have thought that a daughter of a simple provincial bobby would end up working for Interpol in Lyon?'

'A simple provincial bobby!' Meadows repeated, amused. 'I'd never have thought of you as *simple*.'

'I am when compared to her,' Paniatowski said. 'She's collating and analysing information from a hundred and ninety-five different countries. It would drive me insane – I just couldn't do it – but she thrives on it.'

'You always said she was the admiral and you were the buccaneer,' Meadows replied.

A man in young-middle-age, wearing a smart business suit, drew level with them and stopped.

'Excuse me,' he said, 'are you DCI Paniatowski?'

It was strange to hear her title being used after all this time, she thought.

'Yes, I'm Monika Paniatowski,' she said.

'I'm called Brough. I was the last landlord of the Drum and Monkey.'

'You must be sorry to see it go,' Paniatowski said, glancing across the road.

'What?' the landlord said, as if he had no idea what she was talking about. Then enlightenment seemed to dawn. 'Oh, I see what you mean. No, I'm not sorry at all, it was very inefficient as a retail unit, and the money raised from the sale of the site will be used to finance the building of a much more cost-effective outlet.'

Jesus God, Paniatowski thought, of course the Drum had been inefficient. Pubs were supposed to be inefficient. It was part of their charm.

'Anyway,' the landlord continued, 'I was going through the store room when I came across this battered old table. I couldn't figure out why it was there, but the father of one of my barmen – who used to be a barman himself – explained to me that it was the table you and your team of detectives used to use in the old days, and that the then-landlord had kept it for sentimental reasons.' He frowned. 'I can't really understand that myself, but the point is that it's there, and I wondered if you'd like it.'

'It's very kind of you, but I don't think so,' Paniatowski said.

The landlord did not seem the least offended that his offer had been spurned.

'Quite understandable,' he said. 'I wouldn't want it myself. But I promised I'd ask.'

'Now that does surprise me,' Meadows said, when he'd gone.

'What surprises you?' asked Paniatowski, patting her pocket for cigarettes.

'That you didn't want the table, of course. There's plenty of room for it in your house.'

'Yes, there is – but not in my mind,' Paniatowski said. 'I enjoy remembering the past now and again, but what I don't want to do is build a shrine to it.' She patted her pockets again. 'It's a terrible waste to keep looking back, Kate. My gaze is firmly directed towards the future.'

'There's a shop just around the corner. Shall I just nip round to it and buy you a packet of cigarettes?' Meadows said, noticing the pocket patting.

Paniatowski shook her head. 'No thanks, I've given them up.' She saw the quizzical look come to Meadows' face, and added, 'I'm setting an example.'

'And is your example being followed?' Meadows asked.

Paniatowski laughed. 'Of course it is – it's bound to be at this stage. But I'm looking towards the future again.' There was a rumbling sound like the hungry growl of a monster, and looking down the road, they saw a large crane with a wrecking ball attached to its arm, making its stately-clumsy progress up the street.

'Granny, Granny,' said an excited voice, and a moment later, two small thin arms were wrapped around Paniatowski's left leg.

'Let go, May, before you have us both over,' Paniatowski said laughingly.

The little girl stepped clear. 'Will there be crumpets for tea? When we go to the zoo, can we see the polar bears? And will you pick me up so I can see better?'

'Yes, there will be crumpets for tea. Yes, I'll make certain we go and see the polar bears. And I will pick you up, but not for long because you're getting quite heavy, and I'm an old lady.'

'No, you're not,' May said. 'You're not an old lady at all. You're my granny, and I live in your house.'

'All right then, here we go,' Paniatowski said, hoisting her up.

'Are you sure you can manage, Mum?' worried Lizzie, who had followed her daughter through the small crowd.

She had asked Monika if she could call her 'Mum' just after the ceremony at Blackheath Prison, when she had become Mrs Paniatowski. Monika had agreed, because, even though she was sure it would feel quite awkward, she hadn't wanted to hurt Lizzie's feelings. But, in actual fact, it had only felt awkward for a while, and then, much to her surprise, she found she rather liked it.

Monika rested May on her hip. 'I can manage five minutes, then I'll have to hand you back to your mum,' she told the child.

She looked across to the Drum and Monkey. She must have seen it a thousand times before, but she had never given it the attention she gave it now. Her eyes roved over the upper floor, and rested for a second on the words spelled out in Accrington brick:

Thwaites and Company
The Drum and Monkey

She examined the upper-floors window, which in their proportions would not have disgraced a Renaissance palace, and the smoked plate-glass window which ran the whole length of the lower floor. No one could have described it objectively as a beautiful building, and yet it seemed to hold some beauty that was all its own.

The wrecking ball struck the second floor, and it collapsed inwards. Paniatowski thought she could see the individual letters flying away, a *C* here and a *k* there, but knew deep down that it was only a fancy.

The roof just hung there for a few seconds, as if wondering where its support had gone, then it too gave way, falling with a crash and throwing up a cloud of dust.

Bits of the second floor were still standing – sticking out like rotting teeth in a diseased mouth – and the crane driver began to systematically attack them.

'I'm going to be a crane driver when I grow up,' May said excitedly.

'Good for you,' Paniatowski replied, as she felt a single tear running down her cheek.

AUTHOR'S NOTE

As most readers will have realized by now, this is the last of the
Monika Paniatowski series. Monika first appeared in *The Golden
Mile to Murder*, way back in 2001. Since then, she has risen
through the ranks, adopted one child and given birth to two more.
She has had her problems along the way, but I like to think she
has emerged from them bloody but unbowed. As a response to
those readers who feel I have heaped just too much misery on her,
I have given her an ending of which I hope they will approve.

It feels as if it has been a very long journey – hardly surprising
since it bloody well has! – and I would like to thank both those
readers who have been with me from the beginning and those who
have joined along the way. Your kind comments have been much
appreciated, and your constructive criticisms have been taken into
account. I'm going to miss you.